A DESPERATE
CHARACTER
AND
OTHER STORIES

A

DESPERATE

CHARACTER

and

Other Stories

IVAN TURGENEV

Translated By: CONSTANCE GARNETT

TARK CLASSIC FICTION
AN IMPRINT OF

MANOR
ROCKVILLE, MARYLAND
2009

ISBN: 978-1-60450-365-4

Published by TARK Classic Fiction
An Imprint of Arc Manor
P. O. Box 10339
Rockville, MD 20849-0339
www.ArcManor.com

Printed in the United States of America/United Kingdom

TO JOSEPH CONRAD
WHOSE ART IN ESSENCE OFTEN RECALLS
THE ART AND ESSENCE OF TURGENEV

CONTENTS

INTRODUCTION

The six tales now translated for the English reader were written by Turgenev at various dates between 1847 and 1881. Their chronological order is:—

- *Pyetushkov, 1847*
- *The Brigadier, 1867*
- *A Strange Story, 1869*
- *Punin and Baburin, 1874*
- *Old Portraits, 1881*
- *A Desperate Character, 1881*

Pyetushkov is the work of a young man of twenty-nine, and its lively, unstrained realism is so bold, intimate, and delicate as to contradict the flattering compliment that the French have paid to one another—that Turgenev had need to dress his art by the aid of French mirrors.

Although *Pyetushkov* shows us, by a certain open *naivete* of style, that a youthful hand is at work, it is the hand of a young master, carrying out the realism of the 'forties'—that of Gogol, Balzac, and Dickens—straightway, with finer point, to find a perfect equilibrium free from any bias or caricature. The whole strength and essence of the realistic method has been developed in *Pyetushkov* to its just limits. The Russians are *instinctive* realists, and carry the warmth of life into their pages, which warmth the French seem to lose in clarifying their impressions and crystallising them in art. *Pyetushkov* is not exquisite: it is irresistible. Note how the reader is transported bodily into Pyetushkov's stuffy room, and how the major fairly boils out of the two pages he lives in! (pp. 301, 302). That is *realism* if you like. A woman will see the point of *Pyetushkov* very quickly. Onisim and Vassilissa and the aunt walk and chatter around the stupid Pyetushkov, and glance at him significantly in a manner that reveals everything about these people's world. All the servants who appear in the tales in this volume are hit off so marvellously that one sees the lower-class world, which is such a mystery to certain refined minds, has no secrets for Turgenev.

Of a different, and to our taste more fascinating, *genre* is *The Brigadier*. It is greater art because life's prosaic growth is revealed not merely realistically, but also poetically, life as a tiny part of the great universe around it. The tale is a microcosm of Turgenev's own nature; his love of Nature, his tender sympathy for all humble, ragged, eccentric, despised human creatures; his unfaltering keenness of gaze into character, his fine sense of proportion, mingle in. *The Brigadier*, to create for us a sense of the pitiableness of man's tiny life, of the mere human seed which springs and spreads a while on earth, and dies under the menacing gaze of the advancing years. 'Out of the sweetness came forth strength' is perhaps the best saying by which one can define Turgenev's peculiar merits in *The Brigadier*.

Punin and Baburin presents to us again one of those ragged ones, one of 'the poor in spirit,' the idealist Punin, a character whose portrait challenges Dostoievsky's skill on the latter's own ground. That delicious Punin! and that terrible grandmother's scene with Baburin! How absolutely Slav is the blending of irony and kindness in the treatment of Punin, Cucumber, and Pyetushkov, few English readers will understand. All the characters in *Punin and Baburin* are so strongly drawn, so intensely alive, that, like Rembrandt's portraits, they make the living people, who stand looking at them, absurdly grey and lifeless by comparison! Baburin is a Nihilist before the times of Nihilism, he is a type of the strong characters that arose later in the movement of the 'eighties.'

A pre-Nihilistic type is also the character of Sophie in *A Strange Story*. But the chief value of this last psychological study is that it gives the English mind a clue to the fundamental distinction that marks off the Russian people from the peoples of the West. Sophie's words—'You spoke of the will—that's what must be broken' (p. 61)—define most admirably the deepest aspiration of the Russian soul. To be lowly and suffering, to be despised, sick, to be under the lash of fate, to be trampled under foot by others, *to be* unworthy, all this secret desire of the Russian soul implies that the Russian has little *will*, that he finds it easier to resign himself than to make the effort to be powerful, triumphant, worthy. It is from the resignation and softness of the Russian nature that all its characteristic virtues spring. Whereas religion with the English mind is largely an anxiety to be moral, to be *right* and righteous, to be 'a chosen vessel of the Lord,' religion with the Russian implies a genuine abasement and loss of self, a bowing before the will of Heaven, and true brotherly love. The Western mind rises to greatness by concentrating the will-power in action, by assertion of all its inner force, by shutting out forcibly whatever might dominate or distract or weaken it. But the Russian mind, through its lack of character, will-power, and hardness, rises to greatness in its acceptance of life, and in its sympathy with all the unfortunate, the wretched, the poor in spirit. Of course in practical life the Russian lacks many of the useful virtues the Western peoples possess and has most of their vices; but certainly his pity, charity, and brotherliness towards men more unfortunate than himself largely spring from his fatalistic acceptance of his own unworthiness and weakness. So in Sophie's case the desire for self-sacrifice, and her impregnable conviction that to suffer and endure is *right*, is truly Russian in the sense of letting the individuality go *with* the stream of fate, not *against* it. And hence the formidable spirit of the youthful generation that sacrificed itself in the Nihilistic movement: the strenuous action of 'the youth' once set in movement, the spirit of self-sacrifice impelled it calmly towards its goal despite all the forces and threats of fate. Sophie is indeed an early Nihilist born before her time.

We have said that the lack of will in the Russian nature is at the root of Russian virtues and vices, and in this connection it is curious to remark that a race's soul seems often to grow out of the race's *aspiration towards what it is not in life*. Is not the French intellect, for example, so cool, clear-headed, so delicately analytic of its own motives, that through the principle of *counterpoise* it strives to lose itself and release itself in continual rhetoric and emotional positions? Is not the German mind so alive to the material facts of life, to the necessity of getting hold of concrete advantages in life, and of not letting them go, that it deliberately slackens the bent bow, and plunges itself and relaxes itself in floods of abstractions, and idealisations, and dreams of sentimentality? Assuredly it is because the Russian is so inwardly discontented with his own actions that he is such a keen and incisive critic of everything *false* and exaggerated, that he despises all French rhetoric and German sentimentalism. And in this sense it is that the Russian's lack of will comes in to deepen his soul. He surrenders himself thereby to the universe, and, as do the Asiatics, does not let the tiny shadow of his fate, dark though it may be, shut out the universe so thoroughly from his consciousness, as does the aggressive struggling will-power of the Western man striving to let his individuality have full play. The Russian's attitude may indeed be compared to a bowl which catches and sustains what life brings it; and the Western man's to a bowl inverted to ward off what drops from the impassive skies. The mental attitude of the Russian peasant indeed implies that in blood he is nearer akin to the Asiatics than Russian ethnologists have wished to allow. Certainly in the inner life of thought, intellectually, morally, and emotionally, he is a half-way house between the Western and Eastern races, just as geographically he spreads over the two continents. By natural law his destiny calls him towards the East. Should he one day spread his rule further and further among the Asiatics and hold the keys of an immense Asiatic empire, well! future English philosophers may feel thereat a curious fatalistic satisfaction.

EDWARD GARNETT. *October 1899.*

A DESPERATE CHARACTER

I

ＷE were a party of eight in the room, and we were talking of contemporary affairs and men.

'I don't understand these men!' observed A.: 'they're such desperate fellows.... Really desperate.... There has never been anything like it before.'

'Yes, there has,' put in P., a man getting on in years, with grey hair, born some time in the twenties of this century: 'there were desperate characters in former days too, only they were not like the desperate fellows of to-day. Of the poet Yazikov some one has said that he had enthusiasm, but not applied to anything—an enthusiasm without an object. So it was with those people—their desperateness was without an object. But there, if you'll allow me, I'll tell you the story of my nephew, or rather cousin, Misha Poltyev. It may serve as an example of the desperate characters of those days.

He came into God's world, I remember, in 1828, at his father's native place and property, in one of the sleepiest corners of a sleepy province of the steppes. Misha's father, Andrei Nikolaevitch Poltyev, I remember well to this day. He was a genuine old-world landowner, a God-fearing, sedate man, fairly—for those days—well educated, just a little cracked, to tell the truth—and, moreover, he suffered from epilepsy.... That too is an old-world, gentlemanly complaint.... Andrei Nikolaevitch's fits were, however, slight, and generally ended in sleep and depression. He was good-hearted, and of an affable demeanour, not without a certain stateliness: I always pictured to myself the tsar Mihail Fedorovitch as like him. The whole life of Andrei Nikolaevitch was passed in the punctual fulfilment of every observance established from old days, in strict conformity with all the usages of the old orthodox holy Russian mode of life. He got up and went to bed, ate his meals, and went to his bath, rejoiced or was wroth (both very rarely, it is true), even smoked his pipe and played cards (two great innovations!), not after his own fancy, not in a way of his own, but according to the custom and ordinance of his fathers—with due decorum and formality. He was tall, well built, and stout; his voice was soft and rather husky, as is so often the case with virtuous people in Russia; he was scrupulously neat in his dress and linen, and wore white cravats and full-skirted snuff-coloured coats, but his noble blood was nevertheless evident; no one could have taken him for a priest's son or a merchant! At all times, on all possible occasions, and in all possible contingencies, Andrei Nikolaevitch knew without fail what ought to be done, what was to be said, and precisely what expressions were to be used; he knew when he ought to take medicine, and just what he ought to take; what omens were to be believed and what might be disregarded ... in fact, he knew everything that ought to be done.... For as everything had been provided for and laid down by one's elders, one had only to be sure not to imagine anything of one's self.... And above all, without God's blessing not a step to be taken!—It must be confessed that a deadly dulness reigned supreme in his house, in those low-pitched, warm, dark rooms, that so often resounded with the singing of liturgies and all-night services, and had the smell of incense and Lenten dishes almost always hanging about them!

Andrei Nikolaevitch—no longer in his first youth—married a young lady of a neighbouring family, without fortune, a very nervous and sickly person, who had had a boarding-school education. She played the piano fairly, spoke boarding-school French, was easily moved to enthusiasm, and still more easily to melancholy and even tears.... She was of unbalanced character, in fact. She regarded her life as wasted, could not care for her husband, who, 'of course,' did not understand her; but she respected him, ... she put up with him; and being perfectly honest and perfectly cold, she never even dreamed of another 'affection.' Besides, she was always completely engrossed in the care, first, of her own really delicate health, secondly, of the health of her husband, whose fits always inspired in her something like superstitious horror, and lastly, of her only son, Misha, whom she brought up herself with great zeal. Andrei Nikolaevitch did not oppose his wife's looking after Misha, on the one condition of his education never over-stepping the lines laid down, once and for all, within which everything must move in his house! Thus, for instance, at Christmas-time, and at New Year, and St. Vassily's eve, it was permissible for Misha to dress up and masquerade with the servant boys—and not only permissible, but even a binding duty.... But, at any other time, God forbid! and so on, and so on.

II

I remember Misha at thirteen. He was a very pretty boy, with rosy little cheeks and soft lips (indeed he was soft and plump-looking all over), with prominent liquid eyes, carefully brushed and combed, caressing and modest—a regular little girl! There was only one thing about him I did not like: he rarely laughed; but when he did laugh, his teeth—large white teeth, pointed like an animal's—showed disagreeably, and the laugh itself had an abrupt, even savage, almost animal sound, and there were unpleasant gleams in his eyes. His mother was always praising him for being so obedient and well behaved, and not caring to make friends with rude boys, but always preferring feminine society. 'A mother's darling, a milksop,' his father, Andrei Nikolaevitch, would call him; 'but he's always ready to go into the house of God.... And that I am glad to see.' Only one old neighbour, who had been a police captain, once said before me, speaking of Misha, 'Mark my words, he'll be a rebel.' And this saying, I remember, surprised me very much at the time. The old police captain, it is true, used to see rebels on all sides.

Just such an exemplary youth Misha continued to be till the eighteenth year of his age, up to the death of his parents, both of whom he lost almost on the same day. As I was all the while living constantly at Moscow, I heard nothing of my young kinsman. An acquaintance coming from his province did, it is true, inform me that Misha had sold the paternal estate for a trifling sum; but this piece of news struck me as too wildly improbable! And behold, all of a sudden, one autumn morning there flew into the courtyard of my house a carriage, with a pair of splendid trotting horses, and a coachman of monstrous size on the box; and in the carriage, wrapped in a cloak of military cut, with a beaver collar two yards deep, and with a foraging cap cocked on one side, *a la diable m'emporte*, sat ... Misha! On catching sight of me (I was standing at the drawing-room window, gazing in astonishment at the flying equipage), he laughed his abrupt laugh, and jauntily flinging back his cloak, he jumped out of the carriage and ran into the house.

'Misha! Mihail Andreevitch!' I was beginning, ... 'Is it you?'

'Call me Misha,'—he interrupted me. 'Yes, it's I, ... I, in my own person.... I have come to Moscow ... to see the world ... and show myself. And here I am, come to see you. What do you say to my horses?... Eh?' he laughed again.

Though it was seven years since I had seen Misha last, I recognised him at once. His face had remained just as youthful and as pretty as ever—there was no moustache even visible; only his cheeks looked a little swollen under his eyes, and a smell of spirits came from his lips. 'Have you been long in Moscow?' I inquired.

'I supposed you were at home in the country, looking after the place.' ...

'Eh! The country I threw up at once! As soon as my parents died—may their souls rest in peace—(Misha crossed himself scrupulously, without a shade of mockery) at once, without a moment's delay, ... *ein, zwei, drei!* ha, ha! I let it go cheap, damn it! A rascally fellow turned up. But it's no matter! Anyway, I am living as I fancy, and amusing other people. But why are you staring at me like that? Was I, really, to go dragging on in the same old round, do you suppose? ... My dear fellow, couldn't I have a glass of something?'

Misha spoke fearfully quick and hurriedly, and, at the same time, as though he were only just waked up from sleep.

'Misha, upon my word!' I wailed; 'have you no fear of God? What do you look like? What an attire! And you ask for a glass too! And to sell such a fine estate for next to nothing....'

'God I fear always, and do not forget,' he broke in.... 'But He is good, you know—God is.... He will forgive! And I am good too.... I have never yet hurt any one in my life. And drink is good too; and as for hurting,... it never hurt any one either. And my get-up is quite the most correct thing.... Uncle, would you like me to show you I can walk straight? Or to do a little dance?'

'Oh, spare me, please! A dance, indeed! You'd better sit down.'

'As to that, I'll sit down with pleasure.... But why do you say nothing of my greys? Just look at them, they're perfect lions! I've got them on hire for the time, but I shall buy them for certain, ... and the coachman too.... It's ever so much cheaper to have one's own horses. And I had the money, but I lost it yesterday at faro. It's no matter, I'll make it up to-morrow. Uncle, ... how about that little glass?'

I was still unable to get over my amazement. 'Really, Misha, how old are you? You ought not to be thinking about horses or cards, ... but going into the university or the service.'

Misha first laughed again, then gave vent to a prolonged whistle.

'Well, uncle, I see you're in a melancholy humour to-day. I'll come back another time. But I tell you what: you come in the evening to So-kolniki. I've a tent pitched there. The gypsies sing, ... such goings-on.... And there's a streamer on the tent, and on the streamer, written in large letters: "The Troupe of Poltyev's Gypsies." The streamer coils like a snake, the letters are of gold, attractive for every one to read. A free entertain-ment—whoever likes to come! ... No refusal! I'm making the dust fly in Moscow ... to my glory! ... Eh? will you come? Ah, I've one girl there ... a serpent! Black as your boot, spiteful as a dog, and eyes ... like living coals!

One can never tell what she's going to do—kiss or bite! ... Will you come, uncle? ... Well, good-bye, till we meet!'

And with a sudden embrace, and a smacking kiss on my shoulder, Misha darted away into the courtyard, and into the carriage, waved his cap over his head, hallooed,—the monstrous coachman leered at him over his beard, the greys dashed off, and all vanished!

The next day I—like a sinner—set off to Sokolniki, and did actually see the tent with the streamer and the inscription. The drapery of the tent was raised; from it came clamour, creaking, and shouting. Crowds of people were thronging round it. On a carpet spread on the ground sat gypsies, men and women, singing and beating drums, and in the midst of them, in a red silk shirt and velvet breeches, was Misha, holding a guitar, dancing a jig. 'Gentlemen! honoured friends! walk in, please! the performance is just beginning! Free to all!' he was shouting in a high, cracked voice. 'Hey! champagne! pop! a pop on the head! pop up to the ceiling! Ha! you rogue there, Paul de Kock!'

Luckily he did not see me, and I hastily made off.

I won't enlarge on my astonishment at the spectacle of this transformation. But, how was it actually possible for that quiet and modest boy to change all at once into a drunken buffoon? Could it all have been latent in him from childhood, and have come to the surface directly the yoke of his parents' control was removed? But that he had made the dust fly in Moscow, as he expressed it—of that, certainly, there could be no doubt. I have seen something of riotous living in my day; but in this there was a sort of violence, a sort of frenzy of self-destruction, a sort of desperation!

III

For two months these diversions continued.... And once more I was standing at my drawing-room window, looking into the courtyard.... All of a sudden—what could it mean? ... there came slowly stepping in at the gate a pilgrim ... a squash hat pulled down on his forehead, his hair combed out straight to right and left below it, a long gown, a leather belt ... Could it be Misha? He it was!

I went to meet him on the steps.... 'What's this masquerade for?' I demanded.

'It's not a masquerade, uncle,' Misha answered with a deep sigh: since all I had I've squandered to the last farthing—and a great repentance too has come upon me—so I have resolved to go to the Sergiev monastery of the Holy Trinity to expiate my sins in prayer. For what refuge was left me? ... And so I have come to you to say good-bye, uncle, like a prodigal son.'

I looked intently at Misha. His face was just the same, rosy and fresh (indeed it remained almost unchanged to the end), and the eyes, liquid, affectionate, and languishing—and the hands, as small and white.... But he smelt of spirits.

'Well,' I pronounced at last, 'it's a good thing to do—since there's nothing else to be done. But why is it you smell of spirits?'

'A relic of the past,' answered Misha, and he suddenly laughed, but immediately pulled himself up, and, making a straight, low bow—a monk's bow—he added: 'Won't you help me on my way? I'm going, see, on foot to the monastery....'

'When?'

'To-day ... at once.'

'Why be in such a hurry?'

'Uncle, my motto always was, "Make haste, make haste!"'

'But what is your motto now?'

'It's the same now.... Only, make haste towards *good!*'

And so Misha went off, leaving me to ponder on the vicissitudes of human destiny.

But he soon reminded me of his existence. Two months after his visit, I got a letter from him, the first of those letters, of which later on he furnished me with so abundant a supply. And note a peculiar fact: I have seldom seen a neater, more legible handwriting than that unbalanced fellow's. And the wording of his letters was exceedingly correct, just a little flowery. Invariable entreaties for assistance, always attended with resolutions to reform, vows, and promises on his honour.... All of it seemed—and perhaps was—sincere. Misha's signature to his letters was always accompanied by peculiar strokes, flourishes, and stops, and he made great use of marks of exclamation. In this first letter Misha informed me of a new 'turn in his fortune.' (Later on he used to refer to these turns as plunges, ... and frequent were the plunges he took.) He was starting for the Caucasus on active service for his tsar and his country in the capacity of a cadet! And, though a certain benevolent aunt had entered into his impecunious position, and had sent him an inconsiderable sum, still he begged me to assist him in getting his equipment. I did what he asked, and for two years I heard nothing more of him.

I must own I had the gravest doubts as to his having gone to the Caucasus. But it turned out that he really had gone there, had, by favour, got into the T—regiment as a cadet, and had been serving in it for those two years. A perfect series of legends had sprung up there about him. An officer of his regiment related them to me.

IV

I learned a great deal which I should never have expected of him.—I was, of course, hardly surprised that as a military man, as an officer, he was not a success, that he was in fact worse than useless; but what I had not anticipated was that he was by no means conspicuous for much bravery; that in battle he had a downcast, woebegone air, seemed half-depressed, half-bewildered. Discipline of every sort worried him, and made him miserable; he was daring to the point of insanity when only his *own personal* safety was in question; no bet was too mad for him to accept; but do harm to others, kill, fight, he could not, possibly because his heart was too good—or possibly because his 'cottonwool' education (so he expressed it), had made him too soft. Himself he was quite ready to murder in any way at any moment.... But others—no. 'There's no making him out,' his comrades said of him; 'he's a flabby creature, a poor stick—and yet such a desperate fellow—a perfect madman!' I chanced in later days to ask Misha what evil spirit drove him, forced him, to drink to excess, risk his life, and so on. He always had one answer—'wretchedness.'

'But why are you wretched?'

'Why! how can you ask? If one comes, anyway, to one's self, begins to feel, to think of the poverty, of the injustice, of Russia.... Well, it's all over with me! ... one's so wretched at once—one wants to put a bullet through one's head! One's forced to start drinking.'

'Why ever do you drag Russia in?'

'How can I help it? Can't be helped! That's why I'm afraid to think.'

'It all comes, and your wretchedness too, from having nothing to do.'

'But I don't know how to do anything, uncle! dear fellow! Take one's life, and stake it on a card—that I can do! Come, you tell me what I ought to do, what to risk my life for? This instant ... I'll ...'

'But you must simply live.... Why risk your life?'

'I can't! You say I act thoughtlessly.... But what else can I do? ... If one starts thinking—good God, all that comes into one's head! It's only Germans who can think! ...'

What use was it talking to him? He was a desperate man, and that's all one can say.

Of the Caucasus legends I have spoken about, I will tell you two or three. One day, in a party of officers, Misha began boasting of a sabre he had got by exchange—'a genuine Persian blade!' The officers expressed doubts as to its genuineness. Misha began disputing. 'Here then,' he cried at last; 'they say the man that knows most about sabres is Abdulka the one-eyed. I'll go to him, and ask.' The officers wondered. 'What Abdulka? Do you mean that lives in the mountains? The rebel never subdued? Abdul-khan?' 'Yes, that's him.' 'Why, but he'll take you for a spy, will put you in a hole full of bugs, or else cut your head off with your own sabre. And, besides, how are you going to get to him? They'll catch you directly.' 'I'll go to him, though, all the same.' 'Bet you won't!' 'Taken!' And Misha promptly saddled his horse and rode off to Abdulka. He disappeared for three days. All felt certain that the crazy fellow had come by his end. But, behold! he came back—drunk, and with a sabre, not the one he had taken, but another. They began questioning him. 'It was all right,' said he; 'Abdulka's a nice fellow. At first, it's true, he ordered them to put irons on my legs, and was even on the point of having me impaled. Only, I explained why I had come, and showed him the sabre. "And you'd better not keep me," said I; "don't expect a ransom for me; I've not a farthing to bless myself with—and I've no relations." Abdulka was surprised; he looked at me with his solitary eye. "Well," said he, "you are a bold one, you Russian; am I to believe you?" "You may believe me," said I; "I never tell a lie." (And this was true; Misha never lied.) Abdulka looked at me again. "And do you know how to drink wine?" "I do," said I; "give me as much as you will, I'll drink it." Abdulka was surprised again; he called on Allah. And he told his—daughter, I suppose—such a pretty creature, only with an eye like a jackal's—to bring a wine-skin. And I began to get to work on it. "But your sabre," said he, "isn't genuine; here, take the real thing. And now we are pledged friends." But you've lost your bet, gentlemen; pay up.'

The second legend of Misha is of this nature. He was passionately fond of cards; but as he had no money, and could never pay his debts at cards (though he was never a card-sharper), no one at last would sit down to a game with him. So one day he began urgently begging one of his comrades among the officers to play with him! 'But if you lose, you don't pay.' 'The money certainly I can't pay, but I'll put a shot through my left hand, see, with this pistol here!' 'But whatever use will that be to me?' 'No use, but still it will be curious.' This conversation took place after a drinking bout in the presence of witnesses. Whether it was that Misha's proposition struck the officer as really curious—anyway he agreed. Cards were brought, the game began. Misha was in luck; he won a hundred roubles. And thereupon his opponent struck his forehead with vexation. 'What an ass I am!' he cried, 'to be taken in like this! As if you'd have shot your hand if you had lost!—a likely story! hold out your purse!' 'That's a lie,' retorted Misha: 'I've won—but I'll shoot my hand.' He snatched up his pistol—and bang, fired at his own hand. The bullet passed right through it ... and in a week the wound had completely healed.

Another time, Misha was riding with his comrades along a road at night ... and they saw close to the roadside a narrow ravine like a deep cleft, dark—so dark you couldn't see the bottom. 'Look,' said one of the officers, 'Misha may be a desperate fellow, but he wouldn't leap into that ravine.' 'Yes, I'd leap in!' 'No, you wouldn't, for I dare say it's seventy feet deep, and you might break your neck.' His friend knew his weak point—vanity.... There was a great deal of it in Misha. 'But I'll leap in anyway! Would you like to bet on it? Ten roubles.' 'Good!' And the officer had hardly uttered the word, when Misha and his horse were off—into the ravine—and crashing down over the stones. All were simply petrified.... A full minute passed, and they heard Misha's voice, dimly, as it were rising up out of the bowels of the earth: 'All right! fell on the sand ... but it was a long flight! Ten roubles you've lost!'

'Climb out!' shouted his comrades. 'Climb out, I dare say!' echoed Misha. 'A likely story! I should like to see you climb out. You'll have to go for torches and ropes now. And, meanwhile, to keep up my spirits while I wait, fling down a flask....'

And so Misha had to stay five hours at the bottom of the ravine; and when they dragged him out, it turned out that his shoulder was dislocated. But that in no way troubled him. The next day a bone-setter, one of the black-smiths, set his shoulder, and he used it as though nothing had been the matter.

His health in general was marvellous, incredible. I have already mentioned that up to the time of his death he kept his almost childishly fresh complexion. Illness was a thing unknown to him, in spite of his excesses; the strength of his constitution never once showed signs of giving way. When any other man would infallibly have been seriously ill, or even have died, he merely shook himself, like a duck in the water, and was more blooming than ever. Once, also in the Caucasus ... *this* legend is really incredible, but one may judge from it what Misha was thought to be capable of.... Well, once, in the Caucasus, in a state of drunkenness, he fell down with the lower half of his body in a stream of water; his head and arms were on the bank, out of water. It was winter-time, there was a hard frost, and when he was found next morning, his legs and body were pulled out from under a thick layer of ice, which had formed over them in the night—and he didn't even catch cold! Another time—this was in Russia (near Orel, and also in a time of severe frost)—he was in a tavern outside the town in company with seven young seminarists (or theological students), and these seminarists were celebrating their final examination, but had invited Misha, as a delightful person, a man of 'inspiration,' as the phrase was then. A very great deal was drunk, and when at last the festive party got ready to depart, Misha, dead drunk, was in an unconscious condition. All the seven seminarists together had but one three-horse sledge with a high back; where were they to stow the unresisting body? Then one of the young men, inspired by classical reminiscences, proposed tying Misha by his feet to the back of the sledge, as Hector was tied to the chariot of Achilles! The proposal met with approval ... and jolting up and down over the holes, sliding sideways down the slopes, with his legs torn and flayed, and his head rolling in the snow, poor Misha travelled on his back for the mile and a half from the tavern to the town, and hadn't as much as a cough afterwards, hadn't turned a hair! Such heroic health had nature bestowed upon him!

V

From the Caucasus he came again to Moscow, in a Circassian dress, a dagger in his sash, a high-peaked cap on his head. This costume he retained to the end, though he was no longer in the army, from which he had been discharged for outstaying his leave. He stayed with me, borrowed a little money ... and forthwith began his 'plunges,' his wanderings, or, as he expressed it, 'his peregrinations from pillar to post,' then came the sudden disappearances and returns, and the showers of beautifully written letters addressed to people of every possible description, from an archbishop down to stable-boys and mid-wives! Then came calls upon persons known and unknown! And this is worth noticing: when he made these calls, he was never abject and cringing, he never worried people by begging, but on the contrary behaved with propriety, and had positively a cheerful and pleasant air, though the inveterate smell of spirits accompanied him everywhere, and his Oriental costume gradually changed into rags. 'Give, and God will reward you, though I don't deserve it,' he would say, with a bright smile and a candid blush; 'if you don't give, you'll be perfectly right, and I shan't blame you for it. I shall find food to eat, God will provide! And there are people poorer than I, and much more deserving of help—plenty, plenty!' Misha was particularly successful with women: he knew how to appeal to their sympathy. But don't suppose that he was or fancied himself a Lovelace....Oh, no! in that way he was very modest. Whether it was that he had inherited a cool temperament from his parents, or whether indeed this too is to be set down to his dislike for doing any one harm—as, according to his notions, relations with a woman meant inevitably doing a woman harm—I won't undertake to decide; only in all his behaviour with the fair sex he was extremely delicate. Women felt this, and were the more ready to sympathise with him and help him, until at last he revolted them by his drunkenness and debauchery, by the desperateness of which I have spoken already.... I can think of no other word for it.

But in other relations he had by that time lost every sort of delicacy, and was gradually sinking to the lowest depths of degradation. He once, in the public assembly at T—, got as far as setting on the table a jug with a notice: 'Any one, to whom it may seem agreeable to give the high-born nobleman Poltyev (authentic documents in proof of his pedigree are herewith exposed) a flip on the nose, may satisfy this inclination on putting a rouble into this jug.' And I am told there were persons found willing to pay for the privilege of flipping a nobleman's nose! It is true that one such person, who put in only one rouble and gave him *two* flips, he first almost strangled, and then forced to apologise; it is true, too, that part of the money gained in this fashion he promptly distributed among other poor devils ... but still, think what a disgrace!

In the course of his 'peregrinations from pillar to post,' he made his way, too, to his ancestral home, which he had sold for next to nothing to a speculator and money-lender well known in those days. The money-lender was at home, and hearing of the presence in the neighbourhood of the former owner, now reduced to vagrancy, he gave orders not to admit him into the house, and even, in case of necessity, to drive him away. Misha announced that he would not for his part consent to enter the house, polluted by the presence of so repulsive a person; that he would permit no one to drive him away, but was going to the churchyard to pay his devotions at the grave of his parents. So in fact he did.

In the churchyard he was joined by an old house-serf, who had once been his nurse. The money-lender had deprived this old man of his monthly allowance, and driven him off the estate; since then his refuge had been a corner in a peasant's hut. Misha had been too short a time in possession of his estate to have left behind him a particularly favourable memory; still the old servant could not resist running to the churchyard as soon as he heard of his young master's being there. He found Misha sitting on the ground between the tombstones, asked for his hand to kiss, as in old times, and even shed tears on seeing the rags which clothed the limbs of his once pampered young charge.

Misha gazed long and silently at the old man. 'Timofay!' he said at last; Timofay started.

'What do you desire?'

'Have you a spade?'

'I can get one.... But what do you want with a spade, Mihailo Andreitch, sir?'

'I want to dig myself a grave, Timofay, and to lie here for time everlasting between my father and mother. There's only this spot left me in the world. Get a spade!'

'Yes, sir,' said Timofay; he went and got it. And Misha began at once digging in the ground, while Timofay stood by, his chin propped in his hand, repeating: 'It's all that's left for you and me, master!'

Misha dug and dug, from time to time observing: 'Life's not worth living, is it, Timofay?'

'It's not indeed, master.'

The hole was already of a good depth. People saw what Misha was about, and ran to tell the new owner about it. The money-lender was at first very angry, wanted to send for the police: 'This is sacrilege,' said he. But afterwards, probably reflecting that it was inconvenient anyway to have to do with such a madman, and that it might lead to a scandal,—he went in his own person to the churchyard, and approaching Misha, still toiling, made him a polite bow. He went on with his digging as though he had not noticed his successor. 'Mihail Andreitch,' began the money-lender, 'allow me to ask what you are doing here?'

'You can see—I am digging myself a grave.'

'Why are you doing so?'

'Because I don't want to live any longer.'

The money-lender fairly threw up his hands in amazement. 'You don't want to live?'

Misha glanced menacingly at the money-lender. 'That surprises you? Aren't you the cause of it all? ... You? ... You? ... Wasn't it you, Judas, who robbed me, taking advantage of my childishness? Aren't you flaying the peasants' skins off their backs? Haven't you taken from this poor old man his crust of dry bread? Wasn't it you? ... O God! everywhere nothing but injustice, and oppression, and evil-doing.... Everything must go to ruin then, and me too! I don't care for life, I don't care for life in Russia!' And the spade moved faster than ever in Misha's hands.

'Here's a devil of a business!' thought the money-lender; 'he's positively burying himself alive.' 'Mihail Andreevitch,' he began again: 'listen. I've been behaving badly to you, indeed; they told me falsely of you.'

Misha went on digging.

24

'But why be desperate?'

Misha still went on digging, and kept throwing the earth at the money-lender's feet, as though to say, 'Here you are, land-grabber.'

'Really, you 're wrong in this. Won't you be pleased to come in to have some lunch, and rest a bit?'

Misha raised his head. 'So that's it now! And anything to drink?'

The money-lender was delighted. 'Why, of course ... I should think so.'

'You invite Timofay too?'

'Well, ... yes, him too.'

Misha pondered. 'Only, mind ... you made me a beggar, you know.... Don't think you can get off with one bottle!'

'Set your mind at rest ... there shall be all you can want.'

Misha got up and flung down the spade.... 'Well, Timosha,' said he to his old nurse; 'let's do honour to our host.... Come along.'

'Yes, sir,' answered the old man.

And all three started off to the house together. The money-lender knew the man he had to deal with. At the first start Misha, it is true, exacted a promise from him to 'grant all sorts of immunities' to the peasants; but an hour later, this same Misha, together with Timofay, both drunk, were dancing a galop in the big apartments, which still seemed pervaded by the God-fearing shade of Andrei Nikolaevitch; and an hour later still, Misha in a dead sleep (he had a very weak head for spirits), laid in a cart with his high cap and dagger, was being driven off to the town, more than twenty miles away, and there was flung under a hedge.... As for Timofay, who could still keep on his legs, and only hiccupped—him, of course, they kicked out of the house; since they couldn't get at the master, they had to be content with the old servant.

VI

Some time passed again, and I heard nothing of Misha.... God knows what he was doing. But one day, as I sat over the samovar at a posting-station on the T—highroad, waiting for horses, I suddenly heard under the open window of the station room a hoarse voice, uttering in French the words: 'Monsieur ... monsieur ... prenez pitie d'un pauvre gentil-homme ruine.' ... I lifted my head, glanced.... The mangy-looking fur cap, the broken ornaments on the ragged Circassian dress, the dagger in the cracked sheath, the swollen, but still rosy face, the dishevelled, but still thick crop of hair.... Mercy on us! Misha! He had come then to begging alms on the high-roads. I could not help crying out. He recognised me, started, turned away, and was about to move away from the window. I stopped him ... but what could I say to him? Give him a lecture? ... In silence I held out a five-rouble note; he, also in silence, took it in his still white and plump, though shaking and dirty hand, and vanished round the corner of the house.

It was a good while before they gave me horses, and I had time to give myself up to gloomy reflections on my unexpected meeting with Misha; I felt ashamed of having let him go so unsympathetically.

At last I set off on my way, and half a mile from the station I observed ahead of me, in the road, a crowd of people moving along with a curious, as it seemed rhythmic, step. I overtook this crowd—and what did I see?

Some dozen or so beggars, with sacks over their shoulders, were walking two by two, singing and leaping about, while in front of them danced Misha, stamping time with his feet, and shouting, 'Natchiki-tchikaldy, tchuk, tchuk, tchuk! ... Natchiki-tchikaldy, tchuk, tchuk, tchuk!' Directly my carriage caught them up, and he saw me, he began at once shouting, 'Hurrah! Stand in position! right about face, guard of the roadside!'

The beggars took up his shout, and halted; while he, with his peculiar laugh, jumped on to the carriage step, and again yelled: Hurrah!

'What's the meaning of this?' I asked with involuntary astonishment.

'This? This is my company, my army—all beggars, God's people, friends of my heart. Every one of them, thanks to you, has had a glass; and now we are all rejoicing and making merry! ... Uncle! Do you know it's only with beggars, God's people, that one can live in the world ... by God, it is!'

I made him no answer ... but at that moment he struck me as such a kind good creature, his face expressed such childlike simple-heartedness.... A light seemed suddenly as it were to dawn upon me, and I felt a pang in my heart.... 'Get into the carriage,' I said to him. He was taken aback....

'What? Into the carriage?'

'Yes, get in, get in,' I repeated; 'I want to make you a suggestion. Sit down.... Come along with me.'

'Well, as you will.' He sat down. 'Well, and you, my honoured friends, my dear comrades,' he added, addressing the beggars, 'fare-well, till we meet again.' Misha took off his high cap, and bowed low. The beggars all seemed overawed.... I told the coachman to whip up the horses, and the carriage rolled off.

The suggestion I wanted to make Misha was this: the idea suddenly occurred to me to take him with me to my home in the country, about five-and-twenty miles from that station, to rescue him, or at least to make an effort to rescue him. 'Listen, Misha,' I said; 'will you come along and live with me? ... You shall have everything provided you; you shall have clothes and linen made you; you shall be properly fitted out, and you shall have money to spend on tobacco, and so on, only on one condition, that you give up drink.... Do you agree?'

Misha was positively aghast with delight; he opened his eyes wide, flushed crimson, and suddenly falling on my shoulder, began kissing me, and repeating in a broken voice, 'Uncle ... benefactor ... God reward you.' ... He burst into tears at last, and taking off his cap fell to wiping his eyes, his nose, his lips with it.

'Mind,' I observed; 'remember the condition, not to touch strong drink.'

'Damnation to it!' he cried, with a wave of both arms, and with this impetuous movement, I was more than ever conscious of the strong smell of spirits with which he seemed always saturated.... 'Uncle, if you knew what my life has been.... If it hadn't been for sorrow, a cruel fate.... But now I swear, I swear, I will mend my ways, I will show you.... Uncle, I've never told a lie—you can ask whom you like.... I'm honest, but I'm an unlucky fellow, uncle; I've known no kindness from any one....'

Here he broke down finally into sobs. I tried to soothe him, and succeeded so far that when we reached home Misha had long been lost in a heavy sleep, with his head on my knees.

VII

He was at once assigned a room for himself, and at once, first thing, taken to the bath, which was absolutely essential. All his clothes, and his dagger and cap and torn boots, were carefully put away in a loft; he was dressed in clean linen, slippers, and some clothes of mine, which, as is always the way with poor relations, at once seemed to adapt themselves to his size and figure. When he came to table, washed, clean, and fresh, he seemed so touched and happy, he beamed all over with such joyful gratitude, that I too felt moved and joyful.... His face was completely transformed.... Boys of twelve have faces like that on Easter Sundays, after the communion, when, thickly pomaded, in new jacket and starched collars, they come to exchange Easter greetings with their parents. Misha was continually— with a sort of cautious incredulity—feeling himself and repeating: 'What does it mean? ... Am I in heaven?' The next day he announced that he had not slept all night, he had been in such ecstasy.

I had living in my house at that time an old aunt with her niece; both of them were extremely disturbed when they heard of Misha's presence; they could not comprehend how I could have asked him into my house! There were very ugly rumours about him. But in the first place, I knew he was always very courteous with ladies; and, secondly, I counted on his promises of amendment. And, in fact, for the first two days of his stay under my roof Misha not merely justified my expectations but surpassed them, while the ladies of the household were simply enchanted with him. He played piquet with the old lady, helped her to wind her worsted, showed her two new games of patience; for the niece, who had a small voice, he played accompaniments on the piano, and read Russian and French poetry. He told both the ladies lively but discreet anecdotes; in fact, he showed them every attention, so that they repeatedly expressed their surprise to me, and the old lady even observed how unjust people sometimes were.... The things—the things they had said of him ... and he such a quiet fellow, and so polite ... poor Misha! It is true that at table 'poor Misha' licked his lips in a rather peculiar, hurried way, if he simply glanced at the bottle. But I had only to shake my finger at him, and he would turn his eyes upwards, and lay his hand on his heart ... as if to say, I have sworn.... 'I am regenerated now,' he assured me.... 'Well, God grant it be so,' was my thought.... But this regeneration did not last long.

The first two days he was very talkative and cheerful. But even on the third day he seemed somehow subdued, though he remained, as before, with the ladies and tried to entertain them. A half mournful, half dreamy expression flitted now and then over his face, and the face itself was paler and looked thinner. 'Are you unwell?' I asked him.

'Yes,' he answered; 'my head aches a little.' On the fourth day he was completely silent; for the most part he sat in a corner, hanging his head disconsolately, and his dejected appearance worked upon the compassionate sympathies of the two ladies, who now, in their turn, tried to amuse him. At table he ate nothing, stared at his plate, and rolled up pellets of bread. On the fifth day the feeling of compassion in the ladies began to be replaced by other emotions—uneasiness and even alarm. Misha was so strange, he held aloof from people, and kept moving along close to the walls, as though trying to steal by unnoticed, and suddenly looking round as though some one had called him. And what had become of his rosy colour? It seemed covered over by a layer of earth. 'Are you still unwell?' I asked him.

'No, I'm all right,' he answered abruptly.

'Are you dull?'

'Why should I be dull?' But he turned away and would not look me in the face.

28

'Or is it that wretchedness come over you again?' To this he made no reply. So passed another twenty-four hours.

Next day my aunt ran into my room in a state of great excitement, declaring that she would leave the house with her niece, if Misha was to remain in it.

'Why so?'

'Why, we are dreadfully scared with him.... He's not a man, he's a wolf,—nothing better than a wolf. He keeps moving and moving about, and doesn't speak—and looks so wild.... He almost gnashes his teeth at me. My Katia, you know, is so nervous.... She was so struck with him the first day.... I'm in terror for her, and indeed for myself too.' ... I didn't know what to say to my aunt. I couldn't, anyway, turn Misha out, after inviting him.

He relieved me himself from my difficult position. The same day,—I was still sitting in my own room,—suddenly I heard behind me a husky and angry voice: 'Nikolai Nikolaitch, Nikolai Nikolaitch!' I looked round; Misha was standing in the doorway with a face that was fearful, black-looking and distorted. 'Nikolai Nikolaitch!' he repeated ... (not 'uncle' now).

'What do you want?'

'Let me go ... at once!'

'Why?'

'Let me go, or I shall do mischief, I shall set the house on fire or cut some one's throat.' Misha suddenly began trembling. 'Tell them to give me back my clothes, and let a cart take me to the highroad, and let me have some money, however little!'

'Are you displeased, then, at anything?'

'I can't live like this!' he shrieked at the top of his voice. 'I can't live in your respectable, thrice-accursed house! It makes me sick, and ashamed to live so quietly! ... How *you* manage to endure it!'

'That is,' I interrupted in my turn, 'you mean—you can't live without drink....'

'Well, yes! yes!' he shrieked again: 'only let me go to my brethren, my friends, to the beggars! ... Away from your respectable, loathsome species!'

I was about to remind him of his sworn promises, but Misha's frenzied look, his breaking voice, the convulsive tremor in his limbs,—it was all so awful, that I made haste to get rid of him; I said that his clothes should be given him at once, and a cart got ready; and taking a note for twenty-five roubles out of a drawer, I laid it on the table. Misha had begun to advance in a menacing way towards me,—but on this, suddenly he stopped, his face worked, flushed, he struck himself on the breast, the tears rushed from his eyes, and muttering, 'Uncle! angel! I know I'm a ruined man! thanks! thanks!' he snatched up the note and ran away.

An hour later he was sitting in the cart dressed once more in his Circassian costume, again rosy and cheerful; and when the horses started, he yelled, tore off the peaked cap, and, waving it over his head, made bow after bow. Just as he was going off, he had given me a long and warm embrace, and whispered, 'Benefactor, benefactor ... there's no saving me!' He even ran to the ladies and kissed their hands, fell on his knees, called upon God, and begged their forgiveness! Katia I found afterwards in tears.

The coachman, with whom Misha had set off, on coming home informed me that he had driven him to the first tavern on the highroad—and that there 'his honour had stuck,' had begun treating every one indiscriminately—and had quickly sunk into unconsciousness. From that day I never came across Misha again, but his ultimate fate I learned in the following manner.

VIII

Three years later, I was again at home in the country; all of a sudden a servant came in and announced that Madame Poltyev was asking to see me. I knew no Madame Poltyev, and the servant, who made this announcement, for some unknown reason smiled sarcastically. To my glance of inquiry, he responded that the lady asking for me was young, poorly dressed, and had come in a peasant's cart with one horse, which she was driving herself! I told him to ask Madame Poltyev up to my room.

I saw a woman of five-and-twenty, in the dress of the small tradesman class, with a large kerchief on her head. Her face was simple, roundish, not without charm; she looked dejected and gloomy, and was shy and awkward in her movements.

'You are Madame Poltyev?' I inquired, and I asked her to sit down.

'Yes,' she answered in a subdued voice, and she did not sit down. 'I am the widow of your nephew, Mihail Andreevitch Poltyev.'

'Is Mihail Andreevitch dead? Has he been dead long? But sit down, I beg.'
She sank into a chair.

'It's two months.'

'And had you been married to him long?'

'I had been a year with him.'

'Where have you come from now?'

'From out Tula way.... There's a village there, Znamenskoe-Glushkovo—perhaps you may know it. I am the daughter of the deacon there.

Mihail Andreitch and I lived there.... He lived in my father's house. We were a whole year together.'

The young woman's lips twitched a little, and she put her hand up to them. She seemed to be on the point of tears, but she controlled herself, and cleared her throat.

'Mihail Andreitch,' she went on: 'before his death enjoined upon me to go to you; "You must be sure to go," said he! And he told me to thank you for all your goodness, and to give you ... this ... see, this little thing (she took a small packet out of her pocket) which he always had about him.... And Mihail Andreitch said, if you would be pleased to accept it in memory of him, if you would not disdain it.... "There's nothing else," said he, "I can give him" ... that is, you....'

In the packet there was a little silver cup with the monogram of Misha's mother. This cup I had often seen in Misha's hands, and once he had even said to me, speaking of some poor fellow, that he really was destitute, since he had neither cup nor bowl, 'while I, see, have this anyway.'

I thanked her, took the cup, and asked:

'Of what complaint had Misha died? No doubt....'

Then I bit my tongue ... but the young woman understood my unuttered hint.... She took a swift glance at me, then looked down again, smiled mournfully, and said at once: 'Oh no! he had quite given that up, ever since he got to know me ... But he had no health at all! ... It was shattered quite. As soon as he gave up drink, he fell into ill health directly. He became so steady; he always wanted to help father in his land or in the garden, ... or any other work there might be ... in spite of his being of noble birth. But how could he get the strength? ... At writing, too, he tried to work; as you know, he could do that work capitally, but his hands shook, and he couldn't hold the pen properly. ... He was always finding fault with himself; "I'm a white-handed poor creature," he would say; "I've never done any good to anybody, never helped, never laboured!" He worried himself very much about that.... He used to say that our people labour,—but what use are we? ... Ah, Nikolai Nikolaitch, he was a good man—and he was fond of me ... and I... Ah, pardon me....'

Here the young woman wept outright. I would have consoled her, but I did not know how.

'Have you a child left you?' I asked at last.

She sighed. 'No, no child.... Is it likely?' And her tears flowed faster than ever.

'And so that was how Misha's troubled wanderings had ended,' the old man P. wound up his narrative. 'You will agree with me, I am sure, that I'm right in calling him a desperate character; but you will most likely agree too that he was not like the desperate characters of to-day; still, a philosopher, you must admit, would find a family likeness between him and them. In him and in them there's the thirst for self-destruction, the wretchedness, the dissatisfaction.... And what it all comes from, I leave the philosopher to decide.'

BOUGIVALLE, *November 1881.*

A STRANGE STORY

Fifteen years ago—began H.—official duties compelled me to spend a few days in the principal town of the province of T—. I stopped at a very fair hotel, which had been established six months before my arrival by a Jewish tailor, who had grown rich. I am told that it did not flourish long, which is often the case with us; but I found it still in its full splendour: the new furniture emitted cracks like pistol-shots at night; the bed-linen, table-cloths, and napkins smelt of soap, and the painted floors reeked of olive oil, which, however, in the opinion of the waiter, an exceedingly elegant but not very clean individual, tended to prevent the spread of insects. This waiter, a former valet of Prince G.'s, was conspicuous for his free-and-easy manners and his self-assurance. He invariably wore a second-hand frockcoat and slippers trodden down at heel, carried a table-napkin under his arm, and had a multitude of pimples on his cheeks. With a free sweeping movement of his moist hands he gave utterance to brief but pregnant observations. He showed a patronising interest in me, as a person capable of appreciating his culture and knowledge of the world; but he regarded his own lot in life with a rather disillusioned eye. 'No doubt about it,' he said to me one day; 'ours is a poor sort of position nowadays. May be sent flying any day!' His name was Ardalion.

I had to make a few visits to official persons in the town. Ardalion procured me a coach and groom, both alike shabby and loose in the joints; but the groom wore livery, the carriage was adorned with an heraldic crest. After making all my official calls, I drove to see a country gentleman, an old friend of my father's, who had been a long time settled in the town.... I had not met him for twenty years; he had had time to get married, to bring up a good-sized family, to be left a widower and to make his fortune. His business was with government monopolies, that is to say, he lent contractors for monopolies loans at heavy interest.... 'There is always honour in risk,' they say, though indeed the risk was small.

In the course of our conversation there came into the room with hesitating steps, but as lightly as though on tiptoe, a young girl of about seventeen, delicate-looking and thin. 'Here,' said my acquaintance, 'is my eldest daughter Sophia; let me introduce you. She takes my poor wife's place, looks after the house, and takes care of her brothers and sisters.' I bowed a second time to the girl who had come in (she meanwhile dropped into a chair without speaking), and thought to myself that she did not look much like housekeeping or looking after children. Her face was quite childish, round, with small, pleasing, but immobile features; the blue eyes, under high, also immobile and irregular eyebrows, had an intent, almost astonished look, as though they had just observed something unexpected; the full little mouth with the lifted upper lip, not only did not smile, but seemed as though altogether innocent of such a practice; the rosy flush under the tender skin stood in soft, diffused patches on the cheeks, and neither paled nor deepened. The fluffy, fair hair hung in light clusters each side of the little head. Her bosom breathed softly, and her arms were pressed somehow awkwardly and severely against her narrow waist. Her blue gown fell without folds—like a child's—to her little feet. The general impression this girl made upon me was not one of morbidity, but of something enigmatical. I saw before me not simply a shy, provincial miss, but a creature of a special type—that I could not make out. This type neither attracted nor repelled me; I did not fully understand it, and only felt that I had never come across a nature more sincere. Pity ... yes! pity was the feeling that rose up within me at the sight of this young, serious, keenly alert life—God knows why! 'Not of this earth,' was my thought, though there was nothing exactly 'ideal' in the expression of the face, and though Mademoiselle Sophie had obviously come into the drawing-room in fulfilment of those duties of lady of the house to which her father had referred.

He began to talk of life in the town of T—, of the social amusements and advantages it offered. 'We're very quiet here,' he observed; 'the governor's a melancholy fellow; the marshal of the province is a bachelor. But there'll be a big ball in the Hall of the Nobility the day after to-morrow. I advise you to go; there are some pretty girls here. And you'll see all our *intelligentsi* too.'

My acquaintance, as a man of university education, was fond of using learned expressions. He pronounced them with irony, but also with respect. Besides, we all know that moneylending, together with respectability, develops a certain thoughtfulness in men.

'Allow me to ask, will you be at the ball?' I said, turning to my friend's daughter. I wanted to hear the sound of her voice.

'Papa intends to go,' she answered, 'and I with him.'

Her voice turned out to be soft and deliberate, and she articulated every syllable fully, as though she were puzzled.

'In that case, allow me to ask you for the first quadrille.'

She bent her head in token of assent, and even then did not smile.

I soon withdrew, and I remember the expression in her eyes, fixed steadily upon me, struck me as so strange that I involuntarily looked over my shoulder to see whether there were not some one or some thing she was looking at behind my back.

I returned to the hotel, and after dining on the never-varied 'soupe-julienne,' cutlets, and green peas, and grouse cooked to a dry, black chip, I sat down on the sofa and gave myself up to reflection. The subject of my meditations was Sophia, this enigmatical daughter of my old acquaintance; but Ardalion, who was clearing the table, explained my thoughtfulness in his own way; he set it down to boredom.

'There is very little in the way of entertainment for visitors in our town,' he began with his usual easy condescension, while he went on at the same time flapping the backs of the chairs with a dirty dinner-napkin—a practice peculiar, as you're doubtless aware, to servants of superior education. 'Very little!'

He paused, and the huge clock on the wall, with a lilac rose on its white face, seemed in its monotonous, sleepy tick, to repeat his words: 'Ve-ry! ve-ry!' it ticked. 'No concerts, nor theatres,' pursued Ardalion (he had travelled abroad with his master, and had all but stayed in Paris; he knew much better than to mispronounce this last word, as the peasants do)—'nor dances, for example; nor evening receptions among the nobility and gentry—there is nothing of the kind whatever.' (He paused a moment, probably to allow me to observe the choiceness of his diction.) 'They positively visit each other but seldom. Every one sits like a pigeon on its perch. And so it comes to pass that visitors have simply nowhere to go.'

Ardalion stole a sidelong glance at me.

'But there is one thing,' he went on, speaking with a drawl, 'in case you should feel that way inclined....'

He glanced at me a second time and positively leered, but I suppose did not observe signs of the requisite inclination in me.

The polished waiter moved towards the door, pondered a moment, came back, and after fidgeting about uneasily a little, bent down to my ear, and with a playful smile said:

'Would you not like to behold the dead?'

I stared at him in perplexity.

'Yes,' he went on, speaking in a whisper; 'there is a man like that here. He's a simple artisan, and can't even read and write, but he does marvellous things. If you, for example, go to him and desire to see any one of your departed friends, he will be sure to show him you.'

'How does he do it?'

'That's his secret. For though he's an uneducated man—to speak bluntly, illiterate—he's very great in godliness! Greatly respected he is among the merchant gentry!'

'And does every one in the town know about this?'

'Those who need to know; but, there, of course—there's danger from the police to be guarded against. Because, say what you will, such doings are forbidden anyway, and for the common people are a temptation; the common people—the mob, we all know, quickly come to blows.'

'Has he shown you the dead?' I asked Ardalion.

Ardalion nodded. 'He has; my father he brought before me as if living.'

I stared at Ardalion. He laughed and played with his dinner-napkin, and condescendingly, but unflinchingly, looked at me.

'But this is very curious!' I cried at last. 'Couldn't I make the acquaintance of this artisan?'

'You can't go straight to him; but one can act through his mother. She's a respectable old woman; she sells pickled apples on the bridge. If you wish it, I will ask her.'

'Please do.'

Ardalion coughed behind his hand. 'And a gratuity, whatever you think fit, nothing much, of course, should also be handed to her—the old lady. And I on my side will make her understand that she has nothing to fear from you, as you are a visitor here, a gentleman—and of course you can understand that this is a secret, and will not in any case get her into any unpleasantness.'

Ardalion took the tray in one hand, and with a graceful swing of the tray and his own person, turned towards the door.

'So I may reckon upon you!' I shouted after him.

'You may trust me!' I heard his self-satisfied voice say: 'We'll talk to the old woman and transmit you her answer exactly.'

I will not enlarge on the train of thought aroused in me by the extraordinary fact Ardalion had related; but I am prepared to admit that I awaited the promised reply with impatience. Late in the evening Ardalion came to me and announced that to his annoyance he could not find the old woman. I handed him, however, by way of encouragement, a three-rouble note. The next morning he appeared again in my room with a beaming countenance; the old woman had consented to see me.

'Hi! boy!' shouted Ardalion in the corridor; 'Hi! apprentice! Come here!' A boy of six came up, grimed all over with soot like a kitten, with a shaved head, perfectly bald in places, in a torn, striped smock, and huge goloshes on his bare feet. 'You take the gentleman, you know where,' said Ardalion, addressing the 'apprentice,' and pointing to me. 'And you, sir, when you arrive, ask for Mastridia Karpovna.'

The boy uttered a hoarse grunt, and we set off.

We walked rather a long while about the unpaved streets of the town of T—; at last in one of them, almost the most deserted and desolate of all, my guide stopped before an old two-story wooden house, and wiping his nose all over his smock-sleeve, said: 'Here; go to the right.' I passed through the porch into the outer passage, stumbled towards my right, a low door creaked on rusty hinges, and I saw before me a stout old woman in a brown jacket lined with hare-skin, with a parti-coloured kerchief on her head.

'Mastridia Karpovna?' I inquired.

'The same, at your service,' the old woman replied in a piping voice. 'Please walk in. Won't you take a chair?'

The room into which the old woman conducted me was so littered up with every sort of rubbish, rags, pillows, feather-beds, sacks, that one could hardly turn round in it. The sunlight barely struggled in through two dusty little windows; in one corner, from behind a heap of boxes piled on one another, there came a feeble whimpering and wailing.... I could not tell from what; perhaps a sick baby, or perhaps a puppy. I sat down on a chair, and the old woman stood up directly facing me. Her face was yellow, half-transparent like wax; her lips were so fallen in that they formed a single straight line in the midst of a multitude of wrinkles; a tuft of white hair stuck out from below the kerchief on her head, but the sunken grey eyes peered out alertly and cleverly from under the bony overhanging brow; and the sharp nose fairly stuck out like a spindle, fairly sniffed the air as if it would say: I'm a smart one! 'Well, you're no fool!' was my thought. At the same time she smelt of spirits.

I explained to her the object of my visit, of which, however, as I observed, she must be aware. She listened to me, blinked her eyes rapidly, and only lifted her nose till it stuck out still more sharply, as though she were making ready to peck.

'To be sure, to be sure,' she said at last; 'Ardalion Matveitch did say something, certainly; my son Vassinka's art you were wanting.... But we can't be sure, my dear sir....'

'Oh, why so?' I interposed. 'As far as I'm concerned, you may feel perfectly easy.... I'm not an informer.'

'Oh, mercy on us,' the old woman caught me up hurriedly, 'what do you mean? Could we dare to suppose such a thing of your honour! And on what ground could one inform against us? Do you suppose it's some sinful contrivance of ours? No, sir, my son's not the one to lend himself to anything wicked ... or give way to any sort of witchcraft.... God forbid indeed, holy Mother of Heaven! (The old woman crossed herself three times.) He's the foremost in prayer and fasting in the whole province; the foremost, your honour, he is! And that's just it: great grace has been vouchsafed to him. Yes, indeed. It's not the work of his hands. It's from on high, my dear; so it is.'

'So you agree?' I asked: 'when can I see your son?'

The old woman blinked again and shifted her rolled up handkerchief from one sleeve to the other.

'Oh, well, sir—well, sir, I can't say.'

'Allow me, Mastridia Karpovna, to hand you this,' I interrupted, and I gave her a ten-rouble note.

The old woman clutched it at once in her fat, crooked fingers, which recalled the fleshy claws of an owl, quickly slipped it into her sleeve, pondered a little, and as though she had suddenly reached a decision, slapped her thighs with her open hand.

'Come here this evening a little after seven,' she said, not in her previous voice, but in quite a different one, more solemn and subdued; 'only not to this room, but kindly go straight up to the floor above, and you'll find a door to your left, and you open that door; and you'll go, your honour, into an empty room, and in that room you'll see a chair. Sit you down on that chair and wait; and whatever you see, don't utter a word and don't do anything; and please don't speak to my son either; for he's but young yet, and he suffers from fits. He's very easily scared; he'll tremble and shake like any chicken ... a sad thing it is!'

I looked at Mastridia. 'You say he's young, but since he's your son ...'

'In the spirit, sir, in the spirit. Many's the orphan I have under my care!' she added, wagging her head in the direction of the corner, from which came the plaintive whimper. 'O—O God Almighty, holy Mother of God! And do you, your honour, before you come here, think well which of your deceased relations or friends—the kingdom of Heaven to them!—you're desirous of seeing. Go over your deceased friends, and whichever you select, keep him in your mind, keep him all the while till my son comes!'

'Why, mustn't I tell your son whom ...'

'Nay, nay, sir, not one word. He will find out what he needs in your thoughts himself. You've only to keep your friend thoroughly in mind; and at your dinner drink a drop of wine—just two or three glasses; wine never comes amiss.' The old woman laughed, licked her lips, passed her hand over her mouth, and sighed.

'So at half-past seven?' I queried, getting up from my chair.

'At half-past seven, your honour, at half-past seven,' Mastridia Karpovna replied reassuringly.

I took leave of the old woman and went back to the hotel. I did not doubt that they were going to make a fool of me, but in what way?—that was what excited my curiosity. With Ardalion I did not exchange more than two or three words. 'Did she see you?' he asked me, knitting his brow, and on my affirmative reply, he exclaimed: 'The old woman's as good as any statesman!' I set to work, in accordance with the 'statesman's' counsel, to run over my deceased friends.

After rather prolonged hesitation I fixed, at last, on an old man who had long been dead, a Frenchman, once my tutor. I selected him not because he had any special attraction for me; but his whole figure was so original, so unlike any figure of to-day, that it would be utterly impossible to imitate it. He had an enormous head, fluffy white hair combed straight back, thick black eyebrows, a hawk nose, and two large warts of a pinkish hue in the middle of the forehead; he used to wear a green frockcoat with smooth brass buttons, a striped waistcoat with a stand-up collar, a jabot and lace cuffs. 'If he shows me my old Dessaire,' I thought, 'well, I shall have to admit that he's a sorcerer!'

At dinner I followed the old dame's behest and drank a bottle of Lafitte, of the first quality, so Ardalion averred, though it had a very strong flavour of burnt cork, and a thick sediment at the bottom of each glass.

Exactly at half-past seven I stood in front of the house where I had conversed with the worthy Mastridia Karpovna. All the shutters of the windows were closed, but the door was open. I went into the house, mounted the shaky staircase to the first story, and opening a door on the left, found myself, as the old woman had said, in a perfectly empty, rather large room; a tallow candle set in the window-sill threw a dim light over the room; against the wall opposite the door stood a wicker-bottomed chair. I snuffed the candle, which had already burnt down enough to form a long smouldering wick, sat down on the chair and began to wait.

The first ten minutes passed rather quickly; in the room itself there was absolutely nothing which could distract my attention, but I listened intently to every rustle, looked intently at the closed door.... My heart was throbbing. After the first ten minutes followed another ten minutes, then half an hour, three-quarters of an hour, and not a stir of any kind around! I coughed several times to make my presence known; I began to feel bored and out of temper; to be made a fool of in just that way had not entered into my calculations. I was on the point of getting up from my seat, taking the candle from the window, and going downstairs.... I looked at it; the wick again wanted snuffing; but as I turned my eyes from the window to the door, I could not help starting; with his back leaning against the door stood a man. He had entered so quickly and noiselessly that I had heard nothing. He wore a simple blue smock; he was of middle height and rather thick-set. With his hands behind his back and his head bent, he was staring at me. In the dim light of the candle I could not distinctly make out his features. I saw nothing but a shaggy mane of matted hair falling on his forehead, and thick, rather drawn lips and whitish eyes. I was nearly speaking to him, but I recollected Mastridia's injunction, and bit my lips. The man, who had come in, continued to gaze at me, and, strange to say, at the same time I felt something like fear, and, as though at the word of command, promptly started thinking of my old tutor. *He* still stood at the door and breathed heavily, as though he had been climbing a mountain or lifting a weight, while his eyes seemed to expand, seemed to come closer to me—and I felt uncomfortable under their obstinate, heavy, menacing stare; at times those eyes glowed with a malignant inward fire, a fire such as I have seen in the eyes of a pointer dog when it 'points' at a hare; and, like a pointer dog, *he* kept *his* eyes intently following mine when I 'tried to double,' that is, tried to turn my eyes away.

So passed I do not know how long—perhaps a minute, perhaps a quarter of an hour. He still gazed at me; I still experienced a certain discomfort and alarm and still thought of the Frenchman. Twice I tried to say to myself, 'What nonsense! what a farce!' I tried to smile, to shrug my shoulders.... It was no use! All initiative had all at once 'frozen up' within me—I can find no other word for it. I was overcome by a sort of numbness. Suddenly I noticed that he had left the door, and was standing a step or two nearer to me; then he gave a slight bound, both feet together, and stood closer still.... Then again ... and again; while the menacing eyes were simply fastened on my whole face, and the hands remained behind, and the broad chest heaved painfully. These leaps struck me as ridiculous, but I felt dread too, and what I could not understand at all, a drowsiness began suddenly to come upon me. My eyelids clung together ... the shaggy figure with the whitish eyes in the blue smock seemed double before me, and suddenly vanished altogether! ... I shook myself; he was again standing between the door and me, but now much nearer.... Then he vanished again—a sort of mist seemed to fall upon him; again he appeared ... vanished again ... appeared again, and always closer, closer ... his hard, almost gasping breathing floated across to me now.... Again the mist fell, and all of a sudden out of this mist the head of old Dessaire began to take distinct shape, beginning with the white, brushed-back hair! Yes: there were his warts, his black eyebrows, his hook nose! There too his green coat with the brass buttons, the striped waistcoat and jabot.... I shrieked, I got up.... The old man vanished, and in his place I saw again the man in the blue smock. He moved staggering to the wall, leaned his head and both arms against it, and heaving like an over-loaded horse, in a husky voice said, 'Tea!' Mastridia Karpovna—how she came there I can't say—flew to him and saying: 'Vassinka! Vassinka!' began anxiously wiping away the sweat, which simply trickled from his face and hair. I was on the point of approaching her, but she, so insistently, in such a heart-rending voice cried: 'Your honour! merciful sir! have pity on us, go away, for Christ's sake!' that I obeyed, while she turned again to her son. 'Bread-winner, darling,' she murmured soothingly: 'you shall have tea directly, directly. And you too, sir, had better take a cup of tea at home!' she shouted after me.

When I got home I obeyed Mastridia and ordered some tea; I felt tired—even weak. 'Well?' Ardalion questioned me, 'have you been? did you see something?'

'He did, certainly, show me something ... which, I'll own, I had not anticipated,' I replied.

'He's a man of marvellous power,' observed Ardalion, carrying off the samovar; 'he is held in high esteem among the merchant gentry.' As I went to bed, and reflected on the incident that had occurred to me, I fancied at last that I had reached some explanation of it. The man doubtless possessed a considerable magnetic power; acting by some means, which I did not understand of course, upon my nerves, he had evoked within me so vividly, so definitely, the image of the old man of whom I was thinking, that at last I fancied that I saw him before my eyes.... Such 'metastases,' such transferences of sensation, are recognised by science. It was all very well; but the force capable of producing such effects still remained, something marvellous and mysterious. 'Say what you will,' I thought, 'I've seen, seen with my own eyes, my dead tutor!'

The next day the ball in the Hall of Nobility took place. Sophia's father called on me and reminded me of the engagement I had made with his daughter. At ten o'clock I was standing by her side in the middle of a ballroom lighted up by a number of copper lamps, and was preparing to execute the not very complicated steps of the French quadrille to the resounding blare of the military band. Crowds of people were there; the ladies were especially numerous and very pretty; but the first place among them would certainly have been given to my partner, if it had not been for the rather strange, even rather wild look in her eyes. I noticed that she hardly ever blinked; the unmistakable expression of sincerity in her eyes did not make up for what was extraordinary in them. But she had a charming figure, and moved gracefully, though with constraint. When she waltzed, and, throwing herself a little back, bent her slender neck towards her right shoulder, as though she wanted to get away from her partner, nothing more touchingly youthful and pure could be imagined. She was all in white, with a turquoise cross on a black ribbon.

I asked her for a mazurka, and tried to talk to her. But her answers were few and reluctant, though she listened attentively, with the same expression of dreamy absorption which had struck me when I first met her. Not the slightest trace of desire to please, at her age, with her appearance, and the absence of a smile, and those eyes, continually fixed directly upon the eyes of the person speaking to her, though they seemed at the same time to see something else, to be absorbed with something different.... What a strange creature! Not knowing, at last, how to thaw her, I bethought me of telling her of my adventure of the previous day.

She heard me to the end with evident interest, but was not, as I had expected, surprised at what I told her, and merely asked whether he was not called Vassily. I recollected that the old woman had called him 'Vassinka.' 'Yes, his name is Vassily,' I answered; 'do you know him?'

'There is a saintly man living here called Vassily,' she observed; 'I wondered whether it was he.'

'Saintliness has nothing to do with this,' I remarked; 'it's simply the action of magnetism—a fact of interest for doctors and students of science.'

I proceeded to expound my views on the peculiar force called magnetism, on the possibility of one man's will being brought under the influence of another's will, and so on; but my explanations—which were, it is true, somewhat confused—seemed to make no impression on her. Sophie listened, dropping her clasped hands on her knees with a fan lying motionless in them; she did not play with it, she did not move her fingers at all, and I felt that all my words rebounded from her as from a statue of stone. She heard them, but clearly she had her own convictions, which nothing could shake or uproot.

'You can hardly admit miracles!' I cried.

'Of course I admit them,' she answered calmly. 'And how can one help admitting them? Are not we told in the gospel that who has but a grain of faith as big as a mustard seed, he can remove mountains? One need only have faith—there will be miracles!'

'It seems there is very little faith nowadays,' I observed; 'anyway, one doesn't hear of miracles.'

'But yet there are miracles; you have seen one yourself. No; faith is not dead nowadays; and the beginning of faith ...'

'The fear of God is the beginning of wisdom,' I interrupted.

'The beginning of faith,' pursued Sophie, nothing daunted, 'is self-abasement ... humiliation.'

'Humiliation even?' I queried.

'Yes. The pride of man, haughtiness, presumption—that is what must be utterly rooted up. You spoke of the will—that's what must be broken.'

I scanned the whole figure of the young girl who was uttering such sentences.... 'My word, the child's in earnest, too,' was my thought. I glanced at our neighbours in the mazurka; they, too, glanced at me, and I fancied that my astonishment amused them; one of them even smiled at me sympathetically, as though he would say: 'Well, what do you think of our queer young lady? every one here knows what she's like.'

'Have you tried to break your will?' I said, turning to Sophie again.

'Every one is bound to do what he thinks right,' she answered in a dogmatic tone. 'Let me ask you,' I began, after a brief silence, 'do you believe in the possibility of calling up the dead?'

Sophie softly shook her head.

'There are no dead.'

'What?'

'There are no dead souls; they are undying and can always appear, when they like.... They are always about us.'

'What? Do you suppose, for instance, that an immortal soul may be at this moment hovering about that garrison major with the red nose?'

'Why not? The sunlight falls on him and his nose, and is not the sunlight, all light, from God? And what does external appearance matter? To the pure all things are pure! Only to find a teacher, to find a leader!'

'But excuse me, excuse me,' I put in, not, I must own, without malicious intent. 'You want a leader ... but what is your priest for?'

Sophie looked coldly at me.

'You mean to laugh at me, I suppose. My priestly father tells me what I ought to do; but what I want is a leader who would show me himself in action how to sacrifice one's self!'

She raised her eyes towards the ceiling. With her childlike face, and that expression of immobile absorption, of secret, continual perplexity, she reminded me of the pre-raphaelite Madonnas....

'I have read somewhere,' she went on, not turning to me, and hardly moving her lips, 'of a grand person who directed that he should be buried under a church porch so that all the people who came in should tread him under foot and trample on him.... That is what one ought to do in life.'

Boom! boom! tra-ra-ra! thundered the drums from the band.... I must own such a conversation at a ball struck me as eccentric in the extreme; the ideas involuntarily kindled within me were of a nature anything but religious. I took advantage of my partner's being invited to one of the figures of the mazurka to avoid renewing our quasi-theological discussion.

A quarter of an hour later I conducted Mademoiselle Sophie to her father, and two days after I left the town of T—, and the image of the girl with the childlike face and the soul impenetrable as stone slipped quickly out of my memory.

Two years passed, and it chanced that that image was recalled again to me. It was like this: I was talking to a colleague who had just returned from a tour in South Russia. He had spent some time in the town of T—, and told me various items of news about the neighbourhood. 'By the way!' he exclaimed, 'you knew V. G. B. very well, I fancy, didn't you?'

'Of course I know him.'

'And his daughter Sophia, do you know her?'

'I've seen her twice.'

'Only fancy, she's run away!'

'How's that?'

'Well, I don't know. Three months ago she disappeared, and nothing's been heard of her. And the astonishing thing is no one can make out whom she's run off with. Fancy, they've not the slightest idea, not the smallest suspicion! She'd refused all the offers made her, and she was most proper in her behaviour. Ah, these quiet, religious girls are the ones! It's made an awful scandal all over the province! B.'s in despair.... And whatever need had she to run away? Her father carried out her wishes in everything. And what's so unaccountable, all the Lovelaces of the province are there all right, not one's missing.'

'And they've not found her up till now?'

'I tell you she might as well be at the bottom of the sea! It's one rich heiress less in the world, that's the worst of it.'

This piece of news greatly astonished me. It did not seem at all in keeping with the recollection I had of Sophia B. But there! anything may happen.

In the autumn of the same year fate brought me—again on official business—into the S—province, which is, as every one knows, next to the province of T—. It was cold and rainy weather; the worn-out posting-horses could scarcely drag my light trap through the black slush of the highroad. One day, I remember, was particularly unlucky: three times we got 'stuck' in the mud up to the axles of the wheels; my driver was continually giving up one rut and with moans and grunts trudging across to the other, and finding things no better with that. In fact, towards evening I was so exhausted that on reaching the posting-station I decided to spend the night at the inn. I was given a room with a broken-down wooden sofa, a sloping floor, and torn paper on the walls; there was a smell in it of kvas, bast-mats, onions, and even turpentine, and swarms of flies were on everything; but at any rate I could find shelter there from the weather, and the rain had set in, as they say, for the whole day. I ordered a samovar to be brought, and, sitting on the sofa, settled down to those cheerless wayside reflections so familiar to travellers in Russia.

They were broken in upon by a heavy knocking that came from the common room, from which my room was separated by a deal partition. This sound was accompanied by an intermittent metallic jingle, like the clank of chains, and a coarse male voice boomed out suddenly: 'The blessing of God on all within this house. The blessing of God! the blessing of God! Amen, amen! Scatter His enemies!' repeated the voice, with a sort of incongruous and savage drawl on the last syllable of each word.... A noisy sigh was heard, and a ponderous body sank on to the bench with the same jingling sound. 'Akulina! servant of God, come here!' the voice began again: 'Behold! Clothed in rags and blessed! ... Ha-ha-ha! Tfoo! Merciful God, merciful God, merciful God!' the voice droned like a deacon in the choir. 'Merciful God, Creator of my body, behold my iniquity.... O-ho-ho! Ha-ha! ... Tfoo! And all abundance be to this house in the seventh hour!'

'Who's that?' I asked the hospitable landlady, who came in with the samovar.

'That, your honour,' she answered me in a hurried whisper, 'is a blessed, holy man. He's not long come into our parts; and here he's graciously pleased to visit us. In such weather! The wet's simply trickling from him, poor dear man, in streams! And you should see the chains on him—such a lot!'

'The blessing of God! the blessing of God!' the voice was heard again. 'Akulina! Hey, Akulina! Akulinushka—friend! where is our paradise? Our fair paradise of bliss? In the wilderness is our paradise, ... para-dise.... And to this house, from beginning of time, great happiness, ... o ... o ... o ...' The voice muttered something inarticulate, and again, after a protracted yawn, there came the hoarse laugh. This laugh broke out every time, as it were, involuntarily, and every time it was followed by vigorous spitting.

'Ah, me! Stepanitch isn't here! That's the worst of it!' the landlady said, as it were to herself, as she stood with every sign of the profoundest attention at the door. 'He will say some word of salvation, and I, foolish woman, may not catch it!'

She went out quickly.

In the partition there was a chink; I applied my eye to it. The crazy pilgrim was sitting on a bench with his back to me; I saw nothing but his shaggy head, as huge as a beer-can, and a broad bent back in a patched and soaking shirt. Before him, on the earth floor, knelt a frail-looking woman in a jacket, such as are worn by women of the artisan class—old and wet through—and with a dark kerchief pulled down almost over her eyes. She was trying to pull the holy man's boots off; her fingers slid off the greasy, slippery leather. The landlady was standing near her, with her arms folded across her bosom, gazing reverently at the 'man of God.' He was, as before, mumbling some inarticulate words.

At last the woman succeeded in tugging off the boots. She almost fell backwards, but recovered herself, and began unwinding the strips of rag which were wrapped round the vagrant's legs. On the sole of his foot there was a wound.... I turned away.

'A cup of tea wouldn't you bid me get you, my dear?' I heard the hostess saying in an obsequious voice.

'What a notion!' responded the holy man. 'To indulge the sinful body.... O-ho-ho! Break all the bones in it ... but she talks of tea! Oh, oh, worthy old woman, Satan is strong within us.... Fight him with hunger, fight him with cold, with the sluice-gates of heaven, the pouring, penetrating rain, and he takes no harm—he is alive still! Remember the day of the Intercession of the Mother of God! You will receive, you will receive in abundance!'

The landlady could not resist uttering a faint groan of admiration.

'Only listen to me! Give all thou hast, give thy head, give thy shirt! If they ask not of thee, yet give! For God is all-seeing! Is it hard for Him to destroy your roof? He has given thee bread in His mercy, and do thou bake it in the oven! He seeth all! Se ... e ... eth! Whose eye is in the triangle? Say, whose?'

The landlady stealthily crossed herself under her neckerchief.

'The old enemy is adamant! A ... da ... mant! A ... da ... mant!' the religious maniac repeated several times, gnashing his teeth. 'The old serpent! But God will arise! Yes, God will arise and scatter His enemies! I will call up all the dead! I will go against His enemy.... Ha-ha-ha! Tfoo!'

'Have you any oil?' said another voice, hardly audible; 'let me put some on the wound.... I have got a clean rag.'

I peeped through the chink again; the woman in the jacket was still busied with the vagrant's sore foot.... 'A Magdalen!' I thought.

'I'll get it directly, my dear,' said the woman, and, coming into my room, she took a spoonful of oil from the lamp burning before the holy picture.

'Who's that waiting on him?' I asked.

'We don't know, sir, who it is; she too, I suppose, is seeking salvation, atoning for her sins. But what a saintly man he is!'

'Akulinushka, my sweet child, my dear daughter,' the crazy pilgrim was repeating meanwhile, and he suddenly burst into tears.

The woman kneeling before him lifted her eyes to him.... Heavens! where had I seen those eyes?

The landlady went up to her with the spoonful of oil. She finished her operation, and, getting up from the floor, asked if there were a clean loft and a little hay.... 'Vassily Nikititch likes to sleep on hay,' she added.

'To be sure there is, come this way,' answered the woman; 'come this way, my dear,' she turned to the holy man, 'and dry yourself and rest.' The man coughed, slowly got up from the bench—his chains clanked again—and turning round with his face to me, looked for the holy pictures, and began crossing himself with a wide movement.

I recognised him instantly: it was the very artisan Vassily, who had once shown me my dead tutor!

His features were little changed; only their expression had become still more unusual, still more terrible.... The lower part of his swollen face was overgrown with unkempt beard. Tattered, filthy, wild-looking, he inspired in me more repugnance than horror. He left off crossing himself, but still his eyes wandered senselessly about the corners of the room, about the floor, as though he were waiting for something....

'Vassily Nikititch, please come,' said the woman in the jacket with a bow. He suddenly threw up his head and turned round, but stumbled and tottered.... His companion flew to him at once, and supported him under the arm. Judging by her voice and figure, she seemed still young; her face it was almost impossible to see.

'Akulinushka, friend!' the vagrant repeated once more in a shaking voice, and opening his mouth wide, and smiting himself on the breast with his fist, he uttered a deep groan, that seemed to come from the bottom of his heart. Both followed the landlady out of the room.

I lay down on my hard sofa and mused a long while on what I had seen. My mesmeriser had become a regular religious maniac. This was what he had been brought to by the power which one could not but recognise in him!

The next morning I was preparing to go on my way. The rain was falling as fast as the day before, but I could not delay any longer. My servant, as he gave me water to wash, wore a special smile on his face, a smile of restrained irony. I knew that smile well; it indicated that my servant had heard something discreditable or even shocking about gentlefolks. He was obviously burning with impatience to communicate it to me.

'Well, what is it?' I asked at last.

'Did your honour see the crazy pilgrim yesterday?' my man began at once.

'Yes; what then?'

'And did you see his companion too?'

'Yes, I saw her.'

'She's a young lady, of noble family.'

'What?'

'It's the truth I'm telling you; some merchants arrived here this morning from T—; they recognised her. They did tell me her name, but I've forgotten it.'

It was like a flash of enlightenment. 'Is the pilgrim still here?' I asked.

'I fancy he's not gone yet. He's been ever so long at the gate, and making such a wonderful wise to-do, that there's no getting by. He's amusing himself with this tomfoolery; he finds it pay, no doubt.'

My man belonged to the same class of educated servants as Ardalion.

'And is the lady with him?'

'Yes. She's in attendance on him.'

I went out on to the steps, and got a view of the crazy pilgrim. He was sitting on a bench at the gate, and, bent down with both his open hands pressed on it, he was shaking his drooping head from right to left, for all the world like a wild beast in a cage. The thick mane of curly hair covered

his eyes, and shook from side to side, and so did his pendulous lips....
A strange, almost unhuman muttering came from them. His companion
had only just finished washing from a pitcher that was hanging on a pole,
and without having yet replaced her kerchief on her head, was making her
way back to the gate along a narrow plank laid across the dark puddles of
the filthy yard. I glanced at her head, which was now entirely uncovered,
and positively threw up my hands with astonishment: before me stood
Sophie B.!

She turned quickly round and fixed upon me her blue eyes, immovable as ever. She was much thinner, her skin looked coarser and had the
yellowish-ruddy tinge of sunburn, her nose was sharper, and her lips were
harder in their lines. But she was not less good-looking; only besides her
old expression of dreamy amazement there was now a different look—resolute, almost bold, intense and exalted. There was not a trace of childishness left in the face now.

I went up to her. 'Sophia Vladimirovna,' I cried, 'can it be you? In such
a dress ... in such company....'

She started, looked still more intently at me, as though anxious to
find out who was speaking to her, and, without saying a word to me, fairly
rushed to her companion.

'Akulinushka,' he faltered, with a heavy sigh, 'our sins, sins ...'

'Vassily Nikititch, let us go at once! Do you hear, at once, at once,' she
said, pulling her kerchief on to her forehead with one hand, while with
the other she supported the pilgrim under the elbow; 'let us go, Vassily
Nikititch: there is danger here.'

'I'm coming, my good girl, I'm coming,' the crazy pilgrim responded
obediently, and, bending his whole body forward, he got up from the seat.
'Here's only this chain to fasten....'

I once more approached Sophia, and told her my name. I began be-
seeching her to listen to me, to say one word to me. I pointed to the rain,
which was coming down in bucketsful. I begged her to have some care
for her health, the health of her companion. I mentioned her father.... But
she seemed possessed by a sort of wrathful, a sort of vindictive excitement:
without paying the slightest attention to me, setting her teeth and breathing hard, she urged on the distracted vagrant in an undertone, in soft
insistent words, girt him up, fastened on his chains, pulled on to his hair
a child's cloth cap with a broken peak, stuck his staff in his hand, slung
a wallet on her own shoulder, and went with him out at the gate into the
street.... To stop her actually I had not the right, and it would have been
of no use; and at my last despairing call she did not even turn round. Sup-
porting the 'man of God' under his arm, she stepped rapidly over the black

mud of the street; and in a few moments, across the dim dusk of the foggy morning, through the thick network of falling raindrops, I saw the last glimpse of the two figures, the crazy pilgrim and Sophie.... They turned the corner of a projecting hut, and vanished for ever.

I went back to my room. I fell to pondering. I could not understand it; I could not understand how such a girl, well brought up, young, and wealthy, could throw up everything and every one, her own home, her family, her friends, break with all her habits, with all the comforts of life, and for what? To follow a half-insane vagrant, to become his servant! I could not for an instant entertain the idea that the explanation of such a step was to be found in any prompting, however depraved, of the heart, in love or passion.... One had but to glance at the repulsive figure of the 'man of God' to dismiss such a notion entirely! No, Sophie had remained pure; and to her all things were pure; I could not understand what Sophie had done; but I did not blame her, as, later on, I have not blamed other girls who too have sacrificed everything for what they thought the truth, for what they held to be their vocation. I could not help regretting that Sophie had chosen just *that* path; but also I could not refuse her admiration, respect even. In good earnest she had talked of self-sacrifice, of abasement ... in *her*, words were not opposed to acts. She had sought a leader, a guide, and had found him, ... and, my God, what a guide!

Yes, she had lain down to be trampled, trodden under foot.... In the process of time, a rumour reached me that her family had succeeded at last in finding out the lost sheep, and bringing her home. But at home she did not live long, and died, like a 'Sister of Silence,' without having spoken a word to any one.

Peace to your heart, poor, enigmatic creature! Vassily Nikititch is probably on his crazy wanderings still; the iron health of such people is truly marvellous. Perhaps, though, his epilepsy may have done for him.

BADEN-BADEN, 1869.

PUNIN AND BABURIN

PIOTR PETROVITCH'S STORY

♦ ♦ ♦ I am old and ill now, and my thoughts brood oftenest upon death, every day coming nearer; rarely I think of the past, rarely I turn the eyes of my soul behind me. Only from time to time—in winter, as I sit motionless before the glowing fire, in summer, as I pace with slow tread along the shady avenue—I recall past years, events, faces; but it is not on my mature years nor on my youth that my thoughts rest at such times. They either carry me back to my earliest childhood, or to the first years of boyhood. Now, for instance, I see myself in the country with my stern and wrathful grandmother—I was only twelve—and two figures rise up before my imagination....

But I will begin my story consecutively, and in proper order.

I

1830

The old footman Filippitch came in, on tiptoe, as usual, with a cravat tied up in a rosette, with tightly compressed lips, 'lest his breath should be smelt,' with a grey tuft of hair standing up in the very middle of his forehead. He came in, bowed, and handed my grandmother on an iron tray a large letter with an heraldic seal. My grandmother put on her spectacles, read the letter through....

'Is he here?' she asked.

'What is my lady pleased ...' Filippitch began timidly.

'Imbecile! The man who brought the letter—is he here?'

'He is here, to be sure he is.... He is sitting in the counting-house.'

My grandmother rattled her amber rosary beads....

'Tell him to come to me.... And you, sir,' she turned to me, 'sit still.'

As it was, I was sitting perfectly still in my corner, on the stool assigned to me.

My grandmother kept me well in hand!

Five minutes later there came into the room a man of five-and-thirty, black-haired and swarthy, with broad cheek-bones, a face marked with smallpox, a hook nose, and thick eyebrows, from under which the small grey eyes looked out with mournful composure. The colour of the eyes and their expression were out of keeping with the Oriental cast of the rest of the face. The man was dressed in a decent, long-skirted coat. He stopped in the doorway, and bowed—only with his head.

'So your name's Baburin?' queried my grandmother, and she added to herself: *'Il a l'air d'un armenien.'*

'Yes, it is,' the man answered in a deep and even voice. At the first brusque sound of my grandmother's voice his eyebrows faintly quivered. Surely he had not expected her to address him as an equal?

'Are you a Russian? orthodox?'

'Yes.'

My grandmother took off her spectacles, and scanned Baburin from head to foot deliberately. He did not drop his eyes, he merely folded his hands behind his back. What particularly struck my fancy was his beard; it was very smoothly shaven, but such blue cheeks and chin I had never seen in my life!

'Yakov Petrovitch,' began my grandmother, 'recommends you strongly in his letter as sober and industrious; why, then, did you leave his service?'

'He needs a different sort of person to manage his estate, madam.'

'A different ... sort? That I don't quite understand.'

My grandmother rattled her beads again. 'Yakov Petrovitch writes to me that there are two peculiarities about you. What peculiarities?'

Baburin shrugged his shoulders slightly.

'I can't tell what he sees fit to call peculiarities. Possibly that I ... don't allow corporal punishment.'

My grandmother was surprised. 'Do you mean to say Yakov Petrovitch wanted to flog you?'

Baburin's swarthy face grew red to the roots of his hair.

'You have not understood me right, madam. I make it a rule not to employ corporal punishment ... with the peasants.'

My grandmother was more surprised than ever; she positively threw up her hands.

'Ah!' she pronounced at last, and putting her head a little on one side, once more she scrutinised Baburin attentively. 'So that's your rule, is it? Well, that's of no consequence whatever to me; I don't want an overseer, but a counting-house clerk, a secretary. What sort of a hand do you write?'

'I write well, without mistakes in spelling.'

'That too is of no consequence to me. The great thing for me is for it to be clear, and without any of those new copybook letters with tails, that I don't like. And what's your other peculiarity?'

Baburin moved uneasily, coughed....

'Perhaps ... the gentleman has referred to the fact that I am not alone.'

'You are married?'

'Oh no ... but ...'

My grandmother knit her brows.

'There is a person living with me ... of the male sex ... a comrade, a poor friend, from whom I have never parted ... for ... let me see ... ten years now.'

'A relation of yours?'

'No, not a relation—a friend. As to work, there can be no possible hindrance occasioned by him,' Baburin made haste to add, as though foreseeing objections. 'He lives at my cost, occupies the same room with me; he is more likely to be of use, as he is well educated—speaking without flattery, extremely so, in fact—and his morals are exemplary.'

My grandmother heard Baburin out, chewing her lips and half closing her eyes.

'He lives at your expense?'

'Yes.'

'You keep him out of charity?'

'As an act of justice ... as it's the duty of one poor man to help another poor man.'

'Indeed! It's the first time I've heard that. I had supposed till now that that was rather the duty of rich people.'

'For the rich, if I may venture to say so, it is an entertainment ... but for such as we ...'

'Well, well, that's enough, that's enough,' my grandmother cut him short; and after a moment's thought she queried, speaking through her nose, which was always a bad sign, 'And what age is he, your protege?'

'About my own age.'

'Really, I imagined that you were bringing him up.'

'Not so; he is my comrade—and besides ...'

'That's enough,' my grandmother cut him short a second time. 'You're a philanthropist, it seems. Yakov Petrovitch is right; for a man in your position it's something very peculiar. But now let's get to business. I'll explain to you what your duties will be. And as regards wages.... *Que faites vous ici?' added my grandmother suddenly, turning her dry, yellow face to me:—'Allez etudier votre devoir de mythologie.'*

I jumped up, went up to kiss my grandmother's hand, and went out,—not to study mythology, but simply into the garden.

The garden on my grandmother's estate was very old and large, and was bounded on one side by a flowing pond, in which there were not only plenty of carp and eels, but even loach were caught, those renowned loach, that have nowadays disappeared almost everywhere. At the head of this pond was a thick clump of willows; further and higher, on both sides of a rising slope, were dense bushes of hazel, elder, honeysuckle, and sloe-thorn, with an undergrowth of heather and clover flowers. Here and there between the bushes were tiny clearings, covered with emerald-green, silky, fine grass, in the midst of which squat funguses peeped out with their comical, variegated pink, lilac, and straw-coloured caps, and golden balls of 'hen-dazzle' blazed in light patches. Here in spring-time the nightingales sang, the blackbirds whistled, the cuckoos called; here in the heat of summer it was always cool—and I loved to make my way into the wilderness and thicket, where I had favourite secret spots, known—so, at least, I imagined—only to me.

On coming out of my grandmother's room I made straight for one of these spots, which I had named 'Switzerland.' But what was my astonishment when, before I had reached 'Switzerland,' I perceived through the delicate network of half-dry twigs and green branches that some one besides me had found it out! A long, long figure in a long, loose coat of yellow frieze and a tall cap was standing in the very spot I loved best of all! I stole up a little nearer, and made out the face, which was utterly unknown to me, also very long and soft, with small reddish eyes, and a very funny nose; drawn out as long as a pod of peas, it positively over-hung the full lips; and these lips, quivering and forming a round O, were giving vent to a shrill little whistle, while the long fingers of the bony hands, placed facing one another on the upper part of the chest, were rapidly moving with a rotatory action. From time to time the motion of the hands subsided, the lips ceased whistling and quivering, the head was bent forward as though listening. I came still nearer, examined him still more closely.... The stranger held in each hand a small flat cup, such as people use to tease canaries and make them sing. A twig snapped under my feet; the stranger started, turned his dim little eyes towards the copse, and was staggering away ... but he stumbled against a tree, uttered an exclamation, and stood still.

I came out into the open space. The stranger smiled.

'Good morning,' said I.

'Good morning, little master!'

I did not like his calling me little master. Such familiarity!

'What are you doing here?' I asked sternly.

'Why, look here,' he responded, never leaving off smiling, 'I'm calling the little birds to sing.' He showed me his little cups. 'The chaffinches answer splendidly! You, at your tender years, take delight, no doubt, in the feathered songsters' notes! Listen, I beg; I will begin chirping, and they'll answer me directly—it's so delightful!'

He began rubbing his little cups. A chaffinch actually did chirp in response from a mountain ash near. The stranger laughed without a sound, and winked at me.

The laugh and the wink—every gesture of the stranger, his weak, lisping voice, his bent knees and thin hands, his very cap and long frieze coat—everything about him suggested good-nature, something innocent and droll.

'Have you been here long?' I asked.

'I came to-day.'

'Why, aren't you the person of whom ...'

'Mr. Baburin spoke to the lady here. The same, the same.'

'Your friend's name's Baburin, and what's yours?'

'I'm Punin. Punin's my name; Punin. He's Baburin and I'm Punin.' He set the little cups humming again. 'Listen, listen to the chaffinch.... How it carols!'

This queer creature took my fancy 'awfully' all at once. Like almost all boys, I was either timid or consequential with strangers, but I felt with this man as if I had known him for ages.

'Come along with me,' I said to him; 'I know a place better than this; there's a seat there; we can sit down, and we can see the dam from there.'

'By all means let us go,' my new friend responded in his singing voice. I let him pass before me. As he walked he rolled from side to side, tripped over his own feet, and his head fell back.

I noticed on the back of his coat, under the collar, there hung a small tassel. 'What's that you've got hanging there?' I asked.

'Where?' he questioned, and he put his hand up to the collar to feel. 'Ah, the tassel? Let it be! I suppose it was sewn there for ornament! It's not in the way.'

I led him to the seat, and sat down; he settled himself beside me. 'It's lovely here!' he commented, and he drew a deep, deep sigh. 'Oh, how lovely! You have a most splendid garden! Oh, o—oh!'

I looked at him from one side. 'What a queer cap you've got!' I couldn't help exclaiming. 'Show it me here!'

'By all means, little master, by all means.' He took off the cap; I was holding out my hand, but I raised my eyes, and—simply burst out laughing. Punin was completely bald; not a single hair was to be seen on the high conical skull, covered with smooth white skin. He passed his open hand over it, and he too laughed. When he laughed he seemed, as it were, to gulp, he opened his mouth wide, closed his eyes—and vertical wrinkles flitted across his forehead in three rows, like waves. 'Eh,' said he at last, 'isn't it quite like an egg?'

'Yes, yes, exactly like an egg!' I agreed with enthusiasm. 'And have you been like that long?'

'Yes, a long while; but what hair I used to have!—A golden fleece like that for which the Argonauts sailed over the watery deeps.'

Though I was only twelve, yet, thanks to my mythological studies, I knew who the Argonauts were; I was the more surprised at hearing the name on the lips of a man dressed almost in rags.

'You must have learned mythology, then?' I queried, as I twisted his cap over and over in my hands. It turned out to be wadded, with a mangy-looking fur trimming, and a broken cardboard peak.

'I have studied that subject, my dear little master; I've had time enough for everything in my life! But now restore to me my covering, it is a protection to the nakedness of my head.'

He put on the cap, and, with a downward slope of his whitish eyebrows, asked me who I was, and who were my parents.

'I'm the grandson of the lady who owns this place,' I answered. 'I live alone with her. Papa and mamma are dead.'

Punin crossed himself. 'May the kingdom of heaven be theirs! So then, you're an orphan; and the heir, too. The noble blood in you is visible at once; it fairly sparkles in your eyes, and plays like this ... sh ... sh ... sh ...' He represented with his fingers the play of the blood. 'Well, and do you know, your noble honour, whether my friend has come to terms with your grandmamma, whether he has obtained the situation he was promised?'

'I don't know.'

Punin cleared his throat. 'Ah! if one could be settled here, if only for a while! Or else one may wander and wander far, and find not a place to rest one's head; the disquieting alarms of life are unceasing, the soul is confounded....'

'Tell me,' I interrupted: 'are you of the clerical profession?'

Punin turned to me and half closed his eyelids. 'And what may be the cause of that question, gentle youth?'

'Why, you talk so—well, as they read in church.'

'Because I use the old scriptural forms of expression? But that ought not to surprise you. Admitting that in ordinary conversation such forms of expression are not always in place; but when one soars on the wings of inspiration, at once the language too grows more exalted. Surely your teacher—the professor of Russian literature—you do have lessons in that, I suppose?—surely he teaches you that, doesn't he?'

'No, he doesn't,' I responded. 'When we stay in the country I have no teacher. In Moscow I have a great many teachers.'

'And will you be staying long in the country?'

'Two months, not longer; grandmother says that I'm spoilt in the country, though I have a governess even here.'

'A French governess?'

'Yes.'

Punin scratched behind his ear. 'A mamselle, that's to say?'

'Yes; she's called Mademoiselle Friquet.' I suddenly felt it disgraceful for me, a boy of twelve, to have not a tutor, but a governess, like a little girl! 'But I don't mind her,' I added contemptuously. 'What do I care!'

Punin shook his head. 'Ah, you gentlefolk, you gentlefolk! you're too fond of foreigners! You have turned away from what is Russian,—towards all that's strange. You've turned your hearts to those that come from foreign parts....'

'Hullo! Are you talking in verse?' I asked.

'Well, and why not? I can do that always, as much as you please; for it comes natural to me....'

But at that very instant there sounded in the garden behind us a loud and shrill whistle. My new acquaintance hurriedly got up from the bench.

'Good-bye, little sir; that's my friend calling me, looking for me.... What has he to tell me? Good-bye—excuse me....'

He plunged into the bushes and vanished, while I sat on some time longer on the seat. I felt perplexity and another feeling, rather an agreeable one ... I had never met nor spoken to any one like this before. Gradually I fell to dreaming, but recollected my mythology and sauntered towards the house.

At home, I learned that my grandmother had arranged to take Baburin; he had been assigned a small room in the servants' quarters, overlooking the stable-yard. He had at once settled in there with his friend.

When I had drunk my tea, next morning, without asking leave of Mademoiselle Friquet, I set off to the servants' quarters. I wanted to have another chat with the queer fellow I had seen the day before. Without knocking at the door—the very idea of doing so would never have occurred to us—I walked straight into the room. I found in it not the man I was looking for, not Punin, but his protector—the philanthropist, Baburin. He was standing before the window, without his outer garment, his legs wide apart. He was busily engaged in rubbing his head and neck with a long towel.

'What do you want?' he observed, keeping his hands still raised, and knitting his brows.

'Punin's not at home, then?' I queried in the most free-and-easy manner, without taking off my cap.

'Mr. Punin, Nikander Vavilitch, at this moment, is not at home, truly,' Baburin responded deliberately; 'but allow me to make an observation, young man: it's not the proper thing to come into another person's room like this, without asking leave.'

I! ... young man! ... how dared he! ... I grew crimson with fury.

'You cannot be aware who I am,' I rejoined, in a manner no longer free-and-easy, but haughty. 'I am the grandson of the mistress here.'

'That's all the same to me,' retorted Baburin, setting to work with his towel again. 'Though you are the seignorial grandson, you have no right to come into other people's rooms.'

'Other people's? What do you mean? I'm—at home here—everywhere.'

'No, excuse me: here—I'm at home; since this room has been assigned to me, by agreement, in exchange for my work.'

'Don't teach me, if you please,' I interrupted: 'I know better than you what ...'

'You must be taught,' he interrupted in his turn, 'for you're at an age when you ... I know my duties, but I know my rights too very well, and if you continue to speak to me in that way, I shall have to ask you to go out of the room....'

There is no knowing how our dispute would have ended if Punin had not at that instant entered, shuffling and shambling from side to side. He most likely guessed from the expression of our faces that some unpleasantness had passed between us, and at once turned to me with the warmest expressions of delight.

'Ah! little master! little master!' he cried, waving his hands wildly, and going off into his noiseless laugh: 'the little dear! come to pay me a visit! here he's come, the little dear!' (What's the meaning of it? I thought: can he be speaking in this familiar way to me?) 'There, come along, come with me into the garden. I've found something there.... Why stay in this stuffiness here! let's go!'

I followed Punin, but in the doorway I thought it as well to turn round and fling a glance of defiance at Baburin, as though to say, I'm not afraid of you!

He responded in the same way, and positively snorted into the towel—probably to make me thoroughly aware how utterly he despised me!

What an insolent fellow your friend is!' I said to Punin, directly the door had closed behind me.

Almost with horror, Punin turned his plump face to me.

'To whom did you apply that expression?' he asked me, with round eyes.

'Why, to him, of course.... What's his name? that ... Baburin.'

'Paramon Semyonevitch?'

'Why, yes; that ... blackfaced fellow.'

'Eh ... eh ... eh ...!' Punin protested, with caressing reproachfulness. 'How can you talk like that, little master! Paramon Semyonevitch is the most estimable man, of the strictest principles, an extraordinary person! To be sure, he won't allow any disrespect to him, because—he knows his own value. That man possesses a vast amount of knowledge—and it's not a place like this he ought to be filling! You must, my dear, behave very courteously to him; do you know, he's ...' here Punin bent down quite to my ear,—'a republican!'

I stared at Punin. This I had not at all expected. From Keidanov's manual and other historical works I had gathered the fact that at some period or other, in ancient times, there had existed republicans, Greeks and Romans. For some unknown reason I had always pictured them all in helmets, with round shields on their arms, and big bare legs; but that in real life, in the actual present, above all, in Russia, in the province of X—, one could come across republicans—that upset all my notions, and utterly confounded them!

'Yes, my dear, yes; Paramon Semyonitch is a republican,' repeated Punin; 'there, so you'll know for the future how one should speak of a man like that! But now let's go into the garden. Fancy what I've found there! A cuckoo's egg in a redstart's nest! a lovely thing!'

I went into the garden with Punin; but mentally I kept repeating: 're-publican! re ... pub ... lican!'

'So,' I decided at last—'that's why he has such a blue chin!'

My attitude to these two persons—Punin and Baburin—took definite shape from that very day. Baburin aroused in me a feeling of hostility with which there was, however, in a short time, mingled something akin to respect. And wasn't I afraid of him! I never got over being afraid of him even when the sharp severity of his manner with me at first had quite disappeared. It is needless to say that of Punin I had no fear; I did not even respect him; I looked upon him—not to put too fine a point on it—as a buffoon; but I loved him with my whole soul! To spend hours at a time in his company, to be alone with him, to listen to his stories, became a genuine delight to me. My grandmother was anything but pleased at this *intimite* with a person of the 'lower classes'—*du commun*; but, whenever I could break away, I flew at once to my queer, amusing, beloved friend. Our meetings became more frequent after the departure of Mademoiselle Friquet, whom my grandmother sent back to Moscow in disgrace because, in conversation with a military staff captain, visiting in the neighbourhood, she had had the insolence to complain of the dulness which reigned in our household. And Punin, for his part, was not bored by long conversations with a boy of twelve; he seemed to seek them of himself. How often have I listened to his stories, sitting with him in the fragrant shade, on the dry, smooth grass, under the canopy of the silver poplars, or among the reeds above the pond, on the coarse, damp sand of the hollow bank, from which the knotted roots protruded, queerly interlaced, like great black veins, like snakes, like creatures emerging from some subterranean region! Punin told me the whole story of his life in minute detail, describing all his happy adventures, and all his misfortunes, with which I always felt the sincerest sympathy! His father had been a deacon;—'a splendid man—but, under the influence of drink, stern to the last extreme.'

Punin himself had received his education in a seminary; but, unable to stand the severe thrashings, and feeling no inclination for the priestly calling, he had become a layman, and in consequence had experienced all sorts of hardships; and, finally, had become a vagrant. 'And had I not met with my benefactor, Paramon Semyonitch,' Punin commonly added (he never spoke of Baburin except in this way), 'I should have sunk into the miry abysses of poverty and vice.' Punin was fond of high-sounding expressions, and had a great propensity, if not for lying, for romancing and exaggeration; he admired everything, fell into ecstasies over everything.... And I, in imitation of him, began to exaggerate and be ecstatic, too. 'What a crazy fellow you've grown! God have mercy on you!' my old nurse used to say to me. Punin's narratives used to interest me extremely; but even better than his stories I loved the readings we used to have together.

It is impossible to describe the feeling I experienced when, snatching a favourable moment, suddenly, like a hermit in a tale or a good fairy, he

appeared before me with a ponderous volume under his arm, and stealthily beckoning with his long crooked finger, and winking mysteriously,
he pointed with his head, his eyebrows, his shoulders, his whole person,
toward the deepest recesses of the garden, whither no one could penetrate
after us, and where it was impossible to find us out. And when we had
succeeded in getting away unnoticed; when we had satisfactorily reached
one of our secret nooks, and were sitting side by side, and, at last, the
book was slowly opened, emitting a pungent odour, inexpressibly sweet
to me then, of mildew and age;—with what a thrill, with what a wave of
dumb expectancy, I gazed at the face, at the lips of Punin, those lips from
which in a moment a stream of such delicious eloquence was to flow! At
last the first sounds of the reading were heard. Everything around me
vanished ... no, not vanished, but grew far away, passed into clouds of
mist, leaving behind only an impression of something friendly and protecting. Those trees, those green leaves, those high grasses screen us, hide
us from all the rest of the world; no one knows where we are, what we are
about—while with us is poetry, we are saturated in it, intoxicated with
it, something solemn, grand, mysterious is happening to us.... Punin, by
preference, kept to poetry, musical, sonorous poetry; he was ready to lay
down his life for poetry. He did not read, he declaimed the verse majestically, in a torrent of rhythm, in a rolling outpour through his nose, like
a man intoxicated, lifted out of himself, like the Pythian priestess. And
another habit he had: first he would lisp the verses through softly, in a
whisper, as it were mumbling them to himself.... This he used to call the
rough sketch of the reading; then he would thunder out the same verse
in its 'fair copy,' and would all at once leap up, throw up his hand, with a
half-supplicating, half-imperious gesture.... In this way we went through
not only Lomonosov, Sumarokov, and Kantemir (the older the poems,
the more they were to Punin's taste), but even Heraskov's *Rossiad*. And,
to tell the truth, it was this same *Rossiad* which aroused my enthusiasm
most. There is in it, among others, a mighty Tatar woman, a gigantic
heroine; I have forgotten even her name now; but in those days my hands
and feet turned cold as soon as it was mentioned. 'Yes,' Punin would say,
nodding his head with great significance, 'Heraskov, he doesn't let one
off easily. At times one comes upon a line, simply heart-breaking.... One
can only stick to it, and do one's best.... One tries to master it, but he
breaks away again and trumpets, trumpets, with the crash of cymbals.
His name's been well bestowed on him—the very word, Herrraskov!' Lomonosov Punin found fault with for too simple and free a style; while to
Derzhavin he maintained an attitude almost of hostility, saying that he
was more of a courtier than a poet. In our house it was not merely that

no attention was given to literature, to poetry; but poetry, especially Russian poetry, was looked upon as something quite undignified and vulgar; my grandmother did not even call it poetry, but 'doggrel verses'; every author of such doggrel was, in her opinion, either a confirmed toper or a perfect idiot. Brought up among such ideas, it was inevitable that I should either turn from Punin with disgust—he was untidy and shabby into the bargain, which was an offence to my seignorial habits—or that, attracted and captivated by him, I should follow his example, and be infected by his passion for poetry.... And so it turned out. I, too, began reading poetry, or, as my grandmother expressed it, poring over doggrel trash.... I even tried my hand at versifying, and composed a poem, descriptive of a barrel-organ, in which occurred the following two lines:

> *'Lo, the barrel turns around,*
> *And the cogs within resound.'*

Punin commended in this effort a certain imitative melody, but disapproved of the subject itself as low and unworthy of lyrical treatment.

Alas! all those efforts and emotions and transports, our solitary readings, our life together, our poetry, all came to an end at once. Trouble broke upon us suddenly, like a clap of thunder.

My grandmother in everything liked cleanliness and order, quite in the spirit of the active generals of those days; cleanliness and order were to be maintained too in our garden. And so from time to time they 'drove' into it poor peasants, who had no families, no land, no beasts of their own, and those among the house serfs who were out of favour or superannuated, and set them to clearing the paths, weeding the borders, breaking up and sifting the earth in the beds, and so on. Well, one day, in the very heat of these operations, my grandmother went into the garden, and took me with her. On all sides, among the trees and about the lawns, we caught glimpses of white, red, and blue smocks; on all sides we heard the scraping and clanging of spades, the dull thud of clods of earth on the slanting sieves. As she passed by the labourers, my grandmother with her eagle eye noticed at once that one of them was working with less energy than the rest, and that he took off his cap, too, with no show of eagerness. This was a youth, still quite young, with a wasted face, and sunken, lustreless eyes. His cotton smock, all torn and patched, scarcely held together over his narrow shoulders.

'Who's that?' my grandmother inquired of Filippitch, who was walking on tiptoe behind her.

'Of whom ... you are pleased ...' Filippitch stammered.

'Oh, fool! I mean the one that looked so sullenly at me. There, standing yonder, not working.'

'Oh, him! Yes ... th ... th ... that's Yermil, son of Pavel Afanasiitch, now deceased.'

Pavel Afanasiitch had been, ten years before, head butler in my grandmother's house, and stood particularly high in her favour. But suddenly falling into disgrace, he was as suddenly degraded to being herdsman, and did not long keep even that position. He sank lower still, and struggled on for a while on a monthly pittance of flour in a little hut far away. At last he had died of paralysis, leaving his family in the most utter destitution.

'Aha!' commented my grandmother; 'it's clear the apple's not fallen far from the tree. Well, we shall have to make arrangements about this fellow too. I've no need of people like that, with scowling faces.'

My grandmother went back to the house—and made arrangements. Three hours later Yermil, completely 'equipped,' was brought under the window of her room. The unfortunate boy was being transported to a settlement; the other side of the fence, a few steps from him, was a little cart loaded with his poor belongings. Such were the times then. Yermil stood without his cap, with downcast head, barefoot, with his boots tied up with a string behind his back; his face, turned towards the seignorial mansion, expressed not despair nor grief, nor even bewilderment; a stupid smile was frozen on his colourless lips; his eyes, dry and half-closed, looked stubbornly on the ground. My grandmother was apprised of his presence. She got up from the sofa, went, with a faint rustle of her silken skirts, to the window of the study, and, holding her golden-rimmed double eyeglass on the bridge of her nose, looked at the new exile. In her room there happened to be at the moment four other persons, the butler, Baburin, the page who waited on my grandmother in the daytime, and I.

My grandmother nodded her head up and down....

'Madam,' a hoarse almost stifled voice was heard suddenly. I looked round. Baburin's face was red ... dark red; under his overhanging brows could be seen little sharp points of light.... There was no doubt about it; it was he, it was Baburin, who had uttered the word 'Madam.'

My grandmother too looked round, and turned her eyeglass from Yermil to Baburin.

'Who is that ... speaking?' she articulated slowly ... through her nose. Baburin moved slightly forward.

'Madam,' he began, 'it is I.... I venture ... I imagine ... I make bold to submit to your honour that you are making a mistake in acting as ... as you are pleased to act at this moment.'

'That is?' my grandmother said, in the same voice, not removing her eyeglass.

'I take the liberty ...' Baburin went on distinctly, uttering every word though with obvious effort—'I am referring to the case of this lad who is being sent away to a settlement ... for no fault of his. Such arrangements, I venture to submit, lead to dissatisfaction, and to other—which God forbid!—consequences, and are nothing else than a transgression of the powers allowed to seignorial proprietors.'

'And where have you studied, pray?' my grandmother asked after a short silence, and she dropped her eyeglass.

Baburin was disconcerted. 'What are you pleased to wish?' he muttered.

'I ask you: where have you studied? You use such learned words.'

'I ... my education ...' Baburin was beginning.

My grandmother shrugged her shoulders contemptuously. 'It seems,' she interrupted, 'that my arrangements are not to your liking. That is of absolutely no consequence to me—among my subjects I am sovereign, and answerable to no one for them, only I am not accustomed to having people criticising me in my presence, and meddling in what is not their business. I have no need of learned philanthropists of nondescript position; I want servants to do my will without question. So I always lived till you came, and so I shall live after you've gone. You do not suit me; you are discharged. Nikolai Antonov,' my grandmother turned to the steward, 'pay this man off; and let him be gone before dinner-time today! D'you hear? Don't put me into a passion. And the other too ... the fool that lives with him—to be sent off too. What's Yermilka waiting for?' she added, looking out of window, 'I have seen him. What more does he want?' My grandmother shook her handkerchief in the direction of the window, as though to drive away an importunate fly. Then she sat down in a low chair, and turning towards us, gave the order grimly: 'Everybody present to leave the room!'

We all withdrew—all, except the day page, to whom my grandmother's words did not apply, because he was nobody.

My grandmother's decree was carried out to the letter. Before dinner, both Baburin and my friend Punin were driving away from the place. I will not undertake to describe my grief, my genuine, truly childish despair. It was so strong that it stifled even the feeling of awe-stricken admiration inspired by the bold action of the republican Baburin. After the conversation with my grandmother, he went at once to his room and began packing up. He did not vouchsafe me one word, one look, though I was the whole time hanging about him, or rather, in reality, about Punin. The latter was utterly distraught, and he too said nothing; but he was continually glancing at me, and tears stood in his eyes ... always the same tears; they neither fell nor dried up. He did not venture to criticise his 'benefactor'—Paramon Semyonitch could not make a mistake,—but great was his distress and dejection. Punin and I made an effort to read something out of the *Rossiad* for the last time; we even locked ourselves up in the lumber-room—it was useless to dream of going into the garden—but at the very first line we both broke down, and I fairly bellowed like a calf, in spite of my twelve years, and my claims to be grown-up.

When he had taken his seat in the carriage Baburin at last turned to me, and with a slight softening of the accustomed sternness of his face, observed: 'It's a lesson for you, young gentleman; remember this incident, and when you grow up, try to put an end to such acts of injustice. Your heart is good, your nature is not yet corrupted.... Mind, be careful; things can't go on like this!' Through my tears, which streamed copiously over my nose, my lips, and my chin, I faltered out that I would ... I would remember, that I promised ... I would do ... I would be sure ... quite sure ...

But at this point, Punin, whom I had before this embraced twenty times (my cheeks were burning from the contact with his unshaven beard, and I was odoriferous of the smell that always clung to him)—at this point a sudden frenzy came over Punin. He jumped up on the seat of the cart, flung both hands up in the air, and began in a voice of thunder (where he got it from!) to declaim the well-known paraphrase of the Psalm of David by Derzhavin,—a poet for this occasion—not a courtier.

> *'God the All-powerful doth arise*
> *And judgeth in the congregation of the mighty! ...*
> *How long, how long, saith the Lord,*
> *Will ye have mercy on the wicked?*
> *"Ye have to keep the laws...."'*

'Sit down!' Baburin said to him.
Punin sat down, but continued:

> *'To save the guiltless and needy,*
> *To give shelter to the afflicted,*
> *To defend the weak from the oppressors.'*

Punin at the word 'oppressors' pointed to the seignorial abode, and then poked the driver in the back.

> *'To deliver the poor out of bondage!*
> *They know not! neither will they understand! ...'*

Nikolai Antonov running out of the seignorial abode, shouted at the top of his voice to the coachman: 'Get away with you! owl! go along! don't stay lingering here!' and the cart rolled away. Only in the distance could still be heard:

'Arise, O Lord God of righteousness! ...
Come forth to judge the unjust—
And be Thou the only Ruler of the nations!'

'What a clown!' remarked Nikolai Antonov.

'He didn't get enough of the rod in his young days,' observed the deacon, appearing on the steps. He had come to inquire what hour it would please the mistress to fix for the night service.

The same day, learning that Yermil was still in the village, and would not till early next morning be despatched to the town for the execution of certain legal formalities, which were intended to check the arbitrary proceedings of the landowners, but served only as a source of additional revenue to the functionaries in superintendence of them, I sought him out, and, for lack of money of my own, handed him a bundle, in which I had tied up two pocket-handkerchiefs, a shabby pair of slippers, a comb, an old night-gown, and a perfectly new silk cravat. Yermil, whom I had to wake up—he was lying on a heap of straw in the back yard, near the cart—Yermil took my present rather indifferently, with some hesitation in fact, did not thank me, promptly poked his head into the straw and fell asleep again. I went home somewhat disappointed. I had imagined that he would be astonished and overjoyed at my visit, would see in it a pledge of my magnanimous intentions for the future—and instead of that ...

'You may say what you like—these people have no feeling,' was my reflection on my homeward way.

My grandmother, who had for some reason left me in peace the whole of that memorable day, looked at me suspiciously when I came after supper to say good-night to her.

'Your eyes are red,' she observed to me in French; 'and there's a smell of the peasant's hut about you. I am not going to enter into an examination of what you've been feeling and doing—I should not like to be obliged to punish you—but I hope you will get over all your foolishness, and begin to conduct yourself once more in a manner befitting a well-bred boy. However, we are soon going back to Moscow, and I shall get you a tutor—as I see you need a man's hand to manage you. You can go.'

We did, as a fact, go back soon after to Moscow.

II

1837

Seven years had passed by. We were living as before at Moscow—but I was by now a student in my second year—and the authority of my grandmoth-er, who had aged very perceptibly in the last years, no longer weighed upon me. Of all my fellow-students the one with whom I was on the friendli-est terms was a light-hearted and good-natured youth called Tarhov. Our habits and our tastes were similar. Tarhov was a great lover of poetry, and himself wrote verses; while in me the seeds sown by Punin had not been without fruit. As is often the case with young people who are very close friends, we had no secrets from one another. But behold, for several days together I noticed a certain excitement and agitation in Tarhov.... He dis-appeared for hours at a time, and I did not know where he had got to—a thing which had never happened before. I was on the point of demanding, in the name of friendship, a full explanation.... He anticipated me.

One day I was sitting in his room.... 'Petya,' he said suddenly, blushing gaily, and looking me straight in the face, 'I must introduce you to my muse.'

'Your muse! how queerly you talk! Like a classicist. (Romanticism was at that time, in 1837, at its full height.) As if I had not known it ever so long—your muse! Have you written a new poem, or what?'

'You don't understand what I mean,' rejoined Tarhov, still laughing and blushing. 'I will introduce you to a living muse.'

'Aha! so that's it! But how is she—yours?'

'Why, because ... But hush, I believe it's she coming here.'

There was the light click of hurrying heels, the door opened, and in the doorway appeared a girl of eighteen, in a chintz cotton gown, with a black cloth cape on her shoulders, and a black straw hat on her fair, rather curly hair. On seeing me she was frightened and disconcerted, and was beating a retreat ... but Tarhov at once rushed to meet her.

'Please, please, Musa Pavlovna, come in! This is my great friend, a splendid fellow—and the soul of discretion. You've no need to be afraid of him. Petya,' he turned to me, 'let me introduce my Musa—Musa Pavlovna Vinogradov, a great friend of mine.'

I bowed.

'How is that ... Musa?' I was beginning.... Tarhov laughed. 'Ah, you didn't know there was such a name in the calendar? I didn't know it either, my boy, till I met this dear young lady. Musa! such a charming name! And suits her so well!'

I bowed again to my comrade's great friend. She left the door, took two steps forward and stood still. She was very attractive, but I could not agree with Tarhov's opinion, and inwardly said to myself: 'Well, she's a strange sort of muse!'

The features of her curved, rosy face were small and delicate; there was an air of fresh, buoyant youth about all her slender, miniature figure; but of the muse, of the personification of the muse, I—and not only I—all the young people of that time had a very different conception! First of all the muse had infallibly to be dark-haired and pale. An expression of scornful pride, a bitter smile, a glance of inspiration, and that 'something'—mysterious, demonic, fateful—that was essential to our conception of the muse, the muse of Byron, who at that time held sovereign sway over men's fancies. There was nothing of that kind to be discerned in the face of the girl who came in. Had I been a little older and more experienced I should probably have paid more attention to her eyes, which were small and deep-set, with full lids, but dark as agate, alert and bright, a thing rare in fair-haired people. Poetical tendencies I should not have detected in their rapid, as it were elusive, glance, but hints of a passionate soul, passionate to self-forgetfulness. But I was very young then.

I held out my hand to Musa Pavlovna—she did not give me hers—she did not notice my movement; she sat down on the chair Tarhov placed for her, but did not take off her hat and cape.

She was, obviously, ill at ease; my presence embarrassed her. She drew deep breaths, at irregular intervals, as though she were gasping for air.

'I've only come to you for one minute, Vladimir Nikolaitch,' she began—her voice was very soft and deep; from her crimson, almost childish lips, it seemed rather strange;—'but our madame would not let me out for more than half an hour. You weren't well the day before yesterday ... and so, I thought ...'

She stammered and hung her head. Under the shade of her thick, low brows her dark eyes darted—to and fro—elusively. There are dark, swift, flashing beetles that flit so in the heat of summer among the blades of dry grass.

'How good you are, Musa, Musotchka!' cried Tarhov. 'But you must stay, you must stay a little.... We'll have the samovar in directly.'

'Oh no, Vladimir Nikolaevitch! it's impossible! I must go away this minute.'

'You must rest a little, anyway. You're out of breath.... You're tired.'

'I'm not tired. It's ... not that ... only ... give me another book; I've finished this one.' She took out of her pocket a tattered grey volume of a Moscow edition.

'Of course, of course. Well, did you like it? *Roslavlev*,' added Tarhov, addressing me.

'Yes. Only I think *Yury Miloslavsky* is much better. Our madame is very strict about books. She says they hinder our working. For, to her thinking ...'

'But, I say, *Yury Miloslavsky*'s not equal to Pushkin's *Gipsies*? Eh? Musa Pavlovna?' Tarhov broke in with a smile.

'No, indeed! The *Gipsies* ...' she murmured slowly. 'Oh yes, another thing, Vladimir Nikolaitch; don't come to-morrow ... you know where.'

'Why not?'

'It's impossible.'

'But why?'

The girl shrugged her shoulders, and all at once, as though she had received a sudden shove, got up from her chair.

'Why, Musa, Musotchka,' Tarhov expostulated plaintively. 'Stay a little!'

'No, no, I can't.' She went quickly to the door, took hold of the handle....

'Well, at least, take the book!'

'Another time.'

Tarhov rushed towards the girl, but at that instant she darted out of the room. He almost knocked his nose against the door. 'What a girl! She's a regular little viper!' he declared with some vexation, and then sank into thought.

I stayed at Tarhov's. I wanted to find out what was the meaning of it all. Tarhov was not disposed to be reserved. He told me that the girl was a milliner; that he had seen her for the first time three weeks before in a fashionable shop, where he had gone on a commission for his sister, who lived in the provinces, to buy a hat; that he had fallen in love with her at first sight, and that next day he had succeeded in speaking to her in the street; that she had herself, it seemed, taken rather a fancy to him.

'Only, please, don't you suppose,' he added with warmth,—'don't you imagine any harm of her. So far, at any rate, there's been nothing of that sort between us.

'Harm!' I caught him up; 'I've no doubt of that; and I've no doubt either that you sincerely deplore the fact, my dear fellow! Have patience—everything will come right'

'I hope so,' Tarhov muttered through his teeth, though with a laugh. 'But really, my boy, that girl ... I tell you—it's a new type, you know. You hadn't time to get a good look at her. She's a shy thing!—oo! such a shy thing! and what a will of her own! But that very shyness is what I like in her. It's a sign of independence! I'm simply over head and ears, my boy!'

Tarhov fell to talking of his 'charmer,' and even read me the beginning of a poem entitled: 'My Muse.' His emotional outpourings were not quite to my taste. I felt secretly jealous of him. I soon left him.

A few days after I happened to be passing through one of the arcades of the Gostinny Dvor. It was Saturday; there were crowds of people shopping; on all sides, in the midst of the pushing and crushing, the shopmen kept shouting to people to buy. Having bought what I wanted, I was thinking of nothing but getting away from their teasing importunity as soon as possible—when all at once I halted involuntarily: in a fruit shop I caught sight of my comrade's charmer—Musa, Musa Pavlovna! She was standing, profile to me, and seemed to be waiting for something. After a moment's hesitation I made up my mind to go up to her and speak. But I had hardly passed through the doorway of the shop and taken off my cap, when she tottered back dismayed, turned quickly to an old man in a frieze cloak, for whom the shopman was weighing out a pound of raisins, and clutched at his arm, as though fleeing to put herself under his protection. The latter, in his turn, wheeled round facing her—and, imagine my amazement, I recognised him as Punin!

Yes, it was he; there were his inflamed eyes, his full lips, his soft, overhanging nose. He had, in fact, changed little during the last seven years; his face was a little flabbier, perhaps.

'Nikander Vavilitch!' I cried. 'Don't you know me?' Punin started, opened his mouth, stared at me....

'I haven't the honour,' he was beginning—and all at once he piped out shrilly: 'The little master of Troitsky (my grandmother's property was called Troitsky)! Can it be the little master of Troitsky?'

The pound of raisins tumbled out of his hands.

'It really is,' I answered, and, picking up Punin's purchase from the ground, I kissed him.

He was breathless with delight and excitement; he almost cried, removed his cap—which enabled me to satisfy myself that the last traces of hair had vanished from his 'egg'—took a handkerchief out of it, blew his nose, poked the cap into his bosom with the raisins, put it on again, again dropped the raisins.... I don't know how Musa was behaving all this time, I tried not to look at her. I don't imagine Punin's agitation proceeded from any extreme attachment to my person; it was simply that his nature could not stand the slightest unexpected shock. The nervous excitability of these poor devils!

'Come and see us, my dear boy,' he faltered at last; 'you won't be too proud to visit our humble nest? You're a student, I see ...'

'On the contrary, I shall be delighted, really.'

'Are you independent now?'

'Perfectly independent.'

'That's capital! How pleased Paramon Semyonitch will be! To-day he'll be home earlier than usual, and madame lets her, too, off for Saturdays. But, stop, excuse me, I am quite forgetting myself. Of course, you don't know our niece!'

I hastened to slip in that I had not yet had the pleasure.

'Of course, of course! How could you know her! Musotchka ... Take note, my dear sir, this girl's name is Musa—and it's not a nickname, but her real name ... Isn't that a predestination? Musotchka, I want to introduce you to Mr. ... Mr. ...'

'B.,' I prompted.

'B.,' he repeated. 'Musotchka, listen! You see before you the most excellent, most delightful of young men. Fate threw us together when he was still in years of boyhood! I beg you to look on him as a friend!'

I swung off a low bow. Musa, red as a poppy, flashed a look on me from under her eyelids, and dropped them immediately.

'Ah!' thought I, 'you 're one of those who in difficult moments don't turn pale, but red; that must be made a note of.'

'You must be indulgent, she's not a fine lady,' observed Punin, and he went out of the shop into the street; Musa and I followed him.

The house in which Punin lodged was a considerable distance from the Gostinny Dvor, being, in fact, in Sadovoy Street. On the way my former preceptor in poetry had time to communicate a good many details of his mode of existence. Since the time of our parting, both he and Baburin had been tossed about holy Russia pretty thoroughly, and had not long—only a year and a half before—found a permanent home in Moscow. Baburin had succeeded in becoming head-clerk in the office of a rich merchant and manufacturer. 'Not a lucrative berth,' Punin observed with a sigh,—'a lot of work, and not much profit ... but what's one to do? One must be thankful to get that! I, too, am trying to earn something by copying and lessons; only my efforts have so far not been crowned with success. My writing, you perhaps recollect, is old-fashioned, not in accordance with the tastes of the day; and as regards lessons—what has been a great obstacle is the absence of befitting attire; moreover, I greatly fear that in the matter of instruction—in the subject of Russian literature—I am also not in harmony

with the tastes of the day; and so it comes about that I am turned away.'
(Punin laughed his sleepy, subdued laugh. He had retained his old, somewhat high-flown manner of speech, and his old weakness for falling into
rhyme.) 'All run after novelties, nothing but innovations! I dare say you,
too, do not honour the old divinities, and fall down before new idols?'

'And you, Nikander Vavilitch, do you really still esteem Heraskov?'

Punin stood still and waved both hands at once. 'In the highest degree,
sir! in the high ... est de ... gree, I do!'

'And you don't read Pushkin? You don't like Pushkin?'

Punin again flung his hands up higher than his head.

'Pushkin? Pushkin is the snake, lying hid in the grass, who is endowed
with the note of the nightingale!'

While Punin and I talked like this, cautiously picking our way over
the unevenly laid brick pavement of so-called 'white-stoned' Moscow—in
which there is not one stone, and which is not white at all—Musa walked
silently beside us on the side further from me. In speaking of her, I called
her 'your niece.' Punin was silent for a little, scratched his head, and informed me in an undertone that he had called her so ... merely as a manner
of speaking; that she was really no relation; that she was an orphan picked
up and cared for by Baburin in the town of Voronezh; but that he, Punin,
might well call her daughter, as he loved her no less than a real daughter.
I had no doubt that, though Punin intentionally dropped his voice, Musa
could hear all he said very well; and she was at once angry, and shy, and
embarrassed; and the lights and shades chased each other over her face,
and everything in it was slightly quivering, the eyelids and brows and lips
and narrow nostrils. All this was very charming, and amusing, and queer.

But at last we reached the 'modest nest.' And modest it certainly was,
the nest. It consisted of a small, one-storied house, that seemed almost
sunk into the ground, with a slanting wooden roof, and four dingy windows in the front. The furniture of the rooms was of the poorest, and not
over tidy, indeed. Between the windows and on the walls hung about a
dozen tiny wooden cages containing larks, canaries, and siskins. 'My subjects!' Punin pronounced triumphantly, pointing his finger at them. We
had hardly time to get in and look about us, Punin had hardly sent Musa
for the samovar, when Baburin himself came in. He seemed to me to have
aged much more than Punin, though his step was as firm as ever, and the
expression of his face altogether was unchanged; but he had grown thin
and bent, his cheeks were sunken, and his thick black shock of hair was
sprinkled with grey. He did not recognise me, and showed no particular

pleasure when Punin mentioned my name; he did not even smile with his eyes, he barely nodded; he asked—very carelessly and drily—whether my *granny* were living—and that was all. 'I'm not over-delighted at a visit from a nobleman,' he seemed to say; 'I don't feel flattered by it.' The republican was a republican still.

Musa came back; a decrepit little old woman followed her, bringing in a tarnished samovar. Punin began fussing about, and pressing me to take things; Baburin sat down to the table, leaned his head on his hands, and looked with weary eyes about him. At tea, however, he began to talk. He was dissatisfied with his position. 'A screw—not a man,' so he spoke of his employer; 'people in a subordinate position are so much dirt to him, of no consequence whatever; and yet it's not so long since he was under the yoke himself. Nothing but cruelty and covetousness. It's a bondage worse than the government's! And all the trade here rests on swindling and flourishes on nothing else!'

Hearing such dispiriting utterances, Punin sighed expressively, assented, shook his head up and down, and from side to side; Musa maintained a stubborn silence.... She was obviously fretted by the doubt, what I was, whether I was a discreet person or a gossip. And if I were discreet, whether it was not with some afterthought in my mind. Her dark, swift, restless eyes fairly flashed to and fro under their half-drooping lids. Only once she glanced at me, but so inquisitively, so searchingly, almost viciously ... I positively started. Baburin scarcely talked to her at all; but whenever he did address her, there was a note of austere, hardly fatherly, tenderness in his voice.

Punin, on the contrary, was continually joking with Musa; she responded unwillingly, however. He called her little snow-maiden, little snowflake.

'Why do you give Musa Pavlovna such names?' I asked.

Punin laughed. 'Because she's such a chilly little thing.'

'Sensible,' put in Baburin: 'as befits a young girl.'

'We may call her the mistress of the house,' cried Punin. 'Hey? Paramon Semyonitch?' Baburin frowned; Musa turned away ... I did not understand the hint at the time.

So passed two hours ... in no very lively fashion, though Punin did his best to 'entertain the honourable company.' For instance, he squatted down in front of the cage of one of the canaries, opened the door, and commanded: 'On the cupola! Begin the concert!' The canary fluttered out at once, perched on the *cupola*, that is to say, on Punin's bald pate, and turning from side to side, and shaking its little wings, carolled with all its might. During the whole time the concert lasted, Punin kept perfectly still, only conducting with his finger, and half closing his eyes. I could not help roaring with laughter ... but neither Baburin nor Musa laughed.

Just as I was leaving, Baburin surprised me by an unexpected question. He wished to ask me, as a man studying at the university, what sort of person Zeno was, and what were my ideas about him.

'What Zeno?' I asked, somewhat puzzled.

'Zeno, the sage of antiquity. Surely he cannot be unknown to you?'

I vaguely recalled the name of Zeno, as the founder of the school of Stoics; but I knew absolutely nothing more about him.

'Yes, he was a philosopher,' I pronounced, at last.

'Zeno,' Baburin resumed in deliberate tones, 'was that wise man, who declared that suffering was not an evil, since fortitude overcomes all things, and that the good in this world is one: justice; and virtue itself is nothing else than justice.'

Punin turned a reverent ear.

'A man living here who has picked up a lot of old books, told me that saying,' continued Baburin; 'it pleased me much. But I see you are not interested in such subjects.'

Baburin was right. In such subjects I certainly was not interested. Since I had entered the university, I had become as much of a republican as Baburin himself. Of Mirabeau, of Robespierre, I would have talked with zest. Robespierre, indeed ... why, I had hanging over my writing-table the lithographed portraits of Fouquier-Tinville and Chalier! But Zeno! Why drag in Zeno?

As he said good-bye to me, Punin insisted very warmly on my visiting them next day, Sunday; Baburin did not invite me at all, and even remarked between his teeth, that talking to plain people of nondescript position could not give me any great pleasure, and would most likely be disagreeable to my *granny*. At that word I interrupted him, however, and gave him to understand that my grandmother had no longer any authority over me.

'Why, you've not come into possession of the property, have you?' queried Baburin.

'No, I haven't,' I answered.

'Well, then, it follows ...' Baburin did not finish his sentence; but I mentally finished it for him: 'it follows that I'm a boy.'

'Good-bye,' I said aloud, and I retired.

I was just going out of the courtyard into the street ... Musa suddenly ran out of the house, and slipping a piece of crumpled paper into my hand, disappeared at once. At the first lamp-post I unfolded the paper. It turned out to be a note. With difficulty I deciphered the pale pencil-marks.

'For God's sake,' Musa had written, 'come to-morrow after matins to the Alexandrovsky garden near the Kutafia tower I shall wait for you don't refuse me don't make me miserable I simply must see you.' There were no mistakes in spelling in this note, but neither was there any punctuation. I returned home in perplexity.

When, a quarter of an hour before the appointed time, next day, I began to get near the Kutafia tower (it was early in April, the buds were swelling, the grass was growing greener, and the sparrows were noisily chirrupping and quarrelling in the bare lilac bushes), considerably to my surprise, I caught sight of Musa a little to one side, not far from the fence. She was there before me. I was going towards her; but she herself came to meet me.

'Let's go to the Kreml wall,' she whispered in a hurried voice, running her downcast eyes over the ground; 'there are people here.'

We went along the path up the hill.

'Musa Pavlovna,' I was beginning.... But she cut me short at once.

'Please,' she began, speaking in the same jerky and subdued voice, 'don't criticise me, don't think any harm of me. I wrote a letter to you, I made an appointment to meet you, because ... I was afraid.... It seemed to me yesterday,—you seemed to be laughing all the time. Listen,' she added, with sudden energy, and she stopped short and turned towards me: 'listen; if you tell with whom ... if you mention at whose room you met me, I'll throw myself in the water, I'll drown myself, I'll make an end of myself!'

At this point, for the first time, she glanced at me with the inquisitive, piercing look I had seen before.

'Why, she, perhaps, really ... would do it,' was my thought.

'Really, Musa Pavlovna,' I protested, hurriedly: 'how can you have such a bad opinion of me? Do you suppose I am capable of betraying my friend and injuring you? Besides, come to that, there's nothing in your relations, as far as I'm aware, deserving of censure.... For goodness' sake, be calm.'

Musa heard me out, without stirring from the spot, or looking at me again.

'There's something else I ought to tell you,' she began, moving forward again along the path, 'or else you may think I'm quite mad! I ought to tell you, that old man wants to marry me!'

'What old man? The bald one? Punin?'

'No—not he! The other ... Paramon Semyonitch.'

'Baburin?'

'Yes.'

'Is it possible? Has he made you an offer?'

'Yes.'

'But you didn't consent, of course?'

'Yes, I did consent ... because I didn't understand what I was about then. Now it's a different matter.'

I flung up my hands. 'Baburin—and you! Why, he must be fifty!'

'He says forty-three. But that makes no difference. If he were five—and—twenty I wouldn't marry him. Much happiness I should find in it! A whole week will go by without his smiling once! Paramon Semyonitch is my benefactor, I am deeply indebted to him; he took care of me, educated me; I should have been utterly lost but for him; I'm bound to look on him as a father.... But be his wife! I'd rather die! I'd rather be in my coffin!'

'Why do you keep talking about death, Musa Pavlovna?'

Musa stopped again.

'Why, is life so sweet, then? Even your friend Vladimir Nikolaitch, I may say, I've come to love from being wretched and dull: and then Paramon Semyonitch with his offers of marriage.... Punin, though he bores me with his verses, he doesn't scare me, anyway; he doesn't make me read Karamzin in the evenings, when my head's ready to drop off my shoulders for weariness! And what are these old men to me? They call me cold, too. With them, is it likely I should be warm? If they try to make me—I shall go. Paramon Semyonitch himself's always saying: Freedom! freedom! All right, I want freedom too. Or else it comes to this! Freedom for every one else, and keeping me in a cage! I'll tell him so myself. But if you betray me, or drop a hint—remember; they'll never set eyes on me again!'

Musa stood in the middle of the path.

'They'll never set eyes on me again!' she repeated sharply. This time, too, she did not raise her eyes to me; she seemed to be aware that she would infallibly betray herself, would show what was in her heart, if any one looked her straight in the face.... And that was just why she did not lift her eyes, except when she was angry or annoyed, and then she stared straight at the person she was speaking to.... But her small pretty face was aglow with indomitable resolution.

'Why, Tarhov was right,' flashed through my head; 'this girl is a new type.'

'You've no need to be afraid of me,' I declared, at last.

'Truly? Even, if ... You said something about our relations.... But even if there were ...' she broke off.

'Even in that case, you would have no need to be afraid, Musa Pavlovna. I am not your judge. Your secret is buried here.' I pointed to my bosom. 'Believe me, I know how to appreciate ...'

'Have you got my letter?' Musa asked suddenly.

'Yes.'

'Where?'

'In my pocket.'

'Give it here ... quick, quick!'

I got out the scrap of paper. Musa snatched it in her rough little hand, stood still a moment facing me, as though she were going to thank me; but suddenly started, looked round, and without even a word at parting, ran quickly down the hill.

I looked in the direction she had taken. At no great distance from the tower I discerned, wrapped in an 'Almaviva' ('Almavivas' were then in the height of fashion), a figure which I recognised at once as Tarhov.

'Aha, my boy,' thought I, 'you must have had notice, then, since you're on the look-out.'

And whistling to myself, I started homewards.

Next morning I had only just drunk my morning tea, when Punin made his appearance. He came into my room with rather an embarrassed face, and began making bows, looking about him, and apologising for his intrusion, as he called it. I made haste to reassure him. I, sinful man, imagined that Punin had come with the intention of borrowing money. But he confined himself to asking for a glass of tea with rum in it, as, luckily, the samovar had not been cleared away. 'It's with some trepidation and sinking of heart that I have come to see you,' he said, as he nibbled a lump of sugar. 'You I do not fear; but I stand in awe of your honoured grandmother! I am abashed too by my attire, as I have already communicated to you.' Punin passed his finger along the frayed edge of his ancient coat. 'At home it's no matter, and in the street, too, it's no harm; but when one finds one's self in gilded palaces, one's poverty stares one in the face, and one feels confused!' I occupied two small rooms on the ground floor, and certainly it would never have entered any one's head to call them palaces, still less gilded; but Punin apparently was referring to the whole of my grandmother's house, though that too was by no means conspicuously sumptuous. He reproached me for not having been to see them the previous day; 'Paramon Semyonitch,' said he, 'expected you, though he did declare that you would be sure not to come. And Musotchka, too, expected you.'

'What? Musa Pavlovna too?' I queried.

'She too. She's a charming girl we have got with us, isn't she? What do you say?'

'Very charming,' I assented. Punin rubbed his bare head with extraordinary rapidity.

'She's a beauty, sir, a pearl or even a diamond—it's the truth I am telling you.' He bent down quite to my ear. 'Noble blood, too,' he whispered to me, 'only—you understand—left-handed; the forbidden fruit was eaten. Well, the parents died, the relations would do nothing for her, and flung her to the hazards of destiny, that's to say, despair, dying of hunger! But at that point Paramon Semyonitch steps forward, known as a deliverer from of old! He took her, clothed her and cared for her, brought up the poor nestling; and she has blossomed into our darling! I tell you, a man of the rarest qualities!'

Punin subsided against the back of the armchair, lifted his hands, and again bending forward, began whispering again, but still more mysteriously: 'You see Paramon Semyonitch himself too.... Didn't you know? he too is of exalted extraction—and on the left side, too. They do say—his father was a powerful Georgian prince, of the line of King David.... What do you make of that? A few words—but how much is said? The blood of King David! What do you think of that? And according to other accounts, the founder of the family of Paramon Semyonitch was an Indian Shah, Babur. Blue blood! That's fine too, isn't it? Eh?'

'Well?' I queried, 'and was he too, Baburin, flung to the hazards of destiny?'

Punin rubbed his pate again. 'To be sure he was! And with even greater cruelty than our little lady! From his earliest childhood nothing but struggling! And, in fact, I will confess that, inspired by Ruban, I composed in allusion to this fact a stanza for the portrait of Paramon Semyonitch. Wait a bit ... how was it? Yes!

> *'E'en from the cradle fate's remorseless blows*
> *Baburin drove towards the abyss of woes!*
> *But as in darkness gleams the light, so now*
> *The conqueror's laurel wreathes his noble brow!'*

Punin delivered these lines in a rhythmic, sing-song voice, with full rounded vowels, as verses should be read.

'So that's how it is he's a republican!' I exclaimed.

'No, that's not why,' Punin answered simply. 'He forgave his father long ago; but he cannot endure injustice of any sort; it's the sorrows of others that trouble him!'

I wanted to turn the conversation on what I had learned from Musa the day before, that is to say, on Baburin's matrimonial project,—but I did not know how to proceed. Punin himself got me out of the difficulty.

78

'Did you notice nothing?' he asked me suddenly, slily screwing up his eyes, 'while you were with us? nothing special?'

'Why, was there anything to notice?' I asked in my turn.

Punin looked over his shoulder, as though anxious to satisfy himself that no one was listening. 'Our little beauty, Musotchka, is shortly to be a married lady!'

'How so?'

'Madame Baburin,' Punin announced with an effort, and slapping his knees several times with his open hands, he nodded his head, like a china mandarin.

'Impossible!' I cried, with assumed astonishment. Punin's head slowly came to rest, and his hands dropped down. 'Why impossible, allow me to ask?'

'Because Paramon Semyonitch is more fit to be your young lady's father; because such a difference in age excludes all likelihood of love—on the girl's side.'

'Excludes?' Punin repeated excitedly. 'But what about gratitude? and pure affection? and tenderness of feeling? Excludes! You must consider this: admitting that Musa's a splendid girl; but then to gain Paramon Semyonitch's affection, to be his comfort, his prop—his spouse, in short! is that not the loftiest possible happiness even for such a girl? And she realises it! You should look, turn an attentive eye! In Paramon Semyonitch's presence Musotchka is all veneration, all tremor and enthusiasm!'

'That's just what's wrong, Nikander Vavilitch, that she is, as you say, all tremor. If you love any one you don't feel tremors in their presence.'

'But with that I can't agree! Here am I, for instance; no one, I suppose, could love Paramon Semyonitch more than I, but I ... tremble before him.'

'Oh, you—that's a different matter.'

'How is it a different matter? how? how?' interrupted Punin. I simply did not know him; he got hot, and serious, almost angry, and quite dropped his rhythmic sing-song in speaking. 'No,' he declared; 'I notice that you have not a good eye for character! No; you can't read people's hearts!' I gave up contradicting him ... and to give another turn to the conversation, proposed, for the sake of old times, that we should read something together.

Punin was silent for a while.

'One of the old poets? The real ones?' he asked at last.

'No; a new one.'

'A new one?' Punin repeated mistrustfully.

'Pushkin,' I answered. I suddenly thought of the *Gypsies* which Tarhov had mentioned not long before. There, by the way, is the ballad about the old husband. Punin grumbled a little, but I sat him down on the sofa, so that he could listen more comfortably, and began to read Pushkin's poem. The passage came at last, 'old husband, cruel husband'; Punin heard the ballad through to the end, and all at once he got up impulsively.

'I can't,' he pronounced, with an intense emotion, which impressed even me;—'excuse me; I cannot hear more of that author. He is an immoral slanderer; he is a liar ... he upsets me. I cannot! Permit me to cut short my visit to-day.'

I began trying to persuade Punin to remain; but he insisted on having his own way with a sort of stupid, scared obstinacy: he repeated several times that he felt upset, and wished to get a breath of fresh air—and all the while his lips were faintly quivering and his eyes avoided mine, as though I had wounded him. So he went away. A little while after, I too went out of the house and set off to see Tarhov.

Without inquiring of any one, with a student's usual lack of ceremony, I walked straight into his lodgings. In the first room there was no one. I called Tarhov by name, and receiving no answer, was just going to retreat; but the door of the adjoining room opened, and my friend appeared. He looked at me rather queerly, and shook hands without speaking. I had come to him to repeat all I had heard from Punin; and though I felt at once that I had called on Tarhov at the wrong moment, still, after talking a little about extraneous matters, I ended by informing him of Baburin's intentions in regard to Musa. This piece of news did not, apparently, surprise him much; he quietly sat down at the table, and fixing his eyes intently upon me, and keeping silent as before, gave to his features an expression ... an expression, as though he would say: 'Well, what more have you to tell? Come, out with your ideas!' I looked more attentively into his face.... It struck me as eager, a little ironical, a little arrogant even. But that did not hinder me from bringing out my ideas. On the contrary. 'You're showing off,' was my thought; 'so I am not going to spare you!' And there and then I proceeded straightway to enlarge upon the mischief of yielding to impulsive feelings, upon the duty of every man to respect the freedom and personal life of another man—in short, I proceeded to enunciate useful and appropriate counsel. Holding forth in this manner, I walked up and down the room, to be more at ease. Tarhov did not interrupt me, and did not stir from his seat; he only played with his fingers on his chin.

'I know,' said I ... (Exactly what was my motive in speaking so, I have no clear idea myself—envy, most likely; it was not devotion to morality, anyway!) 'I know,' said I, 'that it's no easy matter, no joking matter; I am sure you love Musa, and that Musa loves you—that it is not a passing fancy on your part.... But, see, let us suppose! (Here I folded my arms on my breast.) ... Let us suppose you gratify your passion—what is to follow? You won't marry her, you know. And at the same time you are wrecking the happiness of an excellent, honest man, her benefactor—and—who knows? (here my face expressed at the same time penetration and sorrow)—possibly her own happiness too....'

And so on, and so on!

For about a quarter of an hour my discourse flowed on. Tarhov was still silent. I began to be disconcerted by this silence. I glanced at him from time to time, not so much to satisfy myself as to the impression my words were making on him, as to find out why he neither objected nor agreed, but sat like a deaf mute. At last I fancied that there was ... yes, there certainly was a change in his face. It began to show signs of uneasiness, agitation, painful agitation.... Yet, strange to say, the eager, bright, laughing something, which had struck me at my first glance at Tarhov, still did not leave that agitated, that troubled face! I could not make up my mind whether or no to congratulate myself on the success of my sermon, when Tarhov suddenly got up, and pressing both my hands, said, speaking very quickly, 'Thank you, thank you. You're right, of course, ... though, on the other side, one might observe ... What is your Baburin you make so much of, after all? An honest fool—and nothing more! You call him a republican—and he's simply a fool! Oo! That's what he is! All his republicanism simply means that he can never get on anywhere!'

'Ah! so that's your idea! A fool! can never get on!—but let me tell you,' I pursued, with sudden heat, 'let me tell you, my dear Vladimir Nikolaitch, that in these days to get on nowhere is a sign of a fine, a noble nature! None but worthless people—bad people—get on anywhere and accommodate themselves to everything. You say Baburin is an honest fool! Why, is it better, then, to your mind, to be dishonest and clever?'

'You distort my words!' cried Tarhov. 'I only wanted to explain how I understand that person. Do you think he's such a rare specimen? Not a bit of it! I've met other people like him in my time. A man sits with an air of importance, silent, obstinate, angular.... O-ho-ho! say you. It shows that there's a great deal in him! But there's nothing in him, not one idea in his head—nothing but a sense of his own dignity.'

'Even if there is nothing else, that's an honourable thing,' I broke in. 'But let me ask where you have managed to study him like this? You don't know him, do you? Or are you describing him ... from what Musa tells you?'

Tarhov shrugged his shoulders. 'Musa and I ... have other things to talk of. I tell you what,' he added, his whole body quivering with impatience,—'I tell you what: if Baburin has such a noble and honest nature, how is it he doesn't see that Musa is not a fit match for him? It's one of two things: either he knows that what he's doing to her is something of the nature of an outrage, all in the name of gratitude ... and if so, what about his honesty?—or he doesn't realise it ... and in that case, what can one call him but a fool?'

I was about to reply, but Tarhov again clutched my hands, and again began talking in a hurried voice. 'Though ... of course ... I confess you are right, a thousand times right.... You are a true friend ... but now leave me alone, please.'

I was puzzled. 'Leave you alone?'

'Yes. I must, don't you see, think over all you've just said, thoroughly.... I have no doubt you are right ... but now leave me alone!'

'You 're in such a state of excitement ...' I was beginning.

'Excitement? I?' Tarhov laughed, but instantly pulled himself up. 'Yes, of course I am. How could I help being? You say yourself it's no joking matter. Yes; I must think about it ... alone.' He was still squeezing my hands. 'Good-bye, my dear fellow, good-bye!'

'Good-bye,' I repeated. 'Good-bye, old boy!' As I was going away I flung a last glance at Tarhov. He seemed pleased. At what? At the fact that I, like a true friend and comrade, had pointed out the danger of the way upon which he had set his foot—or that I was going? Ideas of the most diverse kind were floating in my head the whole day till evening—till the very instant when I entered the house occupied by Punin and Baburin, for I went to see them the same day. I am bound to confess that some of Tarhov's phrases had sunk deep into my soul ... and were ringing in my ears.... In truth, was it possible Baburin ... was it possible he did not see she was not a fit match for him?

But could this possibly be: Baburin, the self-sacrificing Baburin—an honest fool!

Punin had said, when he came to see me, that I had been expected there the day before. That may have been so, but on this day, it is certain, no one expected me.... I found every one at home, and every one was surprised at my visit. Baburin and Punin were both unwell: Punin had a headache, and he was lying curled up on the sofa, with his head tied up in a spotted handkerchief, and strips of cucumber applied to his temples. Baburin was suffering from a bilious attack; all yellow, almost dusky, with dark rings round his eyes, with scowling brow and unshaven chin—he did not look much like a bridegroom! I tried to go away.... But they would not let me go, and even made tea. I spent anything but a cheerful evening. Musa, it is true, had no ailment, and was less shy than usual too, but she was obviously vexed, angry.... At last she could not restrain herself, and, as she handed me a cup of tea, she whispered hurriedly: 'You can say what you like, you may try your utmost, you won't make any difference.... So there!' I looked at her in astonishment, and, seizing a favourable moment, asked her, also in a whisper, 'What's the meaning of your words?' 'I'll tell you,' she answered, and her black eyes, gleaming angrily under her frowning brows, were fastened for an instant on my face, and turned away at once: 'the meaning is that I heard all you said there to-day, and thank you for nothing, and things won't be as you 'd have them, anyway.' 'You were there,' broke from me unconsciously.... But at this point Baburin's attention was caught, and he glanced in our direction. Musa walked away from me.

Ten minutes later she managed to come near me again. She seemed to enjoy saying bold and dangerous things to me, and saying them in the presence of her protector, under his vigilant eye, only exercising barely enough caution not to arouse his suspicions. It is well known that walking on the brink, on the very edge, of the precipice is woman's favourite pastime. 'Yes, I was there,' whispered Musa, without any change of countenance, except that her nostrils were faintly quivering and her lips twitching. 'Yes, and if Paramon Semyonitch asks me what I am whispering about with you, I'd tell him this minute. What do I care?'

'Be more careful,' I besought her. 'I really believe they are noticing.'

'I tell you, I'm quite ready to tell them everything. And who's noticing? One's stretching his neck off the pillow, like a sick duck, and hears nothing; and the other's deep in philosophy. Don't you be afraid!' Musa's voice rose a little, and her cheeks gradually flushed a sort of malignant, dusky red; and this suited her marvellously, and never had she been so pretty. As she cleared the table, and set the cups and saucers in their places, she moved swiftly about the room; there was something challenging about her light, free and easy movement. 'You may criticise me as you like,' she seemed to say; 'but I'm going my own way, and I'm not afraid of you.'

I cannot disguise the fact that I found Musa bewitching just that evening. 'Yes,' I mused; 'she's a little spitfire—she's a new type.... She's—exquisite. Those hands know how to deal a blow, I dare say.... What of it! No matter!'

'Paramon Semyonitch,' she cried suddenly, 'isn't a republic an empire in which every one does as he chooses?'

'A republic is not an empire,' answered Baburin, raising his head, and contracting his brows; 'it is a ... form of society in which everything rests on law and justice.'

'Then,' Musa pursued, 'in a republic no one can oppress any one else?'

'No.'

'And every one is free to dispose of himself?'

'Quite free.'

'Ah! that's all I wanted to know.'

'Why do you want to know?'

'Oh, I wanted to—I wanted *you* to tell me that.'

'Our young lady is anxious to learn,' Punin observed from the sofa.

When I went out into the passage Musa accompanied me, not, of course, from politeness, but with the same malicious intent. I asked her, as I took leave, 'Can you really love him so much?'

'Whether I love him, or whether I don't, that's *my* affair,' she answered. 'What is to be, will be.'

'Mind what you're about; don't play with fire ... you'll get burnt.'

'Better be burnt than frozen. You ... with your good advice! And how can you tell he won't marry me? How do you know I so particularly want to get married? If I am ruined ... what business is it of yours?'

She slammed the door after me.

I remember that on the way home I reflected with some pleasure that my friend Vladimir Tarhov might find things rather hot for him with his new type.... He ought to have to pay something for his happiness!

That he would be happy, I was—regretfully—unable to doubt.

Three days passed by. I was sitting in my room at my writing-table, and not so much working as getting myself ready for lunch.... I heard a rustle, lifted my head, and I was stupefied. Before me—rigid, terrible, white as chalk, stood an apparition ... Punin. His half-closed eyes were looking at me, blinking slowly; they expressed a senseless terror, the terror of a frightened hare, and his arms hung at his sides like sticks.

'Nikander Vavilitch! what is the matter with you? How did you come here? Did no one see you? What has happened? Do speak!'

'She has run away,' Punin articulated in a hoarse, hardly audible voice.

'What do you say?'

'She has run away,' he repeated.

'Who?'

'Musa. She went away in the night, and left a note.'

'A note?'

'Yes. "I thank you," she said, "but I am not coming back again. Don't look for me." We ran up and down; we questioned the cook; she knew nothing. I can't speak loud; you must excuse me. I've lost my voice.'

'Musa Pavlovna has left you!' I exclaimed. 'Nonsense! Mr. Baburin must be in despair. What does he intend to do now?'

'He has no intention of doing anything. I wanted to run to the Governor-general: he forbade it. I wanted to give information to the police; he forbade that too, and got very angry. He says, "She's free." He says, "I don't want to constrain her." He has even gone to work, to his office. But he looks more dead than alive. He loved her terribly....Oh, oh, we both loved her!'

Here Punin for the first time showed that he was not a wooden image, but a live man; he lifted both his fists in the air, and brought them down on his pate, which shone like ivory.

'Ungrateful girl!' he groaned; 'who was it gave you food and drink, clothed you, and brought you up? who cared for you, would have given all his life, all his soul ... And you have forgotten it all? To cast me off, truly, were no great matter, but Paramon Semyonitch, Paramon ...'

I begged him to sit down, to rest.

Punin shook his head. 'No, I won't. I have come to you ... I don't know what for. I'm like one distraught; to stay at home alone is fearful; what am I to do with myself? I stand in the middle of the room, shut my eyes, and call, "Musa! Musotchka!" That's the way to go out of one's mind. But no, why am I talking nonsense? I know why I have come to you. You know, the other day you read me that thrice-accursed poem ... you remember, where there is talk of an old husband. What did you do that for? Did you know something then ... or guessed something?' Punin glanced at me. 'Piotr Petrovitch,' he cried suddenly, and he began trembling all over, 'you know, perhaps, where she is. Kind friend, tell me whom she has gone to!'

I was disconcerted, and could not help dropping my eyes....

'Perhaps she said something in her letter,' I began....

'She said she was leaving us because she loved some one else! Dear, good friend, you know, surely, where she is? Save her, let us go to her; we will persuade her. Only think what a man she's bringing to ruin.'

Punin all at once flushed crimson, the blood seemed to rush to his head, he plumped heavily down on his knees. 'Save us, friend, let us go to her.'

My servant appeared in the doorway, and stood still in amazement.

I had no little trouble to get Punin on to his feet again, to convince him that, even if I did suspect something, still it would not do to act like that, on the spur of the moment, especially both together—that would only spoil all our efforts—that I was ready to do my best, but would not answer for anything. Punin did not oppose me, nor did he indeed hear me; he only repeated from time to time in his broken voice, 'Save her, save her and Paramon Semyonitch.' At last he began to cry. 'Tell me at least one thing,' he asked ... 'is *he* handsome, young?'

'Yes, he is young,' I answered.

'He is young,' repeated Punin, smearing the tears over his cheeks; 'and she is young.... It's from that that all the trouble's sprung!'

This rhyme came by chance; poor Punin was in no mood for versifying. I would have given a good deal to hear his rhapsodical eloquence again, or even his almost noiseless laugh.... Alas! his eloquence was quenched for ever, and I never heard his laugh again.

I promised to let him know, as soon as I should find out anything positive.... Tarhov's name I did not, however, mention. Punin suddenly collapsed completely. 'Very good, very good, sir, thank you,' he said with a pitiful face, using the word 'sir,' which he had never done before; 'only mind, sir, do not say anything to Paramon Semyonitch ... or he'll be angry. In one word, he has forbidden it. Good-bye, sir.'

As he got up and turned his back to me, Punin struck me as such a poor feeble creature, that I positively marvelled; he limped with both legs, and doubled up at each step....

'It's a bad look-out. It's the end of him, that's what it means,' I thought.

Though I had promised Punin to trace Musa, yet as I set off the same day to Tarhov's, I had not the slightest expectation of learning anything, as I considered it certain that either I should not find him at home, or that he would refuse to see me. My supposition turned out to be a mistaken one. I found Tarhov at home; he received me, and I found out indeed all I wanted to know; but there was nothing gained by that. Directly I crossed the threshold of his door, Tarhov came resolutely, rapidly, to meet me, and his eyes sparkling and glowing, his face grown handsomer and radiant, he said firmly and briskly: 'Listen, Petya, my boy; I guess what you've come for, and what you want to talk about; but I give you warning, if you say a single word about her, or about her action, or about what, according to you, is the course dictated to me by common sense, we're friends no longer, we're not even acquainted, and I shall beg you to treat me as a stranger.'

I looked at Tarhov; he was quivering all over inwardly, like a tightly drawn harpstring; he was tingling all over, hardly could he hold back the tide of brimming youth and passion; violent, ecstatic happiness had burst into his soul, and had taken full possession of him—and he of it.

'Is that your final decision?' I pronounced mournfully.

'Yes, Petya, my boy, it's final.'

'In that case, there's nothing for me but to say good-bye.'

Tarhov faintly dropped his eyelids.... He was too happy at that moment.

86

'Good-bye, Petya, old boy,' he said, a little through his nose, with a candid smile and a gay flash of all his white teeth.

What was I to do? I left him to his 'happiness.' As I slammed the door after me, the other door of the room slammed also—I heard it.

It was with a heavy heart that I trudged off next day to see my luckless acquaintances. I secretly hoped—such is human weakness—that I should not find them at home, and again I was mistaken. Both were at home. The change that had taken place in them during the last three days must have struck any one. Punin looked ghastly white and flabby. His talkativeness had completely vanished. He spoke listlessly, feebly, still in the same husky voice, and looked somehow lost and bewildered. Baburin, on the contrary, seemed shrunk into himself, and blacker than ever; taciturn at the best of times, he uttered nothing now but a few abrupt sounds; an expression of stony severity seemed to have frozen on his countenance.

I felt it impossible to be silent; but what was there to say? I confined myself to whispering to Punin, 'I have discovered nothing, and my advice to you is to give up all hope.' Punin glanced at me with his swollen, red little eyes—the only red left in his face—muttered something inaudible, and hobbled away. Baburin most likely guessed what I had been speaking about to Punin, and opening his lips, which were tightly compressed, as though glued together, he pronounced, in a deliberate voice, 'My dear sir, since your last visit to us, something disagreeable has happened to us; our young friend, Musa Pavlovna Vinogradov, finding it no longer convenient to live with us, has decided to leave us, and has given us a written communication to that effect. Not considering that we have any right to hinder her doing so, we have left her to act according to her own views of what is best. We trust that she may be happy,' he added, with some effort; 'and I humbly beg you not to allude to the subject, as any such references are useless, and even painful.'

'So he too, like Tarhov, forbids my speaking of Musa,' was the thought that struck me, and I could not help wondering inwardly. He might well prize Zeno so highly. I wished to impart to him some facts about that sage, but my tongue would not form the words, and it did well.

I soon went about my business. At parting neither Punin nor Baburin said, 'Till we meet!' both with one voice pronounced, 'Good-bye.'

Punin even returned me a volume of the *Telegraph* I had brought him, as much as to say, 'he had no need of anything of that kind now.'

A week later I had a curious encounter. An early spring had set in abruptly; at midday the heat rose to eighteen degrees Reaumur. Everything was turning green, and shooting up out of the spongy, damp earth. I hired a horse at the riding-school, and went out for a ride into the outskirts of the town, towards the Vorobyov hills. On the road I was met by a little cart, drawn by a pair of spirited ponies, splashed with mud up to their ears, with plaited tails, and red ribbons in their manes and forelocks. Their harness was such as sportsmen affect, with copper discs and tassels; they were being driven by a smart young driver, in a blue tunic without sleeves, a yellow striped silk shirt, and a low felt hat with peacock's feathers round the crown. Beside him sat a girl of the artisan or merchant class, in a flowered silk jacket, with a big blue handkerchief on her head—and she was simply bubbling over with mirth. The driver was laughing too. I drew my horse on one side, but did not, however, take particular notice of the swiftly passing, merry couple, when, all at once, the young man shouted to his ponies.... Why, that was Tarhov's voice! I looked round.... Yes, it was he; unmistakably he, dressed up as a peasant, and beside him—wasn't it Musa?

But at that instant their ponies quickened their pace, and they were out of my sight in a minute. I tried to put my horse into a gallop in pursuit of them, but it was an old riding school hack, that shambled from side to side as it moved; it went more slowly galloping than trotting.

'Enjoy yourselves, my dear friends!' I muttered through my teeth.

I ought to observe that I had not seen Tarhov during the whole week, though I had been three times to his rooms. He was never at home. Baburin and Punin I had not seen either.... I had not been to see them.

I caught cold on my ride; though it was very warm, there was a piercing wind. I was dangerously ill, and when I recovered I went with my grandmother into the country 'to feed up,' by the doctor's advice. I did not get to Moscow again; in the autumn I was transferred to the Petersburg university.

III

1849

Not seven, but fully twelve years had passed by, and I was in my thirty-second year. My grandmother had long been dead; I was living in Petersburg, with a post in the Department of Home Affairs. Tarhov I had lost sight of; he had gone into the army, and lived almost always in the provinces.

We had met twice, as old friends, glad to see each other; but we had not touched on the past in our talk. At the time of our last meeting he was, if I remember right, already a married man.

One sultry summer day I was sauntering along Gorohov Street, cursing my official duties for keeping me in Petersburg, and the heat and stench and dust of the city. A funeral barred my way. It consisted of a solitary car, that is, to be accurate, of a decrepit hearse, on which a poor-looking wooden coffin, half-covered with a threadbare black cloth, was shaking up and down as it was jolted violently over the uneven pavement. An old man with a white head was walking alone after the hearse.

I looked at him.... His face seemed familiar.... He too turned his eyes upon me.... Merciful heavens! it was Baburin! I took off my hat, went up to him, mentioned my name, and walked along beside him.

'Whom are you burying?' I asked.

'Nikander Vavilitch Punin,' he answered.

I felt, I knew beforehand, that he would utter that name, and yet it set my heart aching. I felt melancholy, and yet I was glad that chance had enabled me to pay my last respects to my old friend....

'May I go with you, Paramon Semyonitch?'

'You may.... I was following him alone; now there'll be two of us.'

Our walk lasted more than an hour. My companion moved forward, without lifting his eyes or opening his lips. He had become quite an old man since I had seen him last; his deeply furrowed, copper-coloured face stood out sharply against his white hair. Signs of a life of toil and suffering, of continual struggle, could be seen in Baburin's whole figure; want and poverty had worked cruel havoc with him. When everything was over, when what was Punin had disappeared for ever in the damp ... yes, undoubtedly damp earth of the Smolensky cemetery, Baburin, after standing a couple of minutes with bowed, uncovered head before the newly risen mound of sandy clay, turned to me his emaciated, as it were embittered, face, his dry, sunken eyes, thanked me grimly, and was about to move away; but I detained him.

'Where do you live, Paramon Semyonitch? Let me come and see you. I had no idea you were living in Petersburg. We could recall old days, and talk of our dead friend.'

Baburin did not answer me at once.

'It's two years since I found my way to Petersburg,' he observed at last; 'I live at the very end of the town. However, if you really care to visit me, come.' He gave me his address. 'Come in the evening; in the evening we are always at home ... both of us.'

'Both of you?'

'I am married. My wife is not very well to-day, and that's why she did not come too. Though, indeed, it's quite enough for one person to go through this empty formality, this ceremony. As if anybody believed in it all!'

I was a little surprised at Baburin's last words, but I said nothing, called a cab, and proposed to Baburin to take him home; but he refused.

The same day I went in the evening to see him. All the way there I was thinking of Punin. I recalled how I had met him the first time, and how ecstatic and amusing he was in those days; and afterwards in Moscow how subdued he had grown—especially the last time I saw him; and now he had made his last reckoning with life;—life is in grim earnest, it seems! Baburin was living in the Viborgsky quarter, in a little house which reminded me of the Moscow 'nest': the Petersburg abode was almost shabbier in appearance. When I went into his room he was sitting on a chair in a corner with his hands on his knees; a tallow candle, burning low, dimly lighted up his bowed, white head. He heard the sound of my footsteps, started up, and welcomed me more warmly than I had expected. A few moments later his wife came in; I recognised her at once as Musa—and only then understood why Baburin had invited me to come; he wanted to show me that he had after all come by his own.

Musa was greatly changed—in face, in voice, and in manners; but her eyes were changed most of all. In old times they had darted about like live creatures, those malicious, beautiful eyes; they had gleamed stealthily, but brilliantly; their glance had pierced, like a pin-prick.... Now they looked at one directly, calmly, steadily; their black centres had lost their lustre. 'I am broken in, I am tame, I am good,' her soft and dull gaze seemed to say. Her continued, submissive smile told the same story. And her dress, too, was subdued; brown, with little spots on it. She came up to me, asked me whether I knew her. She obviously felt no embarrassment, and not because she had lost a sense of shame or memory of the past, but simply because all petty self-consciousness had left her.

Musa talked a great deal about Punin, talked in an even voice, which too had lost its fire. I learned that of late years he had become very feeble, had almost sunk into childishness, so much so that he was miserable if he had not toys to play with; they persuaded him, it is true, that he made them out of waste stuff for sale ... but he really played with them himself. His passion for poetry, however, never died out, and he kept his memory for nothing but verses; a few days before his death he recited a passage from the *Rossiad*; but Pushkin he feared, as children fear bogies. His devotion to Baburin had also remained undiminished; he worshipped him as much as ever, and even at the last, wrapped about by the chill and dark of the end, he had faltered with halting tongue, 'benefactor!' I learned also from Musa that soon after the Moscow episode, it had been Baburin's fate once more to wander all over Russia, continually tossed from one private situation to another; that in Petersburg, too, he had been again in a situation, in a private business, which situation he had, however, been obliged to leave a few days before, owing to some unpleasantness with his employer: Baburin had ventured to stand up for the workpeople.... The invariable smile, with which Musa accompanied her words, set me musing mournfully; it put the finishing touch to the impression made on me by her husband's appearance. They had hard work, the two of them, to make a bare living—there was no doubt of it. He took very little part in our conversation; he seemed more preoccupied than grieved.... Something was worrying him.

'Paramon Semyonitch, come here,' said the cook, suddenly appearing in the doorway.

'What is it? what's wanted?' he asked in alarm.

'Come here,' the cook repeated insistently and meaningly. Baburin buttoned up his coat and went out.

When I was left alone with Musa, she looked at me with a somewhat changed glance, and observed in a voice which was also changed, and with no smile: 'I don't know, Piotr Petrovitch, what you think of me now, but I dare say you remember what I used to be.... I was self-confident, light-hearted ... and not good; I wanted to live for my own pleasure. But I want to tell you this: when I was abandoned, and was like one lost, and was only waiting for God to take me, or to pluck up spirit to make an end of myself,—once more, just as in Voronezh, I met with Paramon Semyonitch—and he saved me once again.... Not a word that could wound me did I hear from him, not a word of reproach; he asked nothing of me—I was not worthy of that; but he loved me ... and I became his wife. What was I to do? I had failed of dying; and I could not live either after my own choice....What was I to do with myself? Even so—it was a mercy to be thankful for. That is all.'

She ceased, turned away for an instant ... the same submissive smile came back to her lips. 'Whether life's easy for me, you needn't ask,' was the meaning I fancied now in that smile.

The conversation passed to ordinary subjects. Musa told me that Punin had left a cat that he had been very fond of, and that ever since his death she had gone up to the attic and stayed there, mewing incessantly, as though she were calling some one ... the neighbours were very much scared, and fancied that it was Punin's soul that had passed into the cat.

'Paramon Semyonitch is worried about something,' I said at last.

'Oh, you noticed it?'—Musa sighed. 'He cannot help being worried. I need hardly tell you that Paramon Semyonitch has remained faithful to his principles.... The present condition of affairs can but strengthen them.' (Musa expressed herself quite differently now from in the old days in Moscow; there was a literary, bookish flavour in her phrases.) 'I don't know, though, whether I can rely upon you, and how you will receive ...'

'Why should you imagine you cannot rely upon me?'

'Well, you are in the government service—you are an official.'

'Well, what of that?'

'You are, consequently, loyal to the government.'

I marvelled inwardly ... at Musa's innocence. 'As to my attitude to the government, which is not even aware of my existence, I won't enlarge upon that,' I observed; 'but you may set your mind at rest. I will make no bad use of your confidence. I sympathise with your husband's ideas ... more than you suppose.'

Musa shook her head.

'Yes; that's all so,' she began, not without hesitation; 'but you see it's like this. Paramon Semyonitch's ideas will shortly, it may be, find expression in action. They can no longer be hidden under a bushel. There are comrades whom we cannot now abandon ...'

Musa suddenly ceased speaking, as though she had bitten her tongue. Her last words had amazed and a little alarmed me. Most likely my face showed what I was feeling—and Musa noticed it.

As I have said already, our interview took place in the year 1849. Many people still remember what a disturbed and difficult time that was, and by what incidents it was signalised in St. Petersburg. I had been struck myself by certain peculiarities in Baburin's behaviour, in his whole demeanour. Twice he had referred to governmental action, to personages in high authority, with such intense bitterness and hatred, with such loathing, that I had been dumbfoundered....

'Well?' he asked me suddenly: 'did you set your peasants free?'

I was obliged to confess I had not.

'Why, I suppose your granny's dead, isn't she?'

I was obliged to admit that she was.

'To be sure, you noble gentlemen,' Baburin muttered between his teeth, '... use other men's hands ... to poke up your fire ... that's what you like.'

In the most conspicuous place in his room hung the well-known lithograph portrait of Belinsky; on the table lay a volume of the old *Polar Star*, edited by Bestuzhev.

A long time passed, and Baburin did not come back after the cook had called him away. Musa looked several times uneasily towards the door by which he had gone out. At last she could bear it no longer; she got up, and with an apology she too went out by the same door. A quarter of an hour later she came back with her husband; the faces of both, so at least I thought, looked troubled. But all of a sudden Baburin's face assumed a different, an intensely bitter, almost frenzied expression.

'What will be the end of it?' he began all at once in a jerky, sobbing voice, utterly unlike him, while his wild eyes shifted restlessly about him. 'One goes on living and living, and hoping that maybe it'll be better, that one will breathe more freely; but it's quite the other way—everything gets worse and worse! They have *squeezed* us right up to the wall! In my youth I bore all with patience; they ... maybe ... beat me ... even ... yes!' he added, turning sharply round on his heels and swooping down as it were, upon me: 'I, a man of full age, was subjected to corporal punishment ... yes;—of other wrongs I will not speak.... But is there really nothing before us but to go back to those old times again? The way they are treating the young people now! ... Yes, it breaks down all endurance at last.... It breaks it down! Yes! Wait a bit!'

I had never seen Baburin in such a condition. Musa turned positively white.... Baburin suddenly cleared his throat, and sank down into a seat. Not wishing to constrain either him or Musa by my presence, I decided to go, and was just saying good-bye to them, when the door into the next room suddenly opened, and a head appeared.... It was not the cook's head, but the dishevelled and terrified-looking head of a young man.

'Something's wrong, Baburin, something's wrong!' he faltered hurriedly, then vanished at once on perceiving my unfamiliar figure.

Baburin rushed after the young man. I pressed Musa's hand warmly, and withdrew, with presentiments of evil in my heart.

'Come to-morrow,' she whispered anxiously.

'I certainly will come,' I answered.

I was still in bed next morning, when my man handed me a letter from Musa.

'Dear Piotr Petrovitch!' she wrote: 'Paramon Semyonitch has been this night arrested by the police and carried off to the fortress, or I don't know where; they did not tell me. They ransacked all our papers, sealed up a great many, and took them away with them. It has been the same with our books and letters. They say a mass of people have been arrested in the town. You can fancy how I feel. It is well Nikander Vavilitch did not live to see it! He was taken just in time. Advise me what I am to do. For myself I am not afraid—I shall not die of starvation—but the thought of Paramon

Semyonitch gives me no rest. Come, please, if only you are not afraid to visit people in our position.

Yours faithfully,
MUSA BABURIN.'

Half an hour later I was with Musa. On seeing me she held out her hand, and, though she did not utter a word, a look of gratitude flitted over her face. She was wearing the same clothes as on the previous day; there was every sign that she had not been to bed or slept all night. Her eyes were red, but from sleeplessness, not from tears. She had not been crying. She was in no mood for weeping. She wanted to act, wanted to struggle with the calamity that had fallen upon them: the old, energetic, self-willed Musa had risen up in her again. She had no time even to be indignant, though she was choking with indignation. How to assist Baburin, to whom to appeal so as to soften his lot—she could think of nothing else. She wanted to go instantly, ... to petition, ... demand.... But where to go, whom to petition, what to demand—this was what she wanted to hear from me, this was what she wanted to consult me about.

I began by counselling her ... to have patience. For the first moment there was nothing left to be done but to wait, and, as far as might be, to make inquiries; and to take any decisive step now when the affair had scarcely begun, and hardly yet taken shape, would be simply senseless, irrational. To hope for any success was irrational, even if I had been a person of much more importance and influence, ... but what could I, a petty official, do? As for her, she was absolutely without any powerful friends....

It was no easy matter to make all this plain to her ... but at last she understood my arguments; she understood, too, that I was not prompted by egoistic feeling, when I showed her the uselessness of all efforts. 'But tell me, Musa Pavlovna,' I began, when she sank at last into a chair (till then she had been standing up, as though on the point of setting off at once to the aid of Baburin),'how Paramon Semyonitch, at his age, comes to be mixed up in such an affair? I feel sure that there are none but young people implicated in it, like the one who came in yesterday to warn you....'

'Those young people are our friends!' cried Musa, and her eyes flashed and darted as of old. Something strong, irrepressible, seemed, as it were, to rise up from the bottom of her soul, ... and I suddenly recalled the expression 'a new type,' which Tarhov had once used of her. 'Years are of no consequence when it is a matter of political principles!' Musa laid a special stress on these last two words. One might fancy that in all her sorrow it was not unpleasing to her to show herself before me in this new, unlooked-for character—in the character of a cultivated and mature woman, fit wife of a republican! ... 'Some old men are younger than some young ones,' she pursued, 'more capable of sacrifice.... But that's not the point.'

'I think, Musa Pavlovna,' I observed, 'that you are exaggerating a little. Knowing the character of Paramon Semyonitch, I should have felt sure beforehand that he would sympathise with every ... sincere impulse; but, on the other hand, I have always regarded him as a man of sense.... Surely he cannot fail to realise all the impracticability, all the absurdity of con-spiracies in Russia? In his position, in his calling ...'

'Oh, of course,' Musa interrupted, with bitterness in her voice, 'he is a working man; and in Russia it is only permissible for noblemen to take part in conspiracies, ... as, for instance, in that of the fourteenth of Decem-ber, ... that's what you meant to say.'

'In that case, what do you complain of now?' almost broke from my lips, ... but I restrained myself. 'Do you consider that the result of the fourteenth of December was such as to encourage other such attempts?' I said aloud.

Musa frowned. 'It is no good talking to you about it,' was what I read in her downcast face.

'Is Paramon Semyonitch very seriously compromised?' I ventured to ask her. Musa made no reply.... A hungry, savage mewing was heard from the attic.

Musa started. 'Ah, it is a good thing Nikander Vavilitch did not see all this!' she moaned almost despairingly. 'He did not see how violently in the night they seized his benefactor, our benefactor—maybe, the best and tru-est man in the whole world,—he did not see how they treated that noble man at his age, how rudely they addressed him, ... how they threatened him, and the threats they used to him!—only because he was a work-ing man! That young officer, too, was no doubt just such an unprincipled, heartless wretch as I have known in my life....'

Musa's voice broke. She was quivering all over like a leaf.

Her long-suppressed indignation broke out at last; old memories stirred up, brought to the surface by the general tumult of her soul, showed themselves alive within her.... But the conviction I carried off at that mo-ment was that the 'new type' was still the same, still the same passionate, impulsive nature.... Only the impulses by which Musa was carried away were not the same as in the days of her youth. What on my first visit I had taken for resignation, for meekness, and what really was so—the subdued, lustreless glance, the cold voice, the quietness and simplicity—all that had significance only in relation to the past, to what would never return....

95

Now it was the present asserted itself.

I tried to soothe Musa, tried to put our conversation on a more practical level. Some steps must be taken that could not be postponed; we must find out exactly where Baburin was; and then secure both for him and for Musa the means of subsistence. All this presented no inconsiderable difficulty; what was needed was not to find money, but work, which is, as we all know, a far more complicated problem....

I left Musa with a perfect swarm of reflections in my head.

I soon learned that Baburin was in the fortress.

The proceedings began, ... dragged on. I saw Musa several times every week. She had several interviews with her husband. But just at the moment of the decision of the whole melancholy affair, I was not in Petersburg. Unforeseen business had obliged me to set off to the south of Russia. During my absence I heard that Baburin had been acquitted at the trial; it appeared that all that could be proved against him was, that young people regarding him as a person unlikely to awaken suspicion, had sometimes held meetings at his house, and he had been present at their meetings; he was, however, by administrative order sent into exile in one of the western provinces of Siberia. Musa went with him.

'Paramon Semyonitch did not wish it,' she wrote to me; 'as, according to his ideas, no one ought to sacrifice self for another person, and not for a cause; but I told him there was no question of sacrifice at all. When I said to him in Moscow that I would be his wife, I thought to myself—for ever, indissolubly! So indissoluble it must be till the end of our days....'

IV

1861

Twelve more years passed by.... Every one in Russia knows, and will ever remember, what passed between the years 1849 and 1861. In my personal life, too, many changes took place, on which, however, there is no need to enlarge. New interests came into it, new cares.... The Baburin couple first fell into the background, then passed out of my mind altogether. Yet I kept up a correspondence with Musa—at very long intervals, however. Sometimes more than a year passed without any tidings of her or of her husband. I heard that soon after 1855 he received permission to return to Russia; but that he preferred to remain in the little Siberian town, where he had been flung by destiny, and where he had apparently made himself a home, and found a haven and a sphere of activity....

And, lo and behold! towards the end of March in 1861, I received the following letter from Musa:—

'It is so long since I have written to you, most honoured Piotr Petrovitch, that I do not even know whether you are still living; and if you are living, have you not forgotten our existence? But no matter; I cannot resist writing to you to-day. Everything till now has gone on with us in the same old way: Paramon Semyonitch and I have been always busy with our schools, which are gradually making good progress; besides that, Paramon Semyonitch was taken up with reading and correspondence and his usual discussions with the Old-believers, members of the clergy, and Polish exiles; his health has been fairly good.... So has mine. But yesterday! the manifesto of the 19th of February reached us! We had long been on the look-out for it. Rumours had reached us long before of what was being done among you in Petersburg, ... but yet I can't describe what it was! You know my husband well; he was not in the least changed by his misfortune; on the contrary, he has grown even stronger and more energetic, and has a will as strong as iron, but at this he could not restrain himself! His hands shook as he read it; then he embraced me three times, and three times he kissed me, tried to say something—but no! he could not! and ended by bursting into tears, which was very astounding to see, and suddenly he shouted, "Hurrah! hurrah! God save the Tsar!" Yes, Piotr Petrovitch, those were his very words! Then he went on: "Now lettest Thou Thy servant depart" ... and again: "This is the first step, others are bound to follow it"; and, just as he was, bareheaded, ran to tell the great news to our friends. There was a bitter frost, and even a snowstorm coming on. I tried to prevent him, but he would not listen to me. And when he came home, he was all covered with snow, his hair, his face, and his beard—he has a beard right down to his chest now—and the tears were positively frozen on his cheeks! But he was very lively and cheerful, and told me to uncork a bottle of home-made champagne, and he drank with our friends that he had brought back with him, to the health of the Tsar and of Russia, and all free Russians; and taking the glass, and fixing his eyes on the ground, he said: "Nikander, Nikander, do you hear? There are no slaves in Russia any more! Rejoice in the grave, old comrade!" And much more he said; to the effect that his "expectations were fulfilled!" He said, too, that now there could be no turning back; that this was in its way a pledge or promise.... I don't remember everything, but it is long since I have seen him so happy. And so I made up my mind to write to you, so that you might know how we have been rejoicing and exulting in the remote Siberian wilds, so that you might rejoice with us....'

This letter I received at the end of March. At the beginning of May another very brief letter arrived from Musa. She informed me that her husband, Paramon Semyonitch Baburin, had taken cold on the very day of the arrival of the manifesto, and died on the 12th of April of inflammation of the lungs, in the 67th year of his age. She added that she intended to remain where his body lay at rest, and to go on with the work he had bequeathed her, since such was the last wish of Paramon Semyonitch, and that was her only law.

Since then I have heard no more of Musa.

PARIS, 1874.

OLD PORTRAITS

About thirty miles from our village there lived, many years ago, a distant cousin of my mother's, a retired officer of the Guards, and rather wealthy landowner, Alexey Sergeitch Teliegin. He lived on his estate and birth-place, Suhodol, did not go out anywhere, and so did not visit us; but I used to be sent, twice a year, to pay him my respects—at first with my tutor, but later on alone. Alexey Sergeitch always gave me a very cordial reception, and I used to stay three or four days at a time with him. He was an old man even when I first made his acquaintance; I was twelve, I remember, on my first visit, and he was then over seventy. He was born in the days of the Empress Elisabeth—in the last year of her reign. He lived alone with his wife, Malania Pavlovna; she was ten years younger than he. They had two daughters; but their daughters had been long married, and rarely visited Suhodol; they were not on the best of terms with their parents, and Alexey Sergeitch hardly ever mentioned their names.

I see, even now, the old-fashioned house, a typical manor-house of the steppes. One story in height, with immense attics, it was built at the beginning of this century, of amazingly thick beams of pine,—such beams came in plenty in those days from the Zhizdrinsky pine-forests; they have passed out of memory now! It was very spacious, and contained a great number of rooms, rather low-pitched and dark, it is true; the windows in the walls had been made small for the sake of greater warmth. In the usual fashion (I ought rather to say, in what was then the usual fashion), the offices and house-serfs' huts surrounded the manorial house on all sides, and the garden was close to it—a small garden, but containing fine fruit-trees, juicy apples, and pipless pears. The flat steppe of rich, black earth stretched for ten miles round. No lofty object for the eye; not a tree, nor even a belfry; somewhere, maybe, jutting up, a windmill, with rents in its sails; truly, well-named Suhodol, or Dry-flat! Inside the house the rooms were filled with ordinary, simple furniture; somewhat unusual was the milestone-post that stood in the window of the drawing-room, with the following inscription:—'If you walk sixty-eight times round this drawing-room you will have gone a mile; if you walk eighty-seven times from the furthest corner of the parlour to the right-hand corner of the billiard-room, you will have gone a mile,' and so on. But what most of all impressed a guest at the house for the first time was the immense collection of pictures hanging on the walls, for the most part works of the so-called Italian masters: all old-fashioned landscapes of a sort, or mythological and religious subjects. But all these pictures were very dark, and even cracked with age;—in one, all that met the eye was some patches of flesh-colour; in another, undulating red draperies on an unseen body; or an arch which seemed to be suspended in the air; or a dishevelled tree with blue foliage; or the bosom of a nymph with an immense breast, like the lid of a soup-tureen; a cut water-melon, with black seeds; a turban, with a feather in it, above a horse's head; or the gigantic brown leg of an apostle, suddenly thrust out, with a muscular calf, and toes turned upwards. In the drawing-room in the place of honour hung a portrait of the Empress Catherine II., full length; a copy of the famous portrait by Lampi—an object of the special reverence, one might say the adoration, of the master of the house. From the ceiling hung glass lustres in bronze settings, very small and very dusty.

Alexey Sergeitch himself was a stumpy, paunchy little old man, with a chubby face of one uniform tint, yet pleasant, with drawn-in lips, and very lively little eyes under high eyebrows. He wore his scanty locks combed to the back of his head; it was only since 1812 that he had given up wearing powder. Alexey Sergeitch invariably wore a grey 'redingote,' with three capes falling over his shoulders, a striped waistcoat, chamois-leather breeches, and high boots of dark red morocco, with heart-shaped scallops and tassels at the tops; he wore a white muslin cravat, a jabot, lace cuffs, and two gold English 'turnip watches,' one in each pocket of his waistcoat. In his right hand he usually carried an enamelled snuff-box full of 'Spanish' snuff, and his left hand leaned on a cane with a silver-chased knob, worn smooth by long use. Alexey Sergeitch had a little nasal, piping voice, and an invariable smile—kindly, but, as it were, condescending, and not without a certain self-complacent dignity. His laugh, too, was kindly—a shrill little laugh that tinkled like glass beads. Courteous and affable he was to the last degree—in the old-fashioned manner of the days of Catherine—and he moved his hands with slow, rounded gestures, also in the old style. His legs were so weak that he could not walk, but ran with hurried little steps from one armchair to another, in which he would suddenly sit down, or rather fall softly, like a cushion.

As I have said already, Alexey Sergeitch went out nowhere, and saw very little of his neighbours, though he liked society, for he was very fond of talking! It is true that he had society in plenty in his own house; various Nikanor Nikanoritchs, Sevastiey Sevastietchs, Fedulitchs, Miheitchs, all poor gentlemen in shabby cossack coats and camisoles, often from the master's wardrobe, lived under his roof, to say nothing of the poor gentlewomen in chintz gowns, black kerchiefs thrown over their shoulders, and worsted reticules in their tightly clenched fingers—all sorts of Avdotia Savishnas, Pelagea Mironovnas, and plain Feklushkas and Arinkas, who found a home in the women's quarters. Never less than fifteen persons sat down to Alexey Sergeitch's table.... He was such a hospitable man! Among all those dependants two were particularly conspicuous: a dwarf, nicknamed Janus, or the Double-faced, of Danish—or, as some maintained, Jewish—extraction, and the mad Prince L. Contrary to what was customary in those days, the dwarf did nothing to amuse the master or mistress, and was not a jester—quite the opposite; he was always silent, had an ill-tempered and sullen appearance, and scowled and gnashed his teeth directly a question was addressed to him. Alexey Sergeitch called him a philosopher, and positively respected him; at table the dishes were handed to him first, after the guests and master and mistress. 'God has afflicted him,' Alexey Sergeitch used to say; 'such is His Divine will; but it's not for me to afflict him further.' 'How is he a philosopher?' I asked him once. (Janus didn't take to me; if I went near him he would fly into a rage, and mutter thickly, 'Stranger! keep off!') 'Eh, God bless me! isn't he a philosopher?' answered Alexey Sergeitch. 'Look ye, little sir, how wisely he holds his tongue!' 'But why is he double-faced?' 'Because, little sir, he has one face on the outside—and so you, surface-gazers, judge him.... But the other, the real face he hides. And that face I know, and no one else—and I love him for it ... because that face is good. You, for instance, look and see nothing ... but I see without a word: he is blaming me for something; for he's a severe critic! And it's always with good reason. That, little sir, you can't understand; but you may believe an old man like me!' The real history of the two-faced Janus—where he came from, and how he came into Alexey Sergeitch's hands—no one knew; but the story of Prince L. was well known to every one. He went, a lad of twenty, of a wealthy and distinguished family, to Petersburg, to serve in a regiment of the Guards. At the first levee the Empress Catherine noticed him, stood still before him, and, pointing at him with her fan, she said aloud, addressing one of her courtiers, who happened to be near, 'Look, Adam Vassilievitch, what a pretty fellow! a perfect doll!' The poor boy's head was completely turned; when he got home he ordered his coach out, and, putting on a ribbon of St. Anne, proceeded to drive all over the town, as though he had reached the pinnacle of fortune. 'Drive over every one,' he shouted to his coachman, 'who does not move out of the way!' All this was promptly reported to the empress: the decree went forth that he should be declared insane, and put under the guardianship of two of his brothers; and they, without a moment's delay, carried him off to the country, and flung him into a stone cell in chains. As they wanted to get the benefit of his property, they did not let the poor wretch out, even when he had completely recovered his balance, and positively kept him locked up till he really did go out of his mind. But their evil doings did not prosper; Prince L. outlived his brothers, and, after long years of adversity, he came into the charge of Alexey Sergeitch, whose kinsman he was. He was a stout, completely bald man, with a long, thin nose and prominent blue eyes. He had quite forgotten how to talk—he simply uttered a sort of inarticulate grumbling; but he sang old-fashioned Russian ballads beautifully, preserving the silvery freshness of his voice to extreme old age; and, while he was singing, he pronounced each word clearly and distinctly. He had attacks at times of a sort of fury, and then he became terrible: he would stand in the corner, with his face to the wall, and all perspiring and red—red all down his bald head and down his neck—he used to go off into vicious chuckles, and, stamping with his feet, order some one—his brothers probably—to be punished. 'Beat 'em!' he growled hoarsely, coughing and choking with laughter; 'flog 'em, don't spare 'em! beat, beat, beat the monsters, my oppressors! That's it! That's it!' On the day before his death he greatly alarmed and astonished Alexey Sergeitch. He came, pale and subdued, into his room, and, making him a low obeisance, first thanked him for his care and kindness, and then asked him to send for a priest, for death had come to him—he had seen death, and he must forgive every one and purify his soul. 'How did you see death?' muttered Alexey Sergeitch in bewilderment at hearing connected speech from him for the first time. 'In what shape? with a scythe?' 'No,' answered Prince L.; 'a simple old woman in a jacket, but with only one eye in her forehead, and that eye without an eyelid.' And the next day Prince L. actually did die, duly performing everything, and taking leave of every one in a rational and affecting manner. 'That's just how I shall die,' Alexey Sergeitch would sometimes observe. And, as a fact, something of the same sort did happen with him—but of that later.

But now let us go back to our story. Of the neighbours, as I have stated already, Alexey Sergeitch saw little; and they did not care much for him, called him a queer fish, stuck up, and a scoffer, and even a 'martiniste' who recognised no authorities, though they had no clear idea of the meaning of this term. To a certain extent the neighbours were right: Alexey Sergeitch had lived in his Suhodol for almost seventy years on end, and had had hardly anything whatever to do with the existing authorities, with the police or the law-courts. 'Police-courts are for the robber, and discipline for the soldier,' he used to say; 'but I, thank God, am neither robber nor soldier!' Rather queer Alexey Sergeitch certainly was, but the soul within him was by no means a petty one. I will tell you something about him.

To tell the truth, I never knew what were his political opinions, if an expression so modern can be used in reference to him; but, in his own way, he was an aristocrat—more an aristocrat than a typical Russian country gentleman. More than once he expressed his regret that God had not given him a son and heir, 'for the honour of our name, to keep up the family.' In his own room there hung on the wall the family-tree of the Teliegins, with many branches, and a multitude of little circles like apples in a golden frame. 'We Teliegins,' he used to say, 'are an ancient line, from long, long ago: however many there've been of us Teliegins, we have never hung about great men's ante-rooms; we've never bent our backs, or stood about in waiting, nor picked up a living in the courts, nor run after decorations; we've never gone trailing off to Moscow, nor intriguing in Petersburg; we've sat at home, each in his hole, his own man on his own land ... home-keeping birds, sir!—I myself, though I did serve in the Guards—but not for long, thank you.' Alexey Sergeitch preferred the old days. 'There was more freedom in those days, more decorum; on my honour, I assure you! but since the year eighteen hundred' (why from that year, precisely, he did not explain), 'militarism, the soldiery, have got the upper hand. Our soldier gentlemen stuck some sort of turbans of cocks' feathers on their heads then, and turned like cocks themselves; began binding their necks up as stiff as could be ... they croak, and roll their eyes—how could they help it, indeed? The other day a police corporal came to me; "I've come to you," says he, "honourable sir," ... (fancy his thinking to surprise me with that! ... I know I'm honourable without his telling me!) "I have business with you." And I said to him, "My good sir, you'd better first unfasten the hooks on your collar. Or else, God have mercy on us—you'll sneeze. Ah, what would happen to you! what would happen to you! You'd break off, like a mushroom ... and I should have to answer for it!" And they do drink, these military gentlemen—oh, oh, oh! I generally order home-made champagne to be given them, because to them, good wine or poor, it's all the same; it runs so smoothly, so quickly, down their throats—how can they distinguish it? And, another thing, they've started sucking at a pap-bottle, smoking a tobacco-pipe. Your military gentleman thrusts his pap-bottle under his moustaches, between his lips, and puffs the smoke out of his nose, his mouth, and even his ears—and fancies himself a hero! There are my sons-in-law—though one of them's a senator, and the other some sort of an administrator over there—they suck the pap-bottle, and they reckon themselves clever fellows too!'

Alexey Sergeitch could not endure smoking; and moreover, he could not endure dogs, especially little dogs. 'If you're a Frenchman, to be sure, you may well keep a lapdog: you run and you skip about here and there, and it runs after you with its tail up ... but what's the use of it to people like us?' He was exceedingly neat and particular. Of the Empress Catherine he never spoke but with enthusiasm, and in exalted, rather bookish phraseology: 'Half divine she was, not human! Only look, little sir, at that smile,' he would add, pointing reverentially to Lampi's portrait, 'and you will agree: half divine! I was so fortunate in my life as to be deemed worthy to behold that smile close, and never will it be effaced from my heart!' And thereupon he would relate anecdotes of the life of Catherine, such as I have never happened to read or hear elsewhere. Here is one of them. Alexey Sergeitch did not permit the slightest allusion to the weaknesses of the great Tsaritsa. 'And, besides,' he exclaimed, 'can one judge of her as of other people?'

One day while she was sitting in her peignoir during her morning toilette, she commanded her hair to be combed.... And what do you think? The lady-in-waiting passed the comb through, and sparks of electricity simply showered out! Then she summoned to her presence the court physician Rogerson, who happened to be in waiting at the court, and said to him: 'I am, I know, censured for certain actions; but do you see this electricity? Consequently, as such is my nature and constitution, you can judge for yourself, as you are a doctor, that it is unjust for them to censure me, and they ought to comprehend me!' The following incident remained indelible in Alexey Sergeitch's memory. He was standing one day on guard indoors, in the palace—he was only sixteen at the time—and behold the empress comes walking past him; he salutes ... 'and she,' Alexey Sergeitch would exclaim at this point with much feeling, 'smiling at my youth and my zeal, deigned to give me her hand to kiss and patted my cheek, and asked me "who I was? where I came from? of what family?" and then' ... here the old man's voice usually broke ... 'then she bade me greet my mother in her name and thank her for having brought up her children so well. And whether I was on earth or in heaven, and how and where she deigned to vanish, whether she floated away into the heights or went her way into the other apartments ... to this day I do not know!'

More than once I tried to question Alexey Sergeitch about those faraway times, about the people who made up the empress's circle.... But for the most part he edged off the subject. 'What's the use of talking about old times?' he used to say ... 'it's only making one's self miserable, remembering that then one was a fine young fellow, and now one hasn't a tooth left in one's head. And what is there to say? They were good old times ... but there, enough of them! And as for those folks—you were asking, you troublesome boy, about the lucky ones!—haven't you seen how a bubble comes up on the water? As long as it lasts and is whole, what colours play upon it! Red, and blue, and yellow—a perfect rainbow or diamond you'd say it was! Only it soon bursts, and there's no trace of it left. And so it was with those folks.'

'But how about Potiomkin?' I once inquired.

Alexey Sergeitch looked grave. 'Potiomkin, Grigory Alexandrovitch, was a statesman, a theologian, a pupil of Catherine's, her cherished creation, one must say.... But enough of that, little sir!'

Alexey Sergeitch was a very devout man, and, though it was a great effort, he attended church regularly. Superstition was not noticeable in him; he laughed at omens, the evil eye, and such 'nonsense,' but he did not like a hare to run across his path, and to meet a priest was not altogether agreeable to him. For all that, he was very respectful to clerical persons, and went up to receive their blessing, and even kissed the priest's hand every time, but he was not willing to enter into conversation with them. 'Such an extremely strong odour comes from them,' he explained: 'and I, poor sinner, am fastidious beyond reason; they've such long hair, and all oily, and they comb it out on all sides—they think they show me respect by so doing, and they clear their throats so loudly when they talk—from shyness may be, or I dare say they want to show respect in that way too. And besides, they make one think of one's last hour. And, I don't know how it is, but I still want to go on living. Only, my little sir, don't you repeat my words; we must respect the clergy—it's only fools that don't respect them; and I'm to blame to babble nonsense in my old age.'

Alexey Sergeitch, like most of the noblemen of his day, had received a very slight education; but he had, to some extent, made good the deficiency himself by reading. He read none but Russian books of the end of last century; the more modern authors he thought insipid and deficient in style.... While he read, he had placed at his side on a round, one-legged table, a silver tankard of frothing spiced kvas of a special sort, which sent an agreeable fragrance all over the house. He used to put on the end of his nose a pair of big, round spectacles, but in latter years he did not so much read as gaze dreamily over the rims of his spectacles, lifting his eyebrows, chewing his lips, and sighing. Once I caught him weeping with a book on his knees, greatly, I own, to my surprise.

He had recalled these lines:

'O pitiful race of man!
Peace is unknown to thee!
Thou canst not find it save
In the dust of the grave....
Bitter, bitter is that sleep!
Rest, rest in death ... but living weep!'

These lines were the composition of a certain Gormitch-Gormitsky, a wandering poet, to whom Alexey Sergeitch had given a home in his house, as he struck him as a man of delicate feeling and even of subtlety; he wore slippers adorned with ribbons, spoke with a broad accent, and frequently sighed, turning his eyes to heaven; in addition to all these qualifications, Gormitch-Gormitsky spoke French decently, having been educated in a Jesuit college, while Alexey Sergeitch only 'followed conversation.' But having once got terribly drunk at the tavern, that same subtle Gormitsky showed a turbulence beyond all bounds; he gave a fearful thrashing to Alexey Sergeitch's valet, the man cook, two laundry-maids who chanced to get in his way, and a carpenter from another village, and he broke several panes in the windows, screaming furiously all the while: 'There, I'll show them, these Russian loafers, rough-hewn billy-goats!'

And the strength the frail-looking creature put forth! It was hard work for eight men to master him! For this violent proceeding Alexey Sergeitch ordered the poet to be turned out of the house, after being put, as a preliminary measure, in the snow—it was winter-time—to sober him.

'Yes,' Alexey Sergeitch used to say, 'my day is over; I was a spirited steed, but I've run my last race now. Then, I used to keep poets at my expense, and I used to buy pictures and books of the Jews, geese of the best breeds, and pouter-pigeons of pure blood.... I used to go in for everything! Though dogs I never did care for keeping, because it goes with drinking, foulness, and buffoonery! I was a young man of spirit, not to be outdone. That there should be anything of Teliegin's and not first-rate ... why, it was not to be thought of! And I had a splendid stud of horses. And my horses came—from what stock do you think, young sir? Why, from none other than the celebrated stables of the Tsar, Ivan Alexeitch, brother of Peter the Great ... it's the truth I'm telling you! All fawn-coloured stallions, sleek—their manes to their knees, their tails to their hoofs.... Lions! And all that was—and is buried in the past. Vanity of vanities—and every kind of vanity! But still—why regret it? Every man has his limits set him. There's no flying above the sky, no living in the water, no getting away from the earth.... We'll live a bit longer, anyway!'

And the old man would smile again and sniff his Spanish snuff.

The peasants liked him; he was, in their words, a kind master, not easily angered. Only they, too, repeated that he was a worn-out steed. In former days Alexey Sergeitch used to go into everything himself—he used to drive out to the fields, and to the mill, and to the dairy, and peep into the granaries and the peasants' huts; every one knew his racing droshky, upholstered in crimson plush, and drawn by a tall mare, with a broad white star all over her forehead, called 'Beacon,' of the same famous breed. Alexey Sergeitch used to drive her himself, the ends of the reins crushed up in his fists. But when his seventieth year came, the old man let everything go, and handed over the management of the estate to the bailiff Antip, of whom he was secretly afraid, and whom he called Micromegas (a reminiscence of Voltaire!), or simply, plunderer. 'Well, plunderer, what have you to say? Have you stacked a great deal in the barn?' he would ask with a smile, looking straight into the plunderer's eyes. 'All, by your good favour, please your honour,' Antip would respond cheerfully. 'Favour's all very well, only you mind what I say, Micromegas! don't you dare touch the peasants, my subjects, out of my sight! If they come to complain ... I've a cane, you see, not far off!' 'Your cane, your honour, Alexey Sergeitch, I always keep well in mind,' Antip Micromegas would respond, stroking his beard. 'All right, don't forget it.' And the master and the bailiff would laugh in each other's faces. With the servants, and with the serfs in general, his 'subjects' (Alexey Sergeitch liked that word) he was gentle in his behaviour. 'Because, think a little, nephew; nothing of their own, but the cross on their neck—and that copper—and daren't hanker after other people's goods ... how can one expect sense of them?' It is needless to state that of the so-called 'serf question' no one even dreamed in those days; it could not disturb the peace of mind of Alexey Sergeitch: he was quite happy in the possession of his 'subjects'; but he was severe in his censure of bad masters, and used to call them the enemies of their order. He divided the nobles generally into three classes: the prudent, 'of whom there are too few'; the prodigal, 'of whom there are quite enough'; and the senseless, 'of whom there are shoals and shoals.'

'And if any one of them is harsh and oppressive with his subjects'—he would say—'then he sins against God, and is guilty before men!'

Yes, the house-serfs had an easy life of it with the old man; the 'subjects out of sight' no doubt fared worse, in spite of the cane with which he threatened Micromegas. And what a lot there were of them, those house-serfs, in his house! And for the most part sinewy, hairy, grumbling old fellows, with stooping shoulders, in long-skirted nankeen coats, belted round the waist, with a strong, sour smell always clinging to them. And on the women's side, one could hear nothing but the patter of bare feet, the swish of petticoats. The chief valet was called Irinarh, and Alexey Sergeitch always called him in a long-drawn-out call: 'I-ri-na-a-arh!' The others he called: 'Boy! Lad! Whoever's there of the men!' Bells he could not endure: 'It's not an eating-house, God forbid!' And what used to surprise me was that whatever time Alexey Sergeitch called his valet, he always promptly made his appearance, as though he had sprung out of the earth, and with a scrape of his heels, his hands behind his back, would stand before his master, a surly, as it were angry, but devoted servant!

Alexey Sergeitch was liberal beyond his means; but he did not like to be called 'benefactor.' 'Benefactor to you, indeed, sir! ... I'm doing myself a benefit, and not you, sir!' (when he was angry or indignant, he always addressed people with greater formality). 'Give to a beggar once,' he used to say, 'and give him twice, and three times.... And—if he should come a fourth time, give to him still—only then you might say too: "It's time, my good man, you found work for something else, not only for your mouth."' 'But, uncle,' one asked, sometimes, 'suppose even after that the beggar came again, a fifth time?' 'Oh, well, give again the fifth time.' He used to have the sick, who came to him for aid, treated at his expense, though he had no faith in doctors himself, and never sent for them. 'My mother,' he declared, 'used to cure illnesses of all sorts with oil and salt—she gave it internally, and rubbed it on too—it always answered splendidly. And who was my mother? She was born in the days of Peter the Great—only fancy that!'

Alexey Sergeitch was a Russian in everything; he liked none but Russian dishes, he was fond of Russian songs, but the harmonica—a 'manufactured contrivance'—he hated; he liked looking at the serf-girls' dances and the peasant-women's jigs; in his youth, I was told, he had been an enthusiastic singer and a dashing dancer; he liked steaming himself in the bath, and steamed himself so vigorously that Irinarh, who, serving him as bathman, used to beat him with a bundle of birch-twigs steeped in beer, to rub him with a handful of tow, and then with a woollen cloth—the truly devoted Irinarh used to say every time, as he crept off his shelf red as a 'new copper image': 'Well, this time I, the servant of God, Irinarh Tolobiev, have come out alive. How will it be next time?'

And Alexey Sergeitch spoke excellent Russian, a little old-fashioned, but choice and pure as spring water, continually interspersing his remarks with favourite expressions: ''Pon my honour, please God, howsoever that may be, sir, and young sir....'

But enough of him. Let us talk a little about Alexey Sergeitch's wife, Malania Pavlovna. Malania Pavlovna was born at Moscow.

She had been famous as the greatest beauty in Moscow—*la Venus de Moscou*. I knew her as a thin old woman with delicate but insignificant features, with crooked teeth, like a hare's, in a tiny little mouth, with a multitude of finely crimped little yellow curls on her forehead, and painted eyebrows. She invariably wore a pyramidal cap with pink ribbons, a high ruff round her neck, a short white dress, and prunella slippers with red heels; and over her dress she wore a jacket of blue satin, with a sleeve hanging loose from her right shoulder. This was precisely the costume in which she was arrayed on St. Peter's Day in the year 1789! On that day she went, being still a girl, with her relations to the Hodinskoe field to see the famous boxing-match arranged by Orlov. 'And Count Alexey Grigorievitch' (oh, how often I used to hear this story!) 'noticing me, approached, bowed very low, taking his hat in both hands, and said: "Peerless beauty," said he, "why have you hung that sleeve from your shoulder? Do you, too, wish to try a tussle with me? ... By all means; only I will tell you beforehand you have vanquished me—I give in! And I am your captive." And every one was looking at us and wondering.' And that very costume she had worn continually ever since. 'Only I didn't wear a cap, but a hat *a la bergere de Trianon*; and though I was powdered, yet my hair shone through it, positively shone through it like gold!' Malania Pavlovna was foolish to the point of 'holy innocence,' as it is called; she chattered quite at random, as though she were hardly aware herself of what dropped from her lips—and mostly about Orlov. Orlov had become, one might say, the principal interest of her life. She usually walked ... or rather swam, into the room with a rhythmic movement of the head, like a peacock, stood still in the middle, with one foot strangely turned out, and two fingers holding the tip of the loose sleeve (I suppose this pose, too, must once have charmed Orlov); she would glance about her with haughty nonchalance, as befits a beauty— and with a positive sniff, and a murmur of 'What next!' as though some importunate gallant were besieging her with compliments, she would go out again, tapping her heels and shrugging her shoulders. She used, too, to take Spanish snuff out of a tiny bonbonniere, picking it up with a tiny golden spoon; and from time to time, especially when any one unknown to her was present, she would hold up—not to her eyes, she had splendid sight, but to her nose—a double eyeglass in the shape of a half-moon, with a coquettish turn of her little white hand, one finger held out separate from the rest. How often has Malania Pavlovna described to me her wedding in the church of the Ascension, in Arbaty—such a fine church!—and how all Moscow was there ... 'and the crush there was!—awful! Carriages with teams, golden coaches, outriders ... one outrider of Count Zavadovsky got run over! and we were married by the archbishop himself—and what a sermon he gave us! every one was crying—wherever I looked I saw tears ... and the governor-general's horses were tawny, like tigers. And the flowers, the flowers that were brought! ... Simply loads of flowers!' And how on that day a foreigner, a wealthy, tremendously wealthy person, had shot himself from love—and how Orlov too had been there.... And going up to Alexey Sergeitch, he had congratulated him and called him a lucky man.... 'A lucky man you are, you silly fellow!' said he. And how in answer to these words Alexey Sergeitch had made a wonderful bow, and had swept the floor from left to right with the plumes of his hat, as if he would say: 'Your Excellency, there is a line now between you and my spouse, which you will not overstep!' And Orlov, Alexey Grigorievitch understood at once, and commended him. 'Oh! that was a man! such a man!' And how, 'One day, Alexis and I were at his house at a ball—I was married then—and he had the most marvellous diamond buttons! And I could not resist it, I admired them. "What marvellous diamonds you have, Count!" said I. And he, taking up a knife from the table, at once cut off a button and presented it to me and said: "In your eyes, my charmer, the diamonds are a hundred times brighter; stand before the looking-glass and compare them." And I stood so, and he stood beside me. "Well, who's right?" said he, while he simply rolled his eyes, looking me up and down. And Alexey Sergeitch was very much put out about it, but I said to him: "Alexis," said I, "please don't you be put out; you ought to know me better!" And he answered me: "Don't disturb yourself, Melanie!" And these very diamonds are now round my medallion of Alexey Grigorievitch—you've seen it, I dare say, my dear;—I wear it on feast-days on a St. George ribbon, because he was a brave hero, a knight of St. George: he burned the Turks.'

For all that, Malania Pavlovna was a very kind-hearted woman; she was easily pleased. 'She's not one to snarl, nor to sneer,' the maids used to say of her. Malania Pavlovna was passionately fond of sweet things—and a special old woman who looked after nothing but the jam, and so was called the jam-maid, would bring her, ten times a day, a china dish with rose-leaves crystallised in sugar, or barberries in honey, or sherbet of ba-nanas. Malania Pavlovna was afraid of solitude—dreadful thoughts are apt to come over one, she would say—and was almost always surrounded by companions, whom she would urgently implore: 'Talk, talk! why do you sit like that, simply keeping your seats warm!' and they would begin twittering like canaries. She was no less devout than Alexey Sergeitch, and was very fond of praying; but as, in her own words, she had never learned to repeat prayers well, she kept for the purpose a poor deacon's widow who prayed with such relish! Never stumbled over a word in her life! And this deacon's widow certainly could utter the words of prayer in a sort of unbroken flow, not interrupting the stream to breathe out or draw breath in, while Malania Pavlovna listened and was much moved. She had another widow in attendance on her—it was her duty to tell her stories in the night. 'But only the old ones,' Malania Pavlovna would beg—'those I know already; the new ones are all so far-fetched.' Malania Pavlovna was flighty in the extreme, and at times she was fanciful too; some ridiculous notion would suddenly come into her head. She did not like the dwarf, Janus, for instance; she was always fancying he would suddenly get up and shout, 'Don't you know who I am? The prince of the Buriats. Mind, you are to obey me!' Or else that he would set fire to the house in a fit of spleen. Malania Pavlovna was as liberal as Alexey Sergeitch; but she never gave money—she did not like to soil her hands—but kerchiefs, bracelets, dresses, ribbons; or she would send pies from the table, or a piece of roast meat, or a bottle of wine. She liked feasting the peasant-women, too, on holidays; they would dance, and she would tap with her heels and throw herself into attitudes.

Alexey Sergeitch was well aware that his wife was a fool; but almost from the first year of his marriage he had schooled himself to keep up the fiction that she was very witty and fond of saying cutting things. Sometimes when her chatter began to get beyond all bounds, he would threaten her with his finger, and say as he did so: 'Ah, the tongue, the tongue! what it will have to answer for in the other world! It will be pierced with a redhot pin!'

Malania Pavlovna was not offended, however, at this; on the contrary, she seemed to feel flattered at hearing a reproof of that sort, as though she would say, 'Well! is it my fault if I'm naturally witty?'

Malania Pavlovna adored her husband, and had been all her life an exemplarily faithful wife; but there had been a romance even in her life—a young cousin, an hussar, killed, as she supposed, in a duel on her account; but, according to more trustworthy reports, killed by a blow on the head from a billiard-cue in a tavern brawl. A water-colour portrait of this object of her affections was kept by her in a secret drawer. Malania Pavlovna always blushed up to her ears when she mentioned Kapiton—such was the name of the young hero—and Alexey Sergeitch would designedly scowl, shake his finger at his wife again, and say: 'No trusting a horse in the field nor a woman in the house. Don't talk to me of Kapiton, he's Cupidon!' Then Malania Pavlovna would be all of a flutter and say: 'Alexis, Alexis, it's too bad of you! In your young days you flirted, I've no doubt, with all sorts of misses and madams—and so now you imagine....' 'Come, that's enough, that's enough, my dear Malania,' Alexey Sergeitch interrupted with a smile. 'Your gown is white—but whiter still your soul!' 'Yes, Alexis, it is whiter!' 'Ah, what a tongue, what a tongue!' Alexis would repeat, patting her hand.

To speak of 'views' in the case of Malania Pavlovna would be even more inappropriate than in the case of Alexey Sergeitch; yet I once chanced to witness a strange manifestation of my aunt's secret feelings. In the course of conversation I once somehow mentioned the famous chief of police, Sheshkovsky; Malania Pavlovna turned suddenly livid—positively livid, green, in spite of her rouge and paint—and in a thick and perfectly unaffected voice (a very rare thing with her—she usually minced a little, intoned, and lisped) she said: 'Oh, what a name to utter! And towards nightfall, too! Don't utter that name!' I was astonished; what kind of significance could his name have for such a harmless and inoffensive creature, incapable—not merely of doing—even of thinking of anything not permissible? Anything but cheerful reflections were aroused in me by this terror, manifesting itself after almost half a century.

Alexey Sergeitch died in his eighty-eighth year—in the year 1848, which apparently disturbed even him. His death, too, was rather strange. He had felt well the same morning, though by that time he never left his easy-chair. And all of a sudden he called his wife: 'Malania, my dear, come here.' 'What is it, Alexis?' 'It's time for me to die, my dear, that's what it is.' 'Mercy on you, Alexey Sergeitch! What for?' 'Because, first of all, one must know when to take leave; and, besides, I was looking the other day at my feet…. Look at my feet … they are not mine … say what you like … look at my hands, look at my stomach … that stomach's not mine—so really I'm using up another man's life. Send for the priest; and meanwhile, put me to bed—from which I shall not get up again.' Malania Pavlovna was terribly upset; however, she put the old man to bed and sent for the priest. Alexey Sergeitch confessed, took the sacrament, said good-bye to his household, and fell asleep. Malania Pavlovna was sitting by his bedside. 'Alexis!' she cried suddenly, 'don't frighten me, don't shut your eyes! Are you in pain?' The old man looked at his wife: 'No, no pain … but it's difficult … difficult to breathe.' Then after a brief silence: 'Malania,' he said, 'so life has slipped by—and do you remember when we were married … what a couple we were?' 'Yes, we were, my handsome, charming Alexis!' The old man was silent again. 'Malania, my dear, shall we meet again in the next world?' 'I will pray God for it, Alexis,' and the old woman burst into tears. 'Come, don't cry, silly; maybe the Lord God will make us young again then—and again we shall be a fine pair!' 'He will make us young, Alexis!' 'With the Lord all things are possible,' observed Alexey Sergeitch. 'He worketh great marvels!—maybe He will make you sensible…. There, my love, I was joking; come, let me kiss your hand.' 'And I yours.' And the two old people kissed each other's hands simultaneously.

Alexey Sergeitch began to grow quieter and to sink into forgetfulness. Malania Pavlovna watched him tenderly, brushing the tears off her eyelashes with her finger-tips. For two hours she continued sitting there. 'Is he asleep?' the old woman with the talent for praying inquired in a whisper, peeping in behind Irinarh, who, immovable as a post, stood in the doorway, gazing intently at his expiring master. 'He is asleep,' answered Malania Pavlovna also in a whisper. And suddenly Alexey Sergeitch opened his eyes. 'My faithful companion,' he faltered, 'my honoured wife, I would bow down at your little feet for all your love and faithfulness—but how to get up? Let me sign you with the cross.' Malania Pavlovna moved closer, bent down.... But the hand he had raised fell back powerless on the quilt, and a few moments later Alexey Sergeitch was no more.

His daughters arrived only on the day of the funeral with their husbands; they had no children either of them. Alexey Sergeitch showed them no animosity in his will, though he never even mentioned them on his death-bed. 'My heart has grown hard to them,' he once said to me. Knowing his kindly nature, I was surprised at his words. It is hard to judge between parents and children. 'A great ravine starts from a little rift,' Alexey Sergeitch said to me once in this connection: 'a wound a yard wide may heal; but once cut off even a finger nail, it will not grow again.'

I fancy the daughters were ashamed of their eccentric old parents.

A month later and Malania Pavlovna too passed away. From the very day of Alexey Sergeitch's death she had hardly risen from her bed, and had not put on her usual attire; but they buried her in the blue jacket, and with Orlov's medallion on her shoulder, only without the diamonds. Those her daughters divided, on the pretext that the diamonds should be used in the setting of some holy pictures; in reality, they used them to adorn their own persons.

And so I can see my old friends as though they were alive and before my eyes, and pleasant is the memory I preserve of them. And yet on my very last visit to them (I was a student by then) an incident occurred which jarred upon the impression of patriarchal harmony always produced in me by the Teliegin household.

Among the house-serfs there was one Ivan, called 'Suhys' Ivan,' a coachman or coach-boy, as they called him on account of his small size, in spite of his being no longer young. He was a tiny little man, brisk, snub-nosed, curly-headed, with an everlastingly smiling, childish face, and little eyes, like a mouse's. He was a great joker, a most comic fellow; he was great at all sorts of tricks—he used to fly kites, let off fireworks and rockets, to play all sorts of games, gallop standing up on the horse's back, fly higher than all the rest in the swing, and could even make Chinese shadows. No one could amuse children better; and he would gladly spend the whole day looking after them. When he started laughing, the whole house would seem to liven up; they would answer him—one would say one thing, one another, but he always made them all merry.... And even if they abused him, they could not but laugh. Ivan danced marvellously, especially the so-called 'fish dance.' When the chorus struck up a dance tune, the fellow would come into the middle of the ring, and then there would begin such a turning and skipping and stamping, and then he would fall flat on the ground, and imitate the movement of a fish brought out of the water on to dry land; such turning and wriggling, the heels positively clapped up to the head; and then he would get up and shriek—the earth seemed simply quivering under him. At times Alexey Sergeitch, who was, as I have said already, exceedingly fond of watching dancing, could not resist shouting, 'Little Vania, here! coach-boy! Dance us the fish, smartly now'; and a minute later he would whisper enthusiastically: 'Ah, what a fellow it is!'

Well, on my last visit, this Ivan Suhih came into my room, and, without saying a word, fell on his knees. 'Ivan, what's the matter?' 'Save me, sir.' 'Why, what is it?' And thereupon Ivan told me his trouble.

He was exchanged, twenty years ago, by 'the Suhy family for a serf of the Teliegins';—simply exchanged without any kind of formality or written deed: the man given in exchange for him had died, but the Suhys had forgotten about Ivan, and he had stayed on in Alexey Sergeitch's house as his own serf; only his nickname had served to recall his origin. But now his former masters were dead; the estate had passed into other hands; and the new owner, who was reported to be a cruel and oppressive man, having learned that one of his serfs was detained without cause or reason at Alexey Sergeitch's, began to demand him back; in case of refusal he threatened legal proceedings, and the threat was not an empty one, as he was himself of the rank of privy councillor, and had great weight in the province. Ivan had rushed in terror to Alexey Sergeitch. The old man was sorry for his dancer, and he offered the privy councillor to buy Ivan for a considerable sum. But the privy councillor would not hear of it; he was a Little Russian, and obstinate as the devil. The poor fellow would have to be given up. 'I have spent my life here, and I'm at home here; I have served here, here I have eaten my bread, and here I want to die,' Ivan said to me—and there was no smile on his face now; on the contrary, it looked turned to stone.... 'And now I am to go to this wretch.... Am I a dog to be flung from one kennel to another with a noose round my neck? ... to be told: "There, get along with you!" Save me, master; beg your uncle, remember how I always amused you.... Or else there'll be harm come of it; it won't end without sin.'

'What sort of sin, Ivan?'

'I shall kill that gentleman. I shall simply go and say to him, "Master, let me go back; or else, mind, be careful of yourself.... I shall kill you."'

If a siskin or a chaffinch could have spoken, and had begun declaring that it would peck another bird to death, it would not have reduced me to greater amazement than did Ivan at that moment. What! Suhys' Vania, that dancing, jesting, comic fellow, the favourite playfellow of children, and a child himself, that kindest-hearted of creatures, a murderer! What ridiculous nonsense! Not for an instant did I believe him; what astonished me to such a degree was that he was capable of saying such a thing. Anyway I appealed to Alexey Sergeitch. I did not repeat what Ivan had said to me, but began asking him whether something couldn't be done. 'My young sir,' the old man answered, 'I should be only too happy—but what's to be done? I offered this Little Russian an immense compensation—I offered him three hundred roubles, 'pon my honour, I tell you! but he—there's no moving him! what's one to do? The transaction was not legal, it was done on trust, in the old-fashioned way ... and now see what mischief's come of it! This Little Russian fellow, you see, will take Ivan by force, do what we will: his arm is powerful, the governor eats cabbage-soup at his table; he'll be sending along soldiers. And I'm afraid of those soldiers! In old days, to be sure, I would have stood up for Ivan, come what might; but now, look at me, what a feeble creature I have grown! How can I make a fight for it?' It was true; on my last visit I found Alexey Sergeitch greatly aged; even the centres of his eyes had that milky colour that babies' eyes have, and his lips wore not his old conscious smile, but that unnatural, mawkish, unconscious grin, which never, even in sleep, leaves the faces of very decrepit old people.

I told Ivan of Alexey Sergeitch's decision. He stood still, was silent for a little, shook his head. 'Well,' said he at last, 'what is to be there's no escaping. Only my mind's made up. There's nothing left, then, but to play the fool to the end. Something for drink, please!' I gave him something; he drank himself drunk, and that day danced the 'fish dance' so that the serf-girls and peasant-women positively shrieked with delight—he surpassed himself in his antics so wonderfully.

Next day I went home, and three months later, in Petersburg, I heard that Ivan had kept his word. He had been sent to his new master; his master had called him into his room, and explained to him that he would be made coachman, that a team of three ponies would be put in his charge, and that he would be severely dealt with if he did not look after them well, and were not punctual in discharging his duties generally. 'I'm not fond of joking.' Ivan heard the master out, first bowed down to his feet, and then announced it was as his honour pleased, but he could not be his servant.

'Let me off for a yearly quit-money, your honour,' said he, 'or send me for a soldier; or else there'll be mischief come of it!'

The master flew into a rage. 'Ah, what a fellow you are! How dare you speak to me like that? In the first place, I'm to be called your excellency, and not your honour; and, secondly, you're beyond the age, and not of a size to be sent for a soldier; and, lastly, what mischief do you threaten me with? Do you mean to set the house on fire, eh?'

'No, your excellency, not the house on fire.'

'Murder me, then, eh?'

Ivan was silent. 'I'm not your servant,' he said at last.

'Oh well, I'll show you,' roared the master, 'whether you 're my servant or not.' And he had Ivan cruelly punished, but yet had the three ponies put into his charge, and made him coachman in the stables.

Ivan apparently submitted; he began driving about as coachman. As he drove well, he soon gained favour with the master, especially as Ivan was very quiet and steady in his behaviour, and the ponies improved so much in his hands; he turned them out as sound and sleek as cucumbers—it was quite a sight to see. The master took to driving out with him oftener than with the other coachmen. Sometimes he would ask him, 'I say, Ivan, do you remember how badly we got on when we met? You've got over all that nonsense, eh?' But Ivan never made any response to such remarks. So one day the master was driving with Ivan to the town in his three-horse sledge with bells and a highback covered with carpet. The horses began to walk up the hill, and Ivan got off the box-seat and went behind the back of the sledge as though he had dropped something. It was a sharp frost; the master sat wrapped up, with a beaver cap pulled down on to his ears. Then Ivan took an axe from under his skirt, came up to the master from behind, knocked off his cap, and saying, 'I warned you, Piotr Petrovitch—you've yourself to blame now!' he struck off his head at one blow. Then he stopped the ponies, put the cap on his dead master, and, getting on the box-seat again, drove him to the town, straight to the courts of justice.

'Here's the Suhinsky general for you, dead; I have killed him. As I told him, so I did to him. Put me in fetters.'

They took Ivan, tried him, sentenced him to the knout, and then to hard labour. The light-hearted, bird-like dancer was sent to the mines, and there passed out of sight for ever....

Yes; one can but repeat, in another sense, Alexey Sergeitch's words: 'They were good old times ... but enough of them!'

1881.

THE BRIGADIER

I

R eader, do you know those little homesteads of country gentlefolks, which were plentiful in our Great Russian Oukraine twenty-five or thirty years ago? Now one rarely comes across them, and in another ten years the last of them will, I suppose, have disappeared for ever. The running pond overgrown with reeds and rushes, the favourite haunt of fussy ducks, among whom one may now and then come across a wary 'teal'; beyond the pond a garden with avenues of lime-trees, the chief beauty and glory of our black-earth plains, with smothered rows of 'Spanish' strawberries, with dense thickets of gooseberries, currants, and raspberries, in the midst of which, in the languid hour of the stagnant noonday heat, one would be sure to catch glimpses of a serf-girl's striped kerchief, and to hear the shrill ring of her voice. Close by would be a summer-house standing on four legs, a conservatory, a neglected kitchen garden, with flocks of sparrows hung on stakes, and a cat curled up on the tumble-down well; a little further, leafy apple-trees in the high grass, which is green below and grey above, straggling cherry-trees, pear-trees, on which there is never any fruit; then flower-beds, poppies, peonies, pansies, milk-wort, 'maids in green,' bushes of Tartar honeysuckle, wild jasmine, lilac and acacia, with the continual hum of bees and wasps among their thick, fragrant, sticky branches. At last comes the manor-house, a one-storied building on a brick foundation, with greenish window-panes in narrow frames, a sloping, once painted roof, a little balcony from which the vases of the balustrade are always jutting out, a crooked gable, and a husky old dog in the recess under the steps at the door. Behind the house a wide yard with nettles, wormwood, and burdocks in the corners, outbuildings with doors that stick, doves and rooks on the thatched roofs, a little store-house with a rusty weathercock, two or three birch-trees with rooks' nests in their bare top branches, and beyond—the road with cushions of soft dust in the ruts and a field and the long hurdles of the hemp patches, and the grey little huts of the village, and the cackle of geese in the far-away rich meadows.... Is all this familiar to you, reader? In the house itself everything is a little awry, a little rickety—but no matter. It stands firm and keeps warm; the stoves are like elephants, the furniture is of all sorts, home-made. Little paths of white footmarks run from the doors over the painted floors. In the hall siskins and larks in tiny cages; in the corner of the dining-room an immense English clock in the form of a tower, with the inscription, 'Strike—silent'; in the drawing-room portraits of the family, painted in oils, with an expression of ill-tempered alarm on the brick-coloured faces, and sometimes too an old warped picture of flowers and fruit or a mythological subject. Everywhere there is the smell of kvas, of apples, of linseed-oil and of leather. Flies buzz and hum about the ceiling and the windows. A daring cockroach suddenly shows his countenance from behind the looking-glass frame.... No matter, one can live here—and live very well too.

II

Just such a homestead it was my lot to visit thirty years ago ... it was in days long past, as you perceive. The little estate in which this house stood belonged to a friend of mine at the university; it had only recently come to him on the death of a bachelor cousin, and he was not living in it himself.... But at no great distance from it there were wide tracts of steppe bog, in which at the time of summer migration, when they are on the wing, there are great numbers of snipe; my friend and I, both enthusiastic sportsmen, agreed therefore to go on St. Peter's day, he from Moscow, I from my own village, to his little house. My friend lingered in Moscow, and was two days late; I did not care to start shooting without him. I was received by an old servant, Narkiz Semyonov, who had had notice of my coming. This old servant was not in the least like 'Savelitch' or 'Caleb'; my friend used to call him in joke 'Marquis.' There was something of conceit, even of affectation, about him; he looked down on us young men with a certain dignity, but cherished no particularly respectful sentiments for other landowners either; of his old master he spoke slightingly, while his own class he simply scorned for their ignorance. He could read and write, expressed himself correctly and with judgment, and did not drink. He seldom went to church, and so was looked upon as a dissenter. In appearance he was thin and tall, had a long and good-looking face, a sharp nose, and over-hanging eyebrows, which he was continually either knitting or lifting; he wore a neat, roomy coat, and boots to his knees with heart-shaped scallops at the tops.

III

On the day of my arrival, Narkiz, having given me lunch and cleared the table, stood in the doorway, looked intently at me, and with some play of the eyebrows observed:

'What are you going to do now, sir?'

'Well, really, I don't know. If Nikolai Petrovitch had kept his word and come, we should have gone shooting together.'

'So you really expected, sir, that he would come at the time he promised?'

'Of course I did.'

'H'm.' Narkiz looked at me again and shook his head as it were with commiseration. 'If you 'd care to amuse yourself with reading,' he continued: 'there are some books left of my old master's; I'll get them you, if you like; only you won't read them, I expect.'

'Why?'

'They're books of no value; not written for the gentlemen of these days.'

'Have you read them?'

'If I hadn't read them, I wouldn't have spoken about them. A dream-book, for instance ... that's not much of a book, is it? There are others too, of course ... only you won't read them either.'

'Why?'

'They are religious books.'

I was silent for a space.... Narkiz was silent too.

'What vexes me most,' I began, 'is staying in the house in such weather.'

'Take a walk in the garden; or go into the copse. We've a copse here beyond the threshing-floor. Are you fond of fishing?'

'Are there fish here?'

'Yes, in the pond. Loaches, sand-eels, and perches are caught there. Now, to be sure, the best time is over; July's here. But anyway, you might try.... Shall I get the tackle ready?'

'Yes, do please.'

'I'll send a boy with you ... to put on the worms. Or maybe I 'd better come myself?' Narkiz obviously doubted whether I knew how to set about things properly by myself.

'Come, please, come along.'

Narkiz, without a word, grinned from ear to ear, then suddenly knitted his brows ... and went out of the room.

IV

Half an hour later we set off to catch fish. Narkiz had put on an extraordinary sort of cap with ears, and was more dignified than ever. He walked in front with a steady, even step; two rods swayed regularly up and down on his shoulders; a bare-legged boy followed him carrying a can and a pot of worms.

'Here, near the dike, there's a seat, put up on the floating platform on purpose,' Narkiz was beginning to explain to me, but he glanced ahead, and suddenly exclaimed: 'Aha! but our poor folk are here already ... they keep it up, it seems.'

I craned my head to look from behind him, and saw on the floating platform, on the very seat of which he had been speaking, two persons sitting with their backs to us; they were placidly fishing.

'Who are they?' I asked.

'Neighbours,' Narkiz responded, with displeasure. 'They've nothing to eat at home, and so here they come to us.'

'Are they allowed to?'

'The old master allowed them.... Nikolai Petrovitch maybe won't give them permission.... The long one is a superannuated deacon—quite a silly creature; and as for the other, that's a little stouter—he's a brigadier.'

'A brigadier?' I repeated, wondering. This 'brigadier's' attire was almost worse than the deacon's.

'I assure you he's a brigadier. And he did have a fine property once. But now he has only a corner given him out of charity, and he lives ... on what God sends him. But, by the way, what are we to do? They've taken the best place.... We shall have to disturb our precious visitors.'

'No, Narkiz, please don't disturb them. We'll sit here a little aside; they won't interfere with us. I should like to make acquaintance with the brigadier.'

'As you like. Only, as far as acquaintance goes ... you needn't expect much satisfaction from it, sir; he's grown very weak in his head, and in conversation he's silly as a little child. As well he may be; he's past his eightieth year.'

'What's his name?'

'Vassily Fomitch. Guskov's his surname.'

'And the deacon?'

'The deacon? ... his nickname's Cucumber. Every one about here calls him so; but what his real name is—God knows! A foolish creature! A regular ne'er-do-well.'

'Do they live together?'

'No; but there—the devil has tied them together, it seems.'

V

We approached the platform. The brigadier cast one glance upon us ... and promptly fixed his eyes on the float; Cucumber jumped up, pulled back his rod, took off his worn-out clerical hat, passed a trembling hand over his rough yellow hair, made a sweeping bow, and gave vent to a feeble little laugh. His bloated face betrayed him an inveterate drunkard; his staring little eyes blinked humbly. He gave his neighbour a poke in the ribs, as though to let him know that they must clear out.... The brigadier began to move on the seat.

'Sit still, I beg; don't disturb yourselves,' I hastened to say. 'You won't interfere with us in the least. We'll take up our position here; sit still.'

Cucumber wrapped his ragged smock round him, twitched his shoulders, his lips, his beard.... Obviously he felt our presence oppressive and he would have been glad to slink away, ... but the brigadier was again lost in the contemplation of his float.... The 'ne'er-do-weel' coughed twice, sat down on the very edge of the seat, put his hat on his knees, and, tucking his bare legs up under him, he discreetly dropped in his line.

'Any bites?' Narkiz inquired haughtily, as in leisurely fashion he unwound his reel.

'We've caught a matter of five loaches,' answered Cucumber in a cracked and husky voice: 'and he took a good-sized perch.'

'Yes, a perch,' repeated the brigadier in a shrill pipe.

VI

I fell to watching closely—not him, but his reflection in the pond. It was as clearly reflected as in a looking-glass—a little darker, a little more silvery. The wide stretch of pond wafted a refreshing coolness upon us; a cool breath of air seemed to rise, too, from the steep, damp bank; and it was the sweeter, as in the dark blue, flooded with gold, above the tree tops, the stagnant sultry heat hung, a burden that could be felt, over our heads. There was no stir in the water near the dike; in the shade cast by the drooping bushes on the bank, water spiders gleamed, like tiny bright buttons, as they described their everlasting circles; at long intervals there was a faint ripple just perceptible round the floats, when a fish was 'playing' with the worm. Very few fish were taken; during a whole hour we drew up only two loaches and an eel. I could not say why the brigadier aroused my curiosity; his rank could not have any influence on me; ruined noblemen were not even at that time looked upon as a rarity, and his appearance presented nothing remarkable. Under the warm cap, which covered the whole upper part of his head down to his ears and his eyebrows, could be seen a smooth, red, clean-shaven, round face, with a little nose, little lips, and small, clear grey eyes. Simplicity and weakness of character, and a sort of long-standing, helpless sorrow, were visible in that meek, almost childish face; the plump, white little hands with short fingers had something helpless, incapable about them too.... I could not conceive how this forlorn old man could once have been an officer, could have maintained discipline, have given his commands—and that, too, in the stern days of Catherine! I watched him; now and then he puffed out his cheeks and uttered a feeble whistle, like a little child; sometimes he screwed up his eyes painfully, with effort, as all decrepit people will. Once he opened his eyes wide and lifted them.... They stared at me from out of the depths of the water—and strangely touching and even full of meaning their dejected glance seemed to me.

VII

I tried to begin a conversation with the brigadier ... but Narkiz had not misinformed me; the poor old man certainly had become weak in his intellect. He asked me my surname, and after repeating his inquiry twice, pondered and pondered, and at last brought out: 'Yes, I fancy there was a judge of that name here. Cucumber, wasn't there a judge about here of that name, hey?' 'To be sure there was, Vassily Fomitch, your honour,' responded Cucumber, who treated him altogether as a child. 'There was, certainly. But let me have your hook; your worm must have been eaten off.... Yes, so it is.'

'Did you know the Lomov family?' the brigadier suddenly asked me in a cracked voice.

'What Lomov family is that?'

'Why, Fiodor Ivanitch, Yevstigney Ivanitch, Alexey Ivanitch the Jew, and Fedulia Ivanovna the plunderer, ... and then, too ...'

The brigadier suddenly broke off and looked down confused.

'They were the people he was most intimate with,' Narkiz whispered, bending towards me; 'it was through them, through that same Alexey Ivanitch, that he called a Jew, and through a sister of Alexey Ivanitch's, Agrafena Ivanovna, as you may say, that he lost all his property.'

'What are you saying there about Agrafena Ivanovna?' the brigadier called out suddenly, and his head was raised, his white eyebrows were frowning.... 'You'd better mind! And why Agrafena, pray? Agrippina Ivanovna—that's what you should call her.'

'There—there—there, sir,' Cucumber was beginning to falter.

'Don't you know the verses the poet Milonov wrote about her?' the old man went on, suddenly getting into a state of excitement, which was a complete surprise to me. 'No hymeneal lights were kindled,' he began chanting, pronouncing all the vowels through his nose, giving the syllables 'an,' 'en,' the nasal sound they have in French; and it was strange to hear this connected speech from his lips: 'No torches ... No, that's not it:

> *"Not vain Corruption's idols frail*
> *Not amaranth nor porphyry*
> *Rejoiced their hearts ...*
> *One thing in them ..."*

'That was about us. Do you hear?

> *"One thing in them unquenchable,*
> *Subduing, sweet, desirable,*
> *To nurse their mutual flame in love!"*

And you talk about Agrafena!'

Narkiz chuckled half-contemptuously, half-indifferently. 'What a queer fish it is!' he said to himself. But the brigadier had again relapsed into dejection, the rod had dropped from his hands and slipped into the water.

VIII

'Well, to my thinking, our fishing is a poor business,' observed Cucumber; 'the fish, see, don't bite at all. It's got fearfully hot, and there's a fit of "mencholy" come over our gentleman. It's clear we must be going home; that will be best.' He cautiously drew out of his pocket a tin bottle with a wooden stopper, uncorked it, scattered snuff on his wrist, and sniffed it up in both nostrils at once.... 'Ah, what good snuff!' he moaned, as he recovered himself. 'It almost made my tooth ache! Now, my dear Vassily Fomitch, get up—it's time to be off!'

The brigadier got up from the bench.

'Do you live far from here?' I asked Cucumber.

'No, our gentleman lives not far ... it won't be as much as a mile.'

'Will you allow me to accompany you?' I said, addressing the brigadier. I felt disinclined to let him go.

Narkiz was surprised at my intention; but I paid no attention to the disapproving shake of his long-eared cap, and walked out of the garden with the brigadier, who was supported by Cucumber. The old man moved fairly quickly, with a motion as though he were on stilts.

IX

We walked along a scarcely trodden path, through a grassy glade between two birch copses. The sun was blazing; the orioles called to each other in the green thicket; corncrakes chattered close to the path; blue butterflies fluttered in crowds about the white, and red flowers of the low-growing clover; in the perfectly still grass bees hung, as though asleep, languidly buzzing. Cucumber seemed to pull himself together, and brightened up; he was afraid of Narkiz—he lived always under his eye; I was a stranger— a new comer—with me he was soon quite at home.

'Here's our gentleman,' he said in a rapid flow; 'he's a small eater and no mistake! but only one perch, is that enough for him? Unless, your honour, you would like to contribute something? Close here round the corner, at the little inn, there are first-rate white wheaten rolls. And if so, please your honour, this poor sinner, too, will gladly drink on this occasion to your health, and may it be of long years and long days.' I gave him a little silver, and was only just in time to pull away my hand, which he was falling upon to kiss. He learned that I was a sportsman, and fell to talking of a very good friend of his, an officer, who had a 'Mindindenger' Swedish gun, with a copper stock, just like a cannon, so that when you fire it off you are almost knocked senseless—it had been left behind by the French—and a dog—simply one of Nature's marvels! that he himself had always had a great passion for the chase, and his priest would have made no trouble about it—he used in fact to catch quails with him—but the ecclesiastical superior had pursued him with endless persecution; 'and as for Narkiz Semyonitch,' he observed in a sing-song tone, 'if according to his notions I'm not a trustworthy person—well, what I say is: he's let his eyebrows grow till he's like a woodcock, and he fancies all the sciences are known to him.' By this time we had reached the inn, a solitary tumble-down, one-roomed little hut without backyard or outbuildings; an emaciated dog lay curled up under the window; a hen was scratching in the dust under his very nose. Cucumber sat the brigadier down on the bank, and darted instantly into the hut. While he was buying the rolls and emptying a glass, I never took my eyes off the brigadier, who, God knows why, struck me as something of an enigma. In the life of this man—so I mused—there must certainly have been something out of the ordinary. But he, it seemed, did not notice me at all. He was sitting huddled up on the bank, and twisting in his fingers some pinks which he had gathered in my friend's garden. Cucumber made his appearance, at last, with a bundle of rolls in his hand; he made his appearance, all red and perspiring, with an expression of gleeful surprise on his face, as though he had just seen something exceedingly agreeable and unexpected. He at once offered the brigadier a roll to eat, and the latter at once ate it. We proceeded on our way.

X

On the strength of the spirits he had drunk, Cucumber quite 'unbent,' as it is called. He began trying to cheer up the brigadier, who was still hurrying forward with a tottering motion as though he were on stilts. 'Why are you so downcast, sir, and hanging your head? Let me sing you a song. That'll cheer you up in a minute.' He turned to me: 'Our gentleman is very fond of a joke, mercy on us, yes! Yesterday, what did I see?—a peasant-woman washing a pair of breeches on the platform, and a great fat woman she was, and he stood behind her, simply all of a shake with laughter—yes, indeed! ... In a minute, allow me: do you know the song of the hare? You mustn't judge me by my looks; there's a gypsy woman living here in the town, a perfect fright, but sings—'pon my soul! one's ready to lie down and die.' He opened wide his moist red lips and began singing, his head on one side, his eyes shut, and his beard quivering:

> *'The hare beneath the bush lies still,*
> *The hunters vainly scour the hill;*
> *The hare lies hid and holds his breath,*
> *His ears pricked up, he lies there still*
> *Waiting for death.*
> *O hunters! what harm have I done,*
> *To vex or injure you? Although*
> *Among the cabbages I run,*
> *One leaf I nibble—only one,*
> *And that's not yours!*
> *Oh, no!'*

Cucumber went on with ever-increasing energy:

> *'Into the forest dark he fled,*
> *His tail he let the hunters see;*
> *"Excuse me, gentlemen," says he,*
> *"That so I turn my back on you—*
> *I am not yours!"'*

Cucumber was not singing now ... he was bellowing:

> *'The hunters hunted day and night,*
> *And still the hare was out of sight.*
> *So, talking over his misdeeds,*
> *They ended by disputing quite—*
> *Alas, the hare is not for us!*
> *The squint-eye is too sharp for us!'*

The first two lines of each stanza Cucumber sang with each syllable drawn out; the other three, on the contrary, very briskly, and accompanied them with little hops and shuffles of his feet; at the conclusion of each verse he cut a caper, in which he kicked himself with his own heels. As he shouted at the top of his voice: 'The squint-eye is too sharp for us!' he turned a somersault.... His expectations were fulfilled. The brigadier suddenly went off into a thin, tearful little chuckle, and laughed so heartily that he could not go on, and stayed still in a half-sitting posture, helplessly slapping his knees with his hands. I looked at his face, flushed crimson, and convulsively working, and felt very sorry for him at that instant especially. Encouraged by his success, Cucumber fell to capering about in a squatting position, singing the refrain of: 'Shildi-budildi!' and 'Natchiki-tchikaldi!' He stumbled at last with his nose in the dust.... The brigadier suddenly ceased laughing and hobbled on.

XI

We went on another quarter of a mile. A little village came into sight on the edge of a not very deep ravine; on one side stood the 'lodge,' with a half-ruined roof and a solitary chimney; in one of the two rooms of this lodge lived the brigadier. The owner of the village, who always resided in Petersburg, the widow of the civil councillor Lomov, had—so I learned later—bestowed this little nook upon the brigadier. She had given orders that he should receive a monthly pension, and had also assigned for his service a half-witted serf-girl living in the same village, who, though she barely understood human speech, was yet capable, in the lady's opinion, of sweeping a floor and cooking cabbage-soup. At the door of the lodge the brigadier again addressed me with the same eighteenth-century smile: would I be pleased to walk into his 'aparte-ment'? We went into this 'apartement.' Everything in it was exceedingly filthy and poor, so filthy and so poor that the brigadier, noticing, probably, by the expression of my face, the impression it made on me, observed, shrugging his shoulders, and half closing his eyelids: 'Ce n'est pas ... oeil de perdrix.' ... What precisely he meant by this remained a mystery to me.... When I addressed him in French, I got no reply from him in that language. Two objects struck me especially in the brigadier's abode: a large officer's cross of St. George in a black frame, under glass, with an inscription in an old-fashioned handwriting: 'Received by the Colonel of the Tchernigov regiment, Vassily Guskov, for the storming of Prague in the year 1794'; and secondly, a half-length portrait in oils of a handsome, black-eyed woman with a long, dark face, hair turned up high and powdered, with postiches on the temple and chin, in a flowered, low-cut bodice, with blue frills, the style of 1780. The portrait was badly painted, but was probably a good likeness; there was a wonderful look of life and will, something extraordinarily living and resolute, about the face. It was not looking at the spectator; it was, as it were, turning away and not smiling; the curve of the thin nose, the regular but flat lips, the almost unbroken straight line of the thick eyebrows, all showed an imperious, haughty, fiery temper. No great effort was needed to picture that face glowing with passion or with rage. Just below the portrait on a little pedestal stood a half-withered bunch of simple wild flowers in a thick glass jar. The brigadier went up to the pedestal, stuck the pinks he was carrying into the jar, and turning to me, and lifting his hand in the direction of the portrait, he observed: 'Agrippina Ivanovna Teliegin, by birth Lomov.' The words of Narkiz came back to my mind; and I looked with redoubled interest at the expressive and evil face of the woman for whose sake the brigadier had lost all his fortune.

'You took part, I see, sir, in the storming of Prague,' I began, pointing to the St. George cross, 'and won a sign of distinction, rare at any time, but particularly so then; you must remember Suvorov?'

'Alexander Vassilitch?' the brigadier answered, after a brief silence, in which he seemed to be pulling his thoughts together; 'to be sure, I remember him; he was a little, brisk old man. Before one could stir a finger, he'd be here and there and everywhere (the brigadier chuckled). He rode into Warsaw on a Cossack horse; he was all in diamonds, and he says to the Poles: "I've no watch, I forgot it in Petersburg—no watch!" and they shouted and huzzaed for him. Queer chaps! Hey! Cucumber! lad!' he added suddenly, changing and raising his voice (the deacon-buffoon had remained standing at the door), 'where's the rolls, eh? And tell Grunka ... to bring some kvas!'

'Directly, your honour,' I heard Cucumber's voice reply. He handed the brigadier the bundle of rolls, and, going out of the lodge, approached a dishevelled creature in rags—the half-witted girl, Grunka, I suppose—and as far as I could make out through the dusty little window, proceeded to demand kvas from her—at least, he several times raised one hand like a funnel to his mouth, and waved the other in our direction.

XII

I made another attempt to get into conversation with the brigadier; but he was evidently tired: he sank, sighing and groaning, on the little couch, and moaning, 'Oy, oy, my poor bones, my poor bones,' untied his garters. I remember I wondered at the time how a man came to be wearing garters. I did not realise that in former days every one wore them. The brigadier began yawning with prolonged, unconcealed yawns, not taking his drowsy eyes off me all the time; so very little children yawn. The poor old man did not even seem quite to understand my question.... And he had taken Prague! He, sword in hand, in the smoke and the dust—at the head of Suvorov's soldiers, the bullet-pierced flag waving above him, the hideous corpses under his feet.... He ... he! Wasn't it wonderful! But yet I could not help fancying that there had been events more extraordinary in the brigadier's life. Cucumber brought white kvas in an iron jug; the brigadier drank greedily—his hands shook. Cucumber supported the bottom of the jug. The old man carefully wiped his toothless mouth with both hands—and again staring at me, fell to chewing and munching his lips. I saw how it was, bowed, and went out of the room.

'Now he'll have a nap,' observed Cucumber, coming out behind me. 'He's terribly knocked up to-day—he went to the grave early this morning.'

'To whose grave?'

'To Agrafena Ivanovna's, to pay his devotions.... She is buried in our parish cemetery here; it'll be four miles from here. Vassily Fomitch visits it every week without fail. Indeed, it was he who buried her and put the fence up at his own expense.'

'Has she been dead long?'

'Well, let's think—twenty years about.'

'Was she a friend of his, or what?'

'Her whole life, you may say, she passed with him ... really. I myself, I must own, never knew the lady, but they do say ... what there was between them ... well, well, well! Sir,' the deacon added hurriedly, seeing I had turned away, 'wouldn't you like to give me something for another drop, for it's time I was home in my hut and rolled up in my blanket?'

I thought it useless to question Cucumber further, so gave him a few coppers, and set off homewards.

XIII

At home I betook myself for further information to Narkiz. He, as I might have anticipated, was somewhat unapproachable, stood a little on his dignity, expressed his surprise that such paltry matters could 'interest' me, and, finally, told me what he knew. I heard the following details.

Vassily Fomitch Guskov had become acquainted with Agrafena Ivanovna Teliegin at Moscow soon after the suppression of the Polish insurrection; her husband had had a post under the governor-general, and Vassily Fomitch was on furlough. He fell in love with her there and then, but did not leave the army at once; he was a man of forty with no family, with a fortune. Her husband soon after died. She was left without children, poor, and in debt.... Vassily Fomitch heard of her position, threw up the service (he received the rank of brigadier on his retirement) and sought out his charming widow, who was not more than five-and-twenty, paid all her debts, redeemed her estate.... From that time he had never parted from her, and finished by living altogether in her house. She, too, seems to have cared for him, but would not marry him. 'She was froward, the deceased lady,' was Narkiz's comment on this: 'My liberty,' she would say, 'is dearer to me than anything.' But as for making use of him—she made use of him 'in every possible way,' and whatever money he had, he dragged to her like an ant. But the frowardness of Agrafena Ivanovna at times assumed extreme proportions; she was not of a mild temper, and somewhat too ready with her hands.... Once she pushed her page-boy down the stairs, and he went and broke two of his ribs and one leg.... Agrafena Ivanovna was frightened ... she promptly ordered the page to be shut up in the lumber-room, and she did not leave the house nor give up the key of the room to any one, till the moans within had ceased.... The page was secretly buried.... 'And had it been in the Empress Catherine's time,' Narkiz added in a whisper, bending down, 'maybe the affair would have ended there—many such deeds were hidden under a bushel in those days, but as ...' here Narkiz drew himself up and raised his voice:' as our righteous Tsar Alexander the Blessed was reigning then ... well, a fuss was made.... A trial followed, the body was dug up ... signs of violence were found on it ... and a great to-do there was. And what do you think? Vassily Fomitch took it all on himself. "I," said he, "am responsible for it all; it was I pushed him down, and I too shut him up." Well, of course, all the judges then, and the lawyers and the police ... fell on him directly ... fell on him and never let him go ... I can assure you ... till the last farthing was out of his purse. They'd leave him in peace for a while, and then attack him again. Down to the very time when the French came into Russia they were worrying at him, and only dropped him then. Well, he managed to provide for Agrafena Ivanovna—to be sure, he saved her—that one must say. Well, and afterwards, up to her death, indeed, he lived with her, and they do say she led him a pretty dance—the brigadier, that is; sent him on foot from Moscow into the country—by God, she did—to get her rents in, I suppose. It was on her account, on account of this same Agrafena Ivanovna—he fought a duel with the English milord Hugh Hughes; and the English milord was forced to make a formal apology too. But later on the brigadier went down hill more and more.... Well, and now he can't be reckoned a man at all.'

'Who was that Alexey Ivanitch the Jew,' I asked, 'through whom he was brought to ruin?'

'Oh, the brother of Agrafena Ivanovna. A grasping creature, Jewish indeed. He lent his sister money at interest, and Vassily Fomitch was her security. He had to pay for it too ... pretty heavily!'

'And Fedulia Ivanovna the plunderer—who was she?'

'Her sister too ... and a sharp one too, as sharp as a lance. A terrible woman!'

XIV

'What a place to find a Werter!' I thought next day, as I set off again towards the brigadier's dwelling. I was at that time very young, and that was possibly why I thought it my duty not to believe in the lasting nature of love. Still, I was impressed and somewhat puzzled by the story I had heard, and felt an intense desire to stir up the old man, to make him talk freely. 'I'll first refer to Suvorov again,' so I resolved within myself; 'there must be some spark of his former fire hidden within him still ... and then, when he's warmed up, I'll turn the conversation on that ... what's her name? ... Agrafena Ivanovna. A queer name for a "Charlotte"—Agrafena!'

I found my Werter-Guskov in the middle of a tiny kitchen-garden, a few steps from the lodge, near the old framework of a never-finished hut, overgrown with nettles. On the mildewed upper beams of this skeleton hut some miserable-looking turkey poults were scrambling, incessantly slipping and flapping their wings and cackling. There was some poor sort of green stuff growing in two or three borders. The brigadier had just pulled a young carrot out of the ground, and rubbing it under his arm 'to clean it,' proceeded to chew its thin tail.... I bowed to him, and inquired after his health.

He obviously did not recognise me, though he returned my greeting—that is to say, touched his cap with his hand, though without leaving off munching the carrot.

'You didn't go fishing to-day?' I began, in the hope of recalling myself to his memory by this question.

'To-day?' he repeated and pondered ... while the carrot, stuck into his mouth, grew shorter and shorter. 'Why, I suppose it's Cucumber fishing! ... But I'm allowed to, too.'

'Of course, of course, most honoured Vassily Fomitch.... I didn't mean that.... But aren't you hot ... like this in the sun.'

The brigadier was wearing a thick wadded dressing-gown.

'Eh? Hot?' he repeated again, as though puzzled over the question, and, having finally swallowed the carrot, he gazed absently upwards.

'Would you care to step into my apartement?' he said suddenly. The poor old man had, it seemed, only this phrase still left him always at his disposal.

We went out of the kitchen-garden ... but there involuntarily I stopped short. Between us and the lodge stood a huge bull. With his head down to the ground, and a malignant gleam in his eyes, he was snorting heavily and furiously, and with a rapid movement of one fore-leg, he tossed the dust up in the air with his broad cleft hoof, lashed his sides with his tail, and suddenly backing a little, shook his shaggy neck stubbornly, and bellowed—not loud, but plaintively, and at the same time menacingly. I was, I confess, alarmed; but Vassily Fomitch stepped forward with perfect composure, and saying in a stern voice, 'Now then, country bumpkin,' shook his handkerchief at him. The bull backed again, bowed his horns ... suddenly rushed to one side and ran away, wagging his head from side to side.

'There's no doubt he took Prague,' I thought.

We went into the room. The brigadier pulled his cap off his hair, which was soaked with perspiration, ejaculated, 'Fa!' ... squatted down on the edge of a chair ... bowed his head gloomily....

'I have come to you, Vassily Fomitch,' I began my diplomatic approaches, 'because, as you have served under the leadership of the great Suvorov—have taken part altogether in such important events—it would be very interesting for me to hear some particulars of your past.'

The brigadier stared at me.... His face kindled strangely—I began to expect, if not a story, at least some word of approval, of sympathy....

'But I, sir, must be going to die soon,' he said in an undertone.

I was utterly nonplussed.

'Why, Vassily Fomitch, 'I brought out at last, 'what makes you ... suppose that?'

The brigadier suddenly flung his arms violently up and down.

'Because, sir ... I, as maybe you know ... often in my dreams see Agrippina Ivanovna—Heaven's peace be with her!—and never can I catch her; I am always running after her—but cannot catch her. But last night—I dreamed—she was standing, as it were, before me, half-turned away, and laughing.... I ran up to her at once and caught her ... and she seemed to turn round quite and said to me: "Well, Vassinka, now you have caught me."'

'What do you conclude from that, Vassily Fomitch?'

'Why, sir, I conclude: it has come, that we shall be together. And glory to God for it, I tell you; glory be to God Almighty, the Father, the Son, and the Holy Ghost (the brigadier fell into a chant): as it was in the beginning, is now and ever shall be, Amen!'

The brigadier began crossing himself. I could get nothing more out of him, so I went away.

XV

The next day my friend arrived.... I mentioned the brigadier, and my visits to him....

'Oh yes! of course! I know his story,' answered my friend; 'I know Madame Lomov very well, the privy councillor's widow, by whose favour he obtained a home here. Oh, wait a minute; I believe there must be preserved here his letter to the privy councillor's widow; it was on the strength of that letter that she assigned him his little cot.' My friend rummaged among his papers and actually found the brigadier's letter. Here it is word for word, with the omission of the mistakes in spelling. The brigadier, like every one of his epoch, was a little hazy in that respect. But to preserve these errors seemed unnecessary; his letter bears the stamp of his age without them.

'HONOURED MADAM, RAISSA PAVLOVNA!

On the decease of my friend, and your aunt, I had the happiness of addressing to you two letters, the first on the first of June, the second on the sixth of July of the year 1815, while she expired on the sixth of May in that year; in them I discovered to you the feelings of my soul and of my heart, which were crushed under deadly wrongs, and they reflected in full my bitter despair, in truth deserving of commiseration; both letters were despatched by the imperial mail registered, and hence I cannot conceive that they have not been perused by your eye. By the genuine candour of my letters, I had counted upon winning your benevolent attention; but the compassionate feelings of your heart were far removed from me in my woe! Left on the loss of my one only friend, Agrippina Ivanovna, in the most distressed and poverty-stricken circumstances, I rested, by her instructions, all my hopes on your bounty; she, aware of her end approaching, said to me in these words, as it were from the grave, and never can I forget them: "My friend, I have been your serpent, and am guilty of all your unhappiness. I feel how much you have sacrificed for me, and in return I leave you in a disastrous and truly destitute situation; on my death have recourse to Raissa Pavlovna"—that is, to you—"and implore her aid, invite her succour! She has a feeling heart, and I have confidence in her, that she will not leave you forlorn." Honoured madam, let me call to witness the all-high Creator of the world that those were her words, and I am speaking with her tongue; and, therefore, trusting firmly in your goodness, to you first of all I addressed myself with my open-hearted and candid letters; but after protracted expectation, receiving no reply to them, I could not conceive otherwise than that your benevolent heart had left me without attention! Such your unfavourable disposition towards me, reduced me to the depths of despair—whither, and to whom, was I to turn in my misfortune I knew not; my soul was troubled, my intellect went astray; at last, for the completion of my ruin, it pleased Providence to chastise me in a still more cruel manner, and to turn my thoughts to your deceased aunt, Fedulia Ivanovna, sister of Agrippina Ivanovna, one in blood, but not one in heart! Having present to myself, before my mind's eye, that I had been for twenty years devoted to the whole family of your kindred, the Lomovs, especially to Fedulia Ivanovna, who never called Agrippina Ivanovna otherwise than "my heart's precious treasure," and me "the most honoured and zealous friend of our family"; picturing all the above, among abundant tears and sighs in the stillness of sorrowful night watches, I thought: "Come, brigadier! so, it seems, it is to be!" and, addressing myself by letter to the said Fedulia Ivanovna, I received a positive assurance that she would share her last crumb with me! The presents sent on by me, more than five hundred roubles' worth in value, were accepted with supreme satisfaction; and afterwards the money too which I brought with me for my maintenance, Fedulia Ivanovna was pleased, on the pretext of guarding it, to take into her care, to the which, to gratify her, I offered no opposition.

If you ask me whence, and on what ground I conceived such confidence—to the above, madam, there is but one reply: she was sister of Agrippina Ivanovna, and a member of the Lomov family! But alas and alas! all the money aforesaid I was very soon deprived of, and the hopes which I had rested on Fedulia Ivanovna—that she would share her last crumb with me—turned out to be empty and vain; on the contrary, the said Fedulia Ivanovna enriched herself with my property. To wit, on her saint's day, the fifth of February, I brought her fifty roubles' worth of green French material, at five roubles the yard; I myself received of all that was promised five roubles' worth of white pique for a waistcoat and a muslin handkerchief for my neck, which gifts were purchased in my presence, as I was aware, with my own money—and that was all that I profited by Fedulia Ivanovna's bounty! So much for the last crumb! And I could further, in all sincerity, disclose the malignant doings of Fedulia Ivanovna to me; and also my expenses, exceeding all reason, as, among the rest, for sweetmeats and fruits, of which Fedulia Ivanovna was exceedingly fond;—but upon all this I am silent, that you may not take such disclosures against the dead in bad part; and also, seeing that God has called her before His judgment seat—and all that I suffered at her hands is blotted out from my heart—and I, as a Christian, forgave her long ago, and pray to God to forgive her!

'But, honoured madam, Raissa Pavlovna! Surely you will not blame me for that I was a true and loyal friend of your family, and that I loved Agrippina Ivanovna with a love so great and so insurmountable that I sacrificed to her my life, my honour, and all my fortune! that I was utterly in her hands, and hence could not dispose of myself nor of my property, and she disposed at her will of me and also of my estate! It is known to you also that, owing to her action with her servant, I suffer, though innocent, a deadly wrong—this affair I brought after her death before the senate, before the sixth department—it is still unsettled now—in consequence of which I was made accomplice with her, my estate put under guardianship, and I am still lying under a criminal charge! In my position, at my age, such disgrace is intolerable to me; and it is only left me to console my heart with the mournful reflection that thus, even after Agrippina Ivanovna's death, I suffer for her sake, and so prove my immutable love and loyal gratitude to her!

'In my letters, above mentioned, to you, I gave you an account with every detail of Agrippina Ivanovna's funeral, and what masses were read for her—my affection and love for her spared no outlay! For all the aforesaid, and for the forty days' requiems, and the reading of the psalter six weeks after for her (in addition to above, fifty roubles of mine were lost, which were given as security for payment for the stone, of which I sent you a description)—on all the aforesaid was spent of my money seven hundred and fifty roubles, in which is included, by way of donation to the church, a hundred and fifty roubles.

'In the goodness of your heart, hear the cry of a desperate man, crushed beneath a load of the crudest calamities! Only your commiseration and humanity can restore the life of a ruined man! Though living— in the suffering of my heart and soul I am as one dead; dead when I think what I was, and what I am; I was a soldier, and served my country in all fidelity and uprightness, as is the bounden duty of a loyal Russian and faithful subject, and was rewarded with the highest honours, and had a fortune befitting my birth and station; and now I must cringe and beg for a morsel of dry bread; dead above all I am when I think what a friend I have lost ... and what is life to me after that? But there is no hastening one's end, and the earth will not open, but rather seems turned to stone! And so I call upon you, in the benevolence of your heart, hush the talk of the people, do not expose yourself to universal censure, that for all my unbounded devotion I have not where to lay my head; confound them by your bounty to me, turn the tongues of the evil speakers and slanderers to glorifying your good works—and I make bold in all humility to add, comfort in the grave your most precious aunt, Agrippina Ivanovna, who can never be forgotten, and who for your speedy succour, in answer to my sinful prayers, will spread her protecting wings about your head, and comfort in his declining days a lonely old man, who had every reason to expect a different fate! ... And, with the most profound respect, I have the honour to be, dear madam, your most devoted servant,

VASSILY GUSKOV,
Brigadier and Cavalier.'

Several years later I paid another visit to my friend's little place....
Vassily Fomitch had long been dead; he died soon after I made his acquaintance. Cucumber was still flourishing. He conducted me to the tomb
of Agrafena Ivanovna. An iron railing enclosed a large slab with a detailed
and enthusiastically laudatory epitaph on the deceased woman; and there,
beside it, as it were at her feet, could be seen a little mound with a slanting
cross on it; the servant of God, the brigadier and cavalier, Vassily Guskov,
lay under this mound.... His ashes found rest at last beside the ashes of the
creature he had loved with such unbounded, almost undying, love.

1867.

PYETUSHKOV

I

In the year 182-... there was living in the town of O—the lieutenant Ivan Afanasiitch Pyetushkov. He was born of poor parents, was left an orphan at five years old, and came into the charge of a guardian. Thanks to this guardian, he found himself with no property whatever; he had a hard struggle to make both ends meet. He was of medium height, and stooped a little; he had a thin face, covered with freckles, but rather pleasing; light brown hair, grey eyes, and a timid expression; his low forehead was furrowed with fine wrinkles. Pyetushkov's whole life had been uneventful in the extreme; at close upon forty he was still youthful and inexperienced as a child. He was shy with acquaintances, and exceedingly mild in his manner with persons over whose lot he could have exerted control....

People condemned by fate to a monotonous and cheerless existence often acquire all sorts of little habits and preferences. Pyetushkov liked to have a new white roll with his tea every morning. He could not do without this dainty. But behold one morning his servant, Onisim, handed him, on a blue-sprigged plate, instead of a roll, three dark red rusks.

Pyetushkov at once asked his servant, with some indignation, what he meant by it.

'The rolls have all been sold out,' answered Onisim, a native of Petersburg, who had been flung by some queer freak of destiny into the very wilds of south Russia.

'Impossible!' exclaimed Ivan Afanasiitch.

'Sold out,' repeated Onisim; 'there's a breakfast at the Marshal's, so they've all gone there, you know.'

Onisim waved his hand in the air, and thrust his right foot forward.

Ivan Afanasiitch walked up and down the room, dressed, and set off himself to the baker's shop. This establishment, the only one of the kind in the town of O—, had been opened ten years before by a German immigrant, had in a short time begun to flourish, and was still flourishing under the guidance of his widow, a fat woman.

Pyetushkov tapped at the window. The fat woman stuck her unhealthy, flabby, sleepy countenance out of the pane that opened.

'A roll, if you please,' Pyetushkov said amiably.

'The rolls are all gone,' piped the fat woman.

'Haven't you any rolls?'

'No.'

'How's that?—really! I take rolls from you every day, and pay for them regularly.'

The woman stared at him in silence. 'Take twists,' she said at last, yawning; 'or a scone.'

'I don't like them,' said Pyetushkov, and he felt positively hurt.

'As you please,' muttered the fat woman, and she slammed to the window-pane.

Ivan Afanasiitch was quite unhinged by his intense vexation. In his perturbation he crossed to the other side of the street, and gave himself up entirely, like a child, to his displeasure.

'Sir!' ... he heard a rather agreeable female voice; 'sir!'

Ivan Afanasiitch raised his eyes. From the open pane of the bakehouse window peeped a girl of about seventeen, holding a white roll in her hand. She had a full round face, rosy cheeks, small hazel eyes, rather a turn-up nose, fair hair, and magnificent shoulders. Her features suggested good-nature, laziness, and carelessness.

'Here's a roll for you, sir,' she said, laughing, 'I'd taken for myself; but take it, please, I'll give it up to you.'

'I thank you most sincerely. Allow me ...'

Pyetushkov began fumbling in his pocket.

'No, no! you are welcome to it.'

She closed the window-pane.

Pyetushkov arrived home in a perfectly agreeable frame of mind.

'You couldn't get any rolls,' he said to his Onisim; 'but here, I've got one, do you see?'

Onisim gave a bitter laugh.

The same day, in the evening, as Ivan Afanasiitch was undressing, he asked his servant, 'Tell me, please, my lad, what's the girl like at the baker's, hey?'

Onisim looked away rather gloomily, and responded, 'What do you want to know for?'

'Oh, nothing,' said Pyetushkov, taking off his boots with his own hands.

'Well, she's a fine girl!' Onisim observed condescendingly.

'Yes, ... she's not bad-looking,' said Ivan Afanasiitch, also looking away. 'And what's her name, do you know?'

'Vassilissa.'

'And do you know her?'

Onisim did not answer for a minute or two.

'We know her.'

Pyetushkov was on the point of opening his mouth again, but he turned over on the other side and fell asleep.

Onisim went out into the passage, took a pinch of snuff, and gave his head a violent shake.

The next day, early in the morning, Pyetushkov called for his clothes. Onisim brought him his everyday coat—an old grass-coloured coat, with huge striped epaulettes. Pyetushkov gazed a long while at Onisim without speaking, then told him to bring him his new coat. Onisim, with some surprise, obeyed. Pyetushkov dressed, and carefully drew on his chamois-leather gloves.

'You needn't go to the baker's to-day,' said he with some hesitation; 'I'm going myself, ... it's on my way.'

'Yes, sir,' responded Onisim, as abruptly as if some one had just given him a shove from behind.

Pyetushkov set off, reached the baker's shop, tapped at the window. The fat woman opened the pane.

'Give me a roll, please,' Ivan Afanasiitch articulated slowly.

The fat woman stuck out an arm, bare to the shoulder—a huge arm, more like a leg than an arm—and thrust the hot bread just under his nose.

Ivan Afanasiitch stood some time under the window, walked once or twice up and down the street, glanced into the courtyard, and at last, ashamed of his childishness, returned home with the roll in his hand. He felt ill at ease the whole day, and even in the evening, contrary to his habit, did not drop into conversation with Onisim.

The next morning it was Onisim who went for the roll.

II

Some weeks went by. Ivan Afanasiitch had completely forgotten Vassilissa, and chatted in a friendly way with his servant as before. One fine morning there came to see him a certain Bublitsyn, an easy-mannered and very agreeable young man. It is true he sometimes hardly knew himself what he was talking about, and was always, as they say, a little wild; but all the same he had the reputation of being an exceedingly agreeable person to talk to. He smoked a great deal with feverish eagerness, with lifted eyebrows and contracted chest—smoked with an expression of intense anxiety, or, one might rather say, with an expression as though, let him have this one more puff at his pipe, and in a minute he would tell you some quite unexpected piece of news; at times he would even give a grunt and a wave of the hand, while himself sucking at his pipe, as though he had suddenly recollected something extraordinarily amusing or important, then he would open his mouth, let off a few rings of smoke, and utter the most commonplace remarks, or even keep silence altogether. After gossiping a little with Ivan Afanasiitch about the neighbours, about horses, the daughters of the gentry around, and other such edifying topics, Mr. Bublitsyn suddenly winked, pulled up his shock of hair, and, with a sly smile, approached the remarkably dim looking-glass which was the solitary ornament of Ivan Afanasiitch's room.

'There's no denying the fact,' he pronounced, stroking his light brown whiskers, 'we've got girls here that beat any of your Venus of Medicis hollow.... Have you seen Vassilissa, the baker girl, for instance?' ... Mr. Bublitsyn sucked at his pipe.

Pyetushkov started.

'But why do I ask you?' pursued Bublitsyn, disappearing in a cloud of smoke,—'you're not the man to notice, don't you know, Ivan Afanasiitch! Goodness knows what you do to occupy yourself, Ivan Afanasiitch!'

'The same as you do,' Pyetushkov replied with some vexation, in a drawling voice.

'Oh no, Ivan Afanasiitch, not a bit of it.... How can you say so?'

'Well, why not?'

'Nonsense, nonsense.'

'Why so, why so?'

Bublitsyn stuck his pipe in the corner of his mouth, and began scrutinising his not very handsome boots. Pyetushkov felt embarrassed.

'Ah, Ivan Afanasiitch, Ivan Afanasiitch!' pursued Bublitsyn, as though sparing his feelings. 'But as to Vassilissa, the baker girl, I can assure you: a very, ve-ry fine girl, ... ve-ry.'

Mr. Bublitsyn dilated his nostrils, and slowly plunged his hands into his pockets.

Strange to relate, Ivan Afanasiitch felt something of the nature of jealousy. He began moving restlessly in his chair, burst into explosive laughter at nothing at all, suddenly blushed, yawned, and, as he yawned, his lower jaw twitched a little. Bublitsyn smoked three more pipes, and withdrew. Ivan Afanasiitch went to the window, sighed, and called for something to drink.

Onisim set a glass of kvas on the table, glanced severely at his master, leaned back against the door, and hung his head dejectedly.

'What are you so thoughtful about?' his master asked him genially, but with some inward trepidation.

'What am I thinking about?' retorted Onisim; 'what am I thinking about? ... it's always about you.'

'About me!'

'Of course it's about you.'

'Why, what is it you are thinking?'

'Why, this is what I'm thinking.' (Here Onisim took a pinch of snuff.) 'You ought to be ashamed, sir—you ought to be ashamed of yourself.'

'Ashamed?'

'Yes, ashamed.... Look at Mr. Bublitsyn, Ivan Afanasiitch.... Tell me if he's not a fine fellow, now.'

'I don't understand you.'

'You don't understand me.... Oh yes, you do understand me.'

Onisim paused.

'Mr. Bublitsyn's a real gentleman—what a gentleman ought to be. But what are you, Ivan Afanasiitch, what are you? Tell me that.'

'Why, I'm a gentleman too.'

'A gentleman, indeed!' ... retorted Onisim, growing indignant. 'A pretty gentleman you are! You're no better, sir, than a hen in a shower of rain, Ivan Afanasiitch, let me tell you. Here you sit sticking at home the whole blessed day ... much good it does you, sitting at home like that! You don't play cards, you don't go and see the gentry, and as for ... well ...'

Onisim waved his hand expressively.

'Now, come ... you really go ... too far ...' Ivan Afanasiitch said hesitatingly, clutching his pipe.

'Too far, indeed, Ivan Afanasiitch, too far, you say! Judge for yourself. Here again, with Vassilissa ... why couldn't you ...'

'But what are you thinking about, Onisim,' Pyetushkov interrupted miserably.

'I know what I'm thinking about. But there—I'd better let you alone! What can you do? Only fancy ... there you ...'

Ivan Afanasiitch got up.

'There, there, if you please, you hold your tongue,' he said quickly, seeming to be searching for Onisim with his eyes; 'I shall really, you know ... I ... what do you mean by it, really? You'd better help me dress.'

Onisim slowly drew off Ivan Afanasiitch's greasy Tartar dressing-gown, gazed with fatherly commiseration at his master, shook his head, put him on his coat, and fell to beating him about the back with a brush.

Pyetushkov went out, and after a not very protracted stroll about the crooked streets of the town, found himself facing the baker's shop. A queer smile was playing about his lips.

He had hardly time to look twice at the too well-known 'establishment,' when suddenly the little gate opened, and Vassilissa ran out with a yellow kerchief on her head and a jacket flung after the Russian fashion on her shoulders. Ivan Afanasiitch at once overtook her.

'Where are you going, my dear?'

Vassilissa glanced swiftly at him, laughed, turned away, and put her hand over her lips.

'Going shopping, I suppose?' queried Ivan Afanasiitch, fidgeting with his feet.

'How inquisitive we are!' retorted Vassilissa.

'Why inquisitive?' said Pyetushkov, hurriedly gesticulating with his hands. 'Quite the contrary.... Oh yes, you know,' he added hastily, as though these last words completely conveyed his meaning.

'Did you eat my roll?'

'To be sure I did,' replied Pyetushkov: 'with special enjoyment.'

Vassilissa continued to walk on and to laugh.

'It's pleasant weather to-day,' pursued Ivan Afanasiitch: 'do you often go out walking?'

'Yes.'

'Ah, how I should like....'

'What say?'

The girls in our district utter those words in a very queer way, with a peculiar sharpness and rapidity.... Partridges call at sunset with just that sound.

'To go out walking, don't you know, with you ... into the country, or ...'

'How can you?'

'Why not?'

'Ah, upon my word, how you do go on!'

'But allow me....'

At this point they were overtaken by a dapper little shopman, with a little goat's beard, and with his fingers held apart like antlers, so as to keep his sleeves from slipping over his hands, in a long-skirted bluish coat, and a warm cap that resembled a bloated water-melon. Pyetushkov, for propriety's sake, fell back a little behind Vassilissa, but quickly came up with her again.

'Well, then, what about our walk?'

Vassilissa looked slily at him and giggled again.

'Do you belong to these parts?'

'Yes.'

Vassilissa passed her hand over her hair and walked a little more slowly. Ivan Afanasiitch smiled, and, his heart inwardly sinking with timidity, he stooped a little on one side and put a trembling arm about the beauty's waist.

Vassilissa uttered a shriek.

'Give over, do, for shame, in the street.'

'Come now, there, there,' muttered Ivan Afanasiitch.

'Give over, I tell you, in the street.... Don't be rude.'

'A ... a ... ah, what a girl you are!' said Pyetushkov reproachfully, while he blushed up to his ears.

Vassilissa stood still.

'Now go along with you, sir—go along, do.'

Pyetushkov obeyed. He got home, and sat for a whole hour without moving from his chair, without even smoking his pipe. At last he took out a sheet of greyish paper, mended a pen, and after long deliberation wrote the following letter.

'DEAR MADAM, VASSILISSA TIMOFYEVNA!

Being naturally a most inoffensive person, how could I have occasioned you annoyance? If I have really been to blame in my conduct to you, then I must tell you: the hints of Mr. Bublitsyn were responsible for this, which was what I never expected. Anyway, I must humbly beg you not to be angry with me. I am a sensitive man, and any kindness I am most sensible of and grateful for. Do not be angry with me, Vassilissa Timofyevna, I beg you most humbly.—I remain respectfully your obedient servant,

IVAN PYETUSHKOV.'

Onisim carried this letter to its address.

III

A fortnight passed. Onisim went every morning as usual to the baker's shop. One day Vassilissa ran out to meet him.

'Good morning, Onisim Sergeitch.'

Onisim put on a gloomy expression, and responded crossly, "Morning.'

'How is it you never come to see us, Onisim Sergeitch?'

Onisim glanced morosely at her.

'What should I come for? you wouldn't give me a cup of tea, no fear.'

'Yes, I would, Onisim Sergeitch, I would. You come and see. Rum in it, too.'

Onisim slowly relaxed into a smile.

'Well, I don't mind if I do, then.'

'When, then—when?'

'When ... well, you are ...'

'To-day—this evening, if you like. Drop in.'

'All right, I'll come along,' replied Onisim, and he sauntered home with his slow, rolling step.

The same evening in a little room, beside a bed covered with a striped eider-down, Onisim was sitting at a clumsy little table, facing Vassilissa. A huge, dingy yellow samovar was hissing and bubbling on the table; a pot of geranium stood in the window; in the other corner near the door there stood aslant an ugly chest with a tiny hanging lock; on the chest lay a shapeless heap of all sorts of old rags; on the walls were black, greasy prints. Onisim and Vassilissa drank their tea in silence, looking straight at each other, turning the lumps of sugar over and over in their hands, as it were reluctantly nibbling them, blinking, screwing up their eyes, and with a hissing sound sucking in the yellowish boiling liquid through their teeth. At last they had emptied the whole samovar, turned upside down the round cups—one with the inscription, 'Take your fill'; the other with the words, 'Cupid's dart hath pierced my heart'—then they cleared their throats, wiped their perspiring brows, and gradually dropped into conversation.

'Onisim Sergeitch, how about your master ...' began Vassilissa, and did not finish her sentence.

'What about my master?' replied Onisim, and he leaned on his hand. 'He's all right. But why do you ask?'

'Oh, I only asked,' answered Vassilissa.

'But I say'—(here Onisim grinned)—'I say, he wrote you a letter, didn't he?'

'Yes, he did.'

Onisim shook his head with an extraordinarily self-satisfied air.

'So he did, did he?' he said huskily, with a smile. 'Well, and what did he say in his letter to you?'

'Oh, all sorts of things. "I didn't mean anything, Madam, Vassilissa Timofyevna," says he, "don't you think anything of it; don't you be offended, madam," and a lot more like that he wrote.... But I say,' she added after a brief silence: 'what's he like?'

'He's all right,' Onisim responded indifferently.

'Does he get angry?'

'He get angry! Not he. Why, do you like him?'

Vassilissa looked down and giggled in her sleeve.

'Come,' grumbled Onisim.

'Oh, what's that to you, Onisim Sergeitch?'

'Oh, come, I tell you.'

'Well,' Vassilissa brought out at last, 'he's ... a gentleman. Of course ... I ... and besides; he ... you know yourself ...'

'Of course I do,' Onisim observed solemnly.

'Of course you're aware, to be sure, Onisim Sergeitch.' ... Vassilissa was obviously becoming agitated.

'You tell him, your master, that I'm ...; say, not angry with him, but that ...'

She stammered.

'We understand,' responded Onisim, and he got up from his seat. 'We understand. Thanks for the entertainment.'

'Come in again some day.'

'All right, all right.'

Onisim approached the door. The fat woman came into the room.

'Good evening to you, Onisim Sergeitch,' she said in a peculiar chant.

'Good evening to you, Praskovia Ivanovna,' he said in the same sing-song.

Both stood still for a little while facing each other.

'Well, good day to you, Praskovia Ivanovna,' Onisim chanted out again.

'Well, good day to you, Onisim Sergeitch,' she responded in the same sing-song.

Onisim arrived home. His master was lying on his bed, gazing at the ceiling.

'Where have you been?'

'Where have I been?' ... (Onisim had the habit of repeating reproachfully the last words of every question.) 'I've been about your business.'

'What business?'

'Why, don't you know? ... I've been to see Vassilissa.'

Pyetushkov blinked and turned over on his bed.

'So that's how it is,' observed Onisim, and he coolly took a pinch of snuff. 'So that's how it is. You're always like that. Vassilissa sends you her duty.'

'Really?'

'Really? So that's all about it. Really! ... She told me to say, Why is it, says she, one never sees him? Why is it, says she, he never comes?'

'Well, and what did you say?'

'What did I say? I told her: You're a silly girl—I told her—as if folks like that are coming to see you! No, you come yourself, I told her.'

'Well, and what did she say?'

'What did she say? ... She said nothing.'

'That is, how do you mean, nothing?'

'Why, nothing, to be sure.'

Pyetushkov said nothing for a little while.

'Well, and is she coming?'

Onisim shook his head.

'She coming! You're in too great a hurry, sir. She coming, indeed! No, you go too fast.' ...

'But you said yourself that ...'

'Oh, well, it's easy to talk.'

Pyetushkov was silent again.

'Well, but how's it to be, then, my lad?'

'How? ... You ought to know best; you 're a gentleman.'

'Oh, nonsense! come now!'

Onisim swayed complacently backwards and forwards.

'Do you know Praskovia Ivanovna?' he asked at last.

'No. What Praskovia Ivanovna?'

'Why, the baker woman!'

'Oh yes, the baker woman. I've seen her; she's very fat.'

'She's a worthy woman. She's own aunt to the other, to your girl.'

'Aunt?'

'Why, didn't you know?'

'No, I didn't know.'

'Well ...'

Onisim was restrained by respect for his master from giving full expression to his feelings.

'That's whom it is you should make friends with.'

'Well, I've no objection.'

Onisim looked approvingly at Ivan Afanasiitch.

'But with what object precisely am I to make friends with her?' inquired Pyetushkov.

'What for, indeed!' answered Onisim serenely.

Ivan Afanasiitch got up, paced up and down the room, stood still before the window, and without turning his head, with some hesitation he articulated:

'Onisim!'

'What say?'

'Won't it be, you know, a little awkward for me with the old woman, eh?'

'Oh, that's as you like.'

'Oh, well, I only thought it might, perhaps. My comrades might notice it; it's a little ... But I'll think it over. Give me my pipe.... So she,' he went on after a short silence—Vassilissa, I mean, says then ...'

But Onisim had no desire to continue the conversation, and he assumed his habitual morose expression.

IV

Ivan Afanasiitch's acquaintance with Praskovia Ivanovna began in the following manner. Five days after his conversation with Onisim, Pyetushkov set off in the evening to the baker's shop. 'Well,' thought he, as he unlatched the creaking gate, 'I don't know how it's to be.' ...

He mounted the steps, opened the door. A huge, crested hen rushed, with a deafening cackle, straight under his feet, and long after was still running about the yard in wild excitement. From a room close by peeped the astonished countenance of the fat woman. Ivan Afanasiitch smiled and nodded. The fat woman bowed to him. Tightly grasping his hat, Pyetushkov approached her. Praskovia Ivanovna was apparently anticipating an honoured guest; her dress was fastened up at every hook. Pyetushkov sat down on a chair; Praskovia Ivanovna seated herself opposite him.

'I have come to you, Praskovia Ivanovna, more on account of....' Ivan Afanasiitch began at last—and then ceased. His lips were twitching spasmodically.

'You are kindly welcome, sir,' responded Praskovia Ivanovna in the proper sing-song, and with a bow. 'Always delighted to see a guest.'

Pyetushkov took courage a little.

'I have long wished, you know, to have the pleasure of making your acquaintance, Praskovia Ivanovna.'

'Much obliged to you, Ivan Afanasiitch.'

Followed a silence. Praskovia Ivanovna wiped her face with a parti-coloured handkerchief; Ivan Afanasiitch continued with intense attention to gaze away to one side. Both were rather uncomfortable. But in merchant and petty shopkeeper society, where even old friends never step outside special angular forms of etiquette, a certain constraint in the behaviour of guests and host to one another not only strikes no one as strange, but,

on the contrary, is regarded as perfectly correct and indispensable, particularly on a first visit. Praskovia Ivanovna was agreeably impressed by
Pyetushkov. He was formal and decorous in his manners, and moreover,
wasn't he a man of some rank, too?

'Praskovia Ivanovna, ma'am, I like your rolls very much,' he said to her.

'Really now, really now.'

'Very good they are, you know, very, indeed.'

'May they do you good, sir, may they do you good. Delighted, to be sure.'

'I've never eaten any like them in Moscow.'

'You don't say so now, you don't say so.'

Again a silence followed.

'Tell me, Praskovia Ivanovna,' began Ivan Afanasiitch; 'that's your
niece, I fancy, isn't it, living with you?'

'My own niece, sir.'

'How comes it ... she's with you?'....

'She's an orphan, so I keep her.'

'And is she a good worker?'

'Such a girl to work ... such a girl, sir ... ay ... ay ... to be sure she is.'

Ivan Afanasiitch thought it discreet not to pursue the subject of the
niece further.

'What bird is that you have in the cage, Praskovia Ivanovna?'

'God knows. A bird of some sort.'

'H'm! Well, so, good day to you, Praskovia Ivanovna.'

'A very good day to your honour. Pray walk in another time, and take
a cup of tea.'

'With the greatest pleasure, Praskovia Ivanovna.'

Pyetushkov walked out. On the steps he met Vassilissa. She giggled.

'Where are you going, my darling?' said Pyetushkov with reckless daring.

'Come, give over, do, you are a one for joking.'

'He, he! And did you get my letter?'

Vassilissa hid the lower part of her face in her sleeve and made no answer.

'And you're not angry with me?'

'Vassilissa!' came the jarring voice of the aunt; 'hey, Vassilissa!'

Vassilissa ran into the house. Pyetushkov returned home. But from
that day he began going often to the baker's shop, and his visits were not
for nothing. Ivan Afanasiitch's hopes, to use the lofty phraseology suitable,
were crowned with success. Usually, the attainment of the goal has a cool-
ing effect on people, but Pyetushkov, on the contrary, grew every day more
and more ardent. Love is a thing of accident, it exists in itself, like art, and,
like nature, needs no reasons to justify it, as some clever man has said who
never loved, himself, but made excellent observations upon love.

Pyetushkov became passionately attached to Vassilissa. He was completely happy. His soul was aglow with bliss. Little by little he carried all his belongings, at any rate all his pipes, to Praskovia Ivanovna's, and for whole days together he sat in her back room. Praskovia Ivanovna charged him something for his dinner and drank his tea, consequently she did not complain of his presence. Vassilissa had grown used to him. She would work, sing, or spin before him, sometimes exchanging a couple of words with him; Pyetushkov watched her, smoked his pipe, swayed to and fro in his chair, laughed, and in leisure hours played 'Fools' with her and Praskovia Ivanovna. Ivan Afanasiitch was happy....

But in this world nothing is perfect, and, small as a man's requirements may be, destiny never quite fulfils them, and positively spoils the whole thing, if possible.... The spoonful of pitch is sure to find its way into the barrel of honey! Ivan Afanasiitch experienced this in his case.

In the first place, from the time of his establishing himself at Vassilissa's, Pyetushkov dropped more than ever out of all intercourse with his comrades. He saw them only when absolutely necessary, and then, to avoid allusions and jeers (in which, however, he was not always successful), he put on the desperately sullen and intensely scared look of a hare in a display of fireworks.

Secondly, Onisim gave him no peace; he had lost every trace of respect for him, he mercilessly persecuted him, put him to shame.

And ... thirdly.... Alas! read further, kindly reader.

V

One day Pyetushkov (who for the reasons given above found little comfort outside Praskovia Ivanovna's doors) was sitting in Vassilissa's room at the back, and was busying himself over some home-brewed concoction, something in the way of jam or syrup. The mistress of the house was not at home. Vassilissa was sitting in the shop singing.

There came a knock at the little pane. Vassilissa got up, went to the window, uttered a little shriek, giggled, and began whispering with some one. On going back to her place, she sighed, and then fell to singing louder than ever.

'Who was that you were talking to?' Pyetushkov asked her.

Vassilissa went on singing carelessly.

'Vassilissa, do you hear? Vassilissa!'

'What do you want?'

'Whom were you talking to?'

'What's that to you?'

'I only asked.'

Pyetushkov came out of the back room in a parti-coloured smoking-jacket with tucked-up sleeves, and a strainer in his hand.

'Oh, a friend of mine,' answered Vassilissa.

'What friend?'

'Oh, Piotr Petrovitch.'

'Piotr Petrovitch? ... what Piotr Petrovitch?'

'He's one of your lot. He's got such a difficult name.'

'Bublitsyn?'

'Yes, yes ... Piotr Petrovitch.'

'And do you know him?'

'Rather!' responded Vassilissa, with a wag of her head.

Pyetushkov, without a word, paced ten times up and down the room.

'I say, Vassilissa,' he said at last, 'that is, how do you know him?'

'How do I know him? ... I know him ... He's such a nice gentleman.'

'How do you mean nice, though? how nice? how nice?'

Vassilissa gazed at Ivan Afanasiitch.

'Nice,' she said slowly and in perplexity. 'You know what I mean.'

Pyetushkov bit his lips and began again pacing the room.

'What were you talking about with him, eh?'

Vassilissa smiled and looked down.

'Speak, speak, speak, I tell you, speak!'

'How cross you are to-day!' observed Vassilissa.

Pyetushkov was silent.

'Come now, Vassilissa,' he began at last; 'no, I won't be cross.... Come, tell me, what were you talking about?'

Vassilissa laughed.

'He is a one to joke, really, that Piotr Petrovitch!'

'Well, what did he say?'

'He is a fellow!'

Pyetushkov was silent again for a little.

'Vassilissa, you love me, don't you?' he asked her.

'Oh, so that's what you're after, too!'

Poor Pyetushkov felt a pang at his heart. Praskovia Ivanovna came in. They sat down to dinner. After dinner Praskovia Ivanovna betook herself to the shelf bed. Ivan Afanasiitch himself lay down on the stove, turned over and dropped asleep. A cautious creak waked him. Ivan Afanasiitch sat up, leaned on his elbow, looked: the door was open. He jumped up—no Vassilissa. He ran into the yard—she was not in the yard; into the street, looked up and down—Vassilissa was nowhere to be seen. He ran without his cap as far as the market—no, Vassilissa was not in sight. Slowly he returned to the baker's shop, clambered on to the stove, and turned with his face to the wall. He felt miserable. Bublitsyn … Bublitsyn … the name was positively ringing in his ears.

'What's the matter, my good sir?' Praskovia Ivanovna asked him in a drowsy voice. 'Why are you groaning?'

'Oh, nothing, ma'am. Nothing. I feel a weight oppressing me.'

'It's the mushrooms,' murmured Praskovia Ivanovna—'it's all those mushrooms.'

O Lord, have mercy on us sinners!

An hour passed, a second—still no Vassilissa. Twenty times Pyetush-kov was on the point of getting up, and twenty times he huddled miser-ably under the sheepskin…. At last he really did get down from the stove and determined to go home, and positively went out into the yard, but came back. Praskovia Ivanovna got up. The hired man, Luka, black as a beetle, though he was a baker, put the bread into the oven. Pyetushkov went again out on to the steps and pondered. The goat that lived in the yard went up to him, and gave him a little friendly poke with his horns. Pyetushkov looked at him, and for some unknown reason said 'Kss, Kss.' Suddenly the low wicket-gate slowly opened and Vassilissa appeared. Ivan Afanasiitch went straight to meet her, took her by the hand, and rather coolly, but resolutely, said to her:

'Come along with me.'

'But, excuse me, Ivan Afanasiitch … I …'

'Come with me,' he repeated.

She obeyed.

Pyetushkov led her to his lodgings. Onisim, as usual, was lying at full length asleep. Ivan Afanasiitch waked him, told him to light a candle. Vassilissa went to the window and sat down in silence. While Onisim was busy getting a light in the anteroom, Pyetushkov stood motionless at the other window, staring into the street. Onisim came in, with the candle in his hands, was beginning to grumble … Ivan Afanasiitch turned quickly round: 'Go along,' he said to him.

Onisim stood still in the middle of the room.

'Go away at once,' Pyetushkov repeated threateningly.

Onisim looked at his master and went out.

Ivan Afanasiitch shouted after him:

'Away, quite away. Out of the house. You can come back in two hours' time.'

Onisim slouched off.

Pyetushkov waited till he heard the gate bang, and at once went up to Vassilissa.

'Where have you been?'

Vassilissa was confused.

'Where have you been? I tell you,' he repeated.

Vassilissa looked round ...

'I am speaking to you ... where have you been?' And Pyetushkov raised his arm ...

'Don't beat me, Ivan Afanasiitch, don't beat me,' Vassilissa whispered in terror.

Pyetushkov turned away.

'Beat you ... No! I'm not going to beat you. Beat you? I beg your pardon, my darling. God bless you! While I supposed you loved me, while I ... I ... '

Ivan Afanasiitch broke off. He gasped for breath.

'Listen, Vassilissa,' he said at last. 'You know I'm a kind-hearted man, you know it, don't you, Vassilissa, don't you?'

'Yes, I do,' she said faltering.

'I do nobody any harm, nobody, nobody in the world. And I deceive nobody. Why are you deceiving me?'

'But I'm not deceiving you, Ivan Afanasiitch.'

'You aren't deceiving me? Oh, very well! Oh, very well! Then tell me where you've been.'

'I went to see Matrona.'

'That's a lie!'

'Really, I've been at Matrona's. You ask her, if you don't believe me.'

'And Bub—what's his name ... have you seen that devil?'

'Yes, I did see him.'

'You did see him! you did see him! Oh! you did see him!'

Pyetushkov turned pale.

'So you were making an appointment with him in the morning at the window—eh? eh?'

'He asked me to come.'

'And so you went.... Thanks very much, my girl, thanks very much!' Pyetushkov made Vassilissa a low bow.

'But, Ivan Afanasiitch, you're maybe fancying ...'

'You'd better not talk to me! And a pretty fool I am! There's nothing to make an outcry for! You may make friends with any one you like. I've nothing to do with you. So there! I don't want to know you even.'

Vassilissa got up.

'That's for you to say, Ivan Afanasiitch.'

'Where are you going?'

'Why, you yourself ...'

'I'm not sending you away,' Pyetushkov interrupted her.

'Oh no, Ivan Afanasiitch.... What's the use of my stopping here?'

Pyetushkov let her get as far as the door.

'So you're going, Vassilissa?'

'You keep on abusing me.'

'I abuse you! You've no fear of God, Vassilissa! When have I abused you? Come, come, say when?'

'Why! Just this minute weren't you all but beating me?'

'Vassilissa, it's wicked of you. Really, it's downright wicked.'

'And then you threw it in my face, that you don't want to know me. "I'm a gentleman," say you.'

Ivan Afanasiitch began wringing his hands speechlessly. Vassilissa got back as far as the middle of the room.

'Well, God be with you, Ivan Afanasiitch. I'll keep myself to myself, and you keep yourself to yourself.'

'Nonsense, Vassilissa, nonsense,' Pyetushkov cut her short. 'You think again; look at me. You see I'm not myself. You see I don't know what I'm saying.... You might have some feeling for me.'

'You keep on abusing me, Ivan Afanasiitch.'

'Ah, Vassilissa! Let bygones be bygones. Isn't that right? Come, you're not angry with me, are you?'

'You keep abusing me,' Vassilissa repeated.

'I won't, my love, I won't. Forgive an old man like me. I'll never do it in future. Come, you've forgiven me, eh?'

'God be with you, Ivan Afanasiitch.'

'Come, laugh then, laugh.'

Vassilissa turned away.

'You laughed, you laughed, my love!' cried Pyetushkov, and he capered about like a child.

VI

The next day Pyetushkov went to the baker's shop as usual. Everything went on as before. But there was a settled ache at his heart. He did not laugh now as often, and sometimes he fell to musing. Sunday came. Praskovia Ivanovna had an attack of lumbago; she did not get down from the shelf bed, except with much difficulty to go to mass. After mass Pyetushkov called Vassilissa into the back room. She had been complaining all the morning of feeling dull. To judge by the expression of Ivan Afanasiitch's countenance, he was revolving in his brain some extraordinary idea, unforeseen even by him.

'You sit down here, Vassilissa,' he said to her, 'and I'll sit here. I want to have a little talk with you.'

Vassilissa sat down.

'Tell me, Vassilissa, can you write?'

'Write?'

'Yes, write?'

'No, I can't.'

'What about reading?'

'I can't read either.'

'Then who read you my letter?'

'The deacon.'

Pyetushkov paused.

'But would you like to learn to read and write?'

'Why, what use would reading and writing be to us, Ivan Afanasiitch?'

'What use? You could read books.'

'But what good is there in books?'

'All sorts of good ... I tell you what, if you like, I'll bring you a book.'

'But I can't read, you see, Ivan Afanasiitch.'

'I'll read to you.'

'But, I say, won't it be dull?'

'Nonsense! dull! On the contrary, it's the best thing to get rid of dulness.'

'Maybe you'll read stories, then.'

'You shall see to-morrow.'

In the evening Pyetushkov returned home, and began rummaging in his boxes. He found several odd numbers of the Library of Good Reading, five grey Moscow novels, Nazarov's arithmetic, a child's geography with a globe on the title-page, the second part of Keydanov's history, two dream-books, an almanack for the year 1819, two numbers of Galatea, Kozlov's *Natalia Dolgorukaia*, and the first part of *Roslavlev*. He pondered a long while which to choose, and finally made up his mind to take Kozlov's poem, and *Roslavlev*.

Next day Pyetushkov dressed in haste, put both the books under the lapel of his coat, went to the baker's shop, and began reading aloud Zagoskin's novel. Vassilissa sat without moving; at first she smiled, then seemed to become absorbed in thought ... then she bent a little forward;

her eyes closed, her mouth slightly opened, her hands fell on her knees; she was dozing. Pyetushkov read quickly, inarticulately, in a thick voice; he raised his eyes ...

'Vassilissa, are you asleep?'

She started, rubbed her face, and stretched. Pyetushkov felt angry with her and with himself....

'It's dull,' said Vassilissa lazily.

'I tell you what, would you like me to read you poetry?'

'What say?'

'Poetry ... good poetry.'

'No, that's enough, really.'

Pyetushkov hurriedly picked up Kozlov's poem, jumped up, crossed the room, ran impulsively up to Vassilissa, and began reading. Vassilissa let her head drop backwards, spread out her hands, stared into Ivan Afanasiitch's face, and suddenly went off into a loud harsh guffaw ... she fairly rolled about with laughing.

Ivan Afanasiitch flung the book on the floor in his annoyance. Vassilissa went on laughing.

'Why, what are you laughing at, silly?'

Vassilissa roared more than ever.

'Laugh away, laugh away,' Pyetushkov muttered between his teeth.

Vassilissa held her sides, gasping.

'But what is it, idiot?' But Vassilissa could only wave her hands.

Ivan Afanasiitch snatched up his cap, and ran out of the house. With rapid, unsteady steps, he walked about the town, walked on and on, and found himself at the city gates. Suddenly there was the rattle of wheels, the tramp of horses along the street.... Some one called him by name. He raised his head and saw a big, old-fashioned wagonette. In the wagonette facing him sat Mr. Bublitsyn between two young ladies, the daughters of Mr. Tiutiurov. Both the girls were dressed exactly alike, as though in outward sign of their immutable affection; both smiled pensively, and carried their heads on one side with a languid grace. On the other side of the carriage appeared the wide straw hat of their excellent papa; and from time to time his round, plump neck presented itself to the gaze of spectators. Beside his straw hat rose the mob-cap of his spouse. The very attitude of both the parents was a sufficient proof of their sincere goodwill towards the young man and their confidence in him. And Bublitsyn obviously was aware of their flattering confidence and appreciated it. He was, of course, sitting in an unconstrained position, and talking and laughing without constraint; but in the very freedom of his manner there could be discerned a shade of tender, touching respectfulness. And the Tiutiurov girls? It is hard to convey in words all that an attentive observer could trace in the faces of the two sisters. Goodwill and gentleness, and discreet gaiety, a melancholy comprehension of life, and a faith, not to be shaken, in themselves, in the lofty and noble destiny of man on earth, courteous attention to their young companion, in intellectual endowments perhaps not fully their equal, but still by the qualities of his heart quite deserving of their indulgence ... such were the characteristics and the feelings reflected at that moment on the faces of the young ladies. Bublitsyn called to Ivan Afanasiitch for no special reason, simply in the fulness of his inner satisfaction; he bowed to him with excessive friendliness and cordiality. The young ladies even looked at him with gentle amiability, as at a man whose acquaintance they would not object to.... The good, sleek, quiet horses went by Ivan Afanasiitch at a gentle trot; the carriage rolled smoothly along the broad road, carrying with it good-humoured, girlish laughter; he caught a final glimpse of Mr. Tiutiurov's hat; the two outer horses turned their heads on each side, jauntily stepping over the short, green grass ... the coachman gave a whistle of approbation and warning, the carriage disappeared behind some willows.

A long while poor Pyetushkov remained standing still.

'I'm a poor lonely creature,' he whispered at last ... 'alone in the world.'

A little boy in tatters stopped before him, looked timidly at him, held out his hand ...

'For Christ's sake, good gentleman.'

Pyetushkov pulled out a copper.

'For your loneliness, poor orphan,' he said with effort, and he walked back to the baker's shop. On the threshold of Vassilissa's room Ivan Afanasiitch stopped.

'Yes,' he thought, 'these are my friends. Here is my family, this is it.... And here Bublitsyn and there Bublitsyn.'

Vassilissa was sitting with her back to him, winding worsted, and carelessly singing to herself; she was wearing a striped cotton gown; her hair was done up anyhow.... The room, insufferably hot, smelt of feather beds and old rags; jaunty, reddish-brown 'Prussians' scurried rapidly here and there across the walls; on the decrepit chest of drawers, with holes in it where the locks should have been, beside a broken jar, lay a woman's shabby slipper.... Kozlov's poem was still where it had fallen on the floor.... Pyetushkov shook his head, folded his arms, and went away. He was hurt.

At home he called for his things to dress. Onisim slouched off after his better coat. Pyetushkov had a great desire to draw Onisim into conversation, but Onisim preserved a sullen silence. At last Ivan Afanasiitch could hold out no longer.

'Why don't you ask me where I'm going?'

'Why, what do I want to know where you're going for?'

'What for? Why, suppose some one comes on urgent business, and asks, "Where's Ivan Afanasiitch?" And then you can tell him, "Ivan Afanasiitch has gone here or there."'

'Urgent business.... But who ever does come to you on urgent business?'

'Why, are you beginning to be rude again? Again, hey?'

Onisim turned away, and fell to brushing the coat.

'Really, Onisim, you are a most disagreeable person.'

Onisim looked up from under his brows at his master.

'And you 're always like this. Yes, positively always.'

Onisim smiled.

'But what's the good of my asking you where you're going, Ivan Afanasiitch? As though I didn't know! To the girl at the baker's shop!'

'There, that's just where you're wrong! that's just where you're mistaken! Not to her at all. I don't intend going to see the girl at the baker's shop any more.'

Onisim dropped his eyelids and brandished the brush. Pyetushkov waited for his approbation; but his servant remained speechless.

'It's not the proper thing,' Pyetushkov went on in a severe voice—'it's unseemly.... Come, tell me what you think?'

'What am I to think? It's for you to say. What business have I to think?'

Pyetushkov put on his coat. 'He doesn't believe me, the beast,' he thought to himself.

He went out of the house, but he did not go to see any one. He walked about the streets. He directed his attention to the sunset. At last a little after eight o'clock he returned home. He wore a smile; he repeatedly shrugged his shoulders, as though marvelling at his own folly. 'Yes,' thought he, 'this is what comes of a strong will....'

Next day Pyetushkov got up rather late. He had not passed a very good night, did not go out all day, and was fearfully bored. Pyetushkov read through all his poor books, and praised aloud one story in the Library of Good Reading. As he went to bed, he told Onisim to give him his pipe. Onisim handed him a wretched pipe. Pyetushkov began smoking; the pipe wheezed like a broken-winded horse.

'How disgusting!' cried Ivan Afanasiitch; 'where's my cherry wood pipe?'

'At the baker's shop,' Onisim responded tranquilly.

Pyetushkov blinked spasmodically.

'Well, you wish me to go for it?'

'No, you needn't; don't go ... no need, don't go, do you hear?'

'Yes, sir.'

The night passed somehow. In the morning Onisim, as usual, gave Pyetushkov on the blue sprigged plate a new white roll. Ivan Afanasiitch looked out of window and asked Onisim:

'You've been to the baker's shop?'

'Who's to go, if I don't?'

'Ah!'

Pyetushkov became plunged in meditation.

'Tell me, please, did you see any one there?'

'Of course I did.'

'Whom did you see there, now, for instance?'

'Why, of course, Vassilissa.'

Ivan Afanasiitch was silent. Onisim cleared the table, and was just going out of the room....

'Onisim,' Pyetushkov cried faintly.

'What is it?'

'Er ... did she ask after me?'

'Of course she didn't.'

Pyetushkov set his teeth. 'Yes,' he thought, 'that's all it's worth, her love, indeed....' His head dropped. 'Absurd I was, to be sure,' he thought again. 'A fine idea to read her poetry. A girl like that! Why, she's a fool! Why, she's good for nothing but to lie on the stove and eat pancakes. Why, she's a post, a perfect post; an uneducated workgirl.'

'She's never come,' he whispered, two hours later, still sitting in the same place, 'she's never come. To think of it; why, she could see that I left her out of temper; why, she might know that I was hurt. There's love for you! And she did not even ask if I were well. Never even said, "Is Ivan Afanasiitch quite well?" She hasn't seen me for two whole days—and not a sign.... She's even again, maybe, thought fit to meet that Bub—Lucky fellow. Ouf, devil take it, what a fool I am!'

Pyetushkov got up, paced up and down the room in silence, stood still, knitted his brows slightly and scratched his neck. 'However,' he said aloud, 'I'll go to see her. I must see what she's about there. I must make her feel ashamed. Most certainly ... I'll go. Onisim! my clothes.'

'Well,' he mused as he dressed, 'we shall see what comes of it. She may, I dare say, be angry with me. And after all, a man keeps coming and coming, and all of a sudden, for no rhyme or reason, goes and gives up coming. Well, we shall see.'

Ivan Afanasiitch went out of the house, and made his way to the baker's shop. He stopped at the little gate, he wanted to straighten himself out and set himself to rights.... Pyetushkov clutched at the folds of his coat with both hands, and almost pulled them out altogether.... Convulsively he twisted his tightly compressed neck, fastened the top hook of his collar, drew a deep breath....

'Why are you standing there?' Praskovia Ivanovna bawled to him from the little window. 'Come in.'

Pyetushkov started, and went in. Praskovia Ivanovna met him in the doorway.

'Why didn't you come to see us yesterday, my good sir? Was it, maybe, some ailment prevented you?'

'Yes, I had something of a headache yesterday....'

'Ah, you should have put cucumber on your temples, my good sir. It would have taken it away in a twinkling. Is your head aching now?'

'No, it's not.'

'Ah well, and thank Thee, O Lord, for it.'

Ivan Afanasiitch went off into the back room. Vassilissa saw him.

'Ah! good day, Ivan Afanasiitch.'

'Good day, Vassilissa Ivanovna.'

'Where have you put the tap, Ivan Afanasiitch?'

'Tap? what tap?'

'The wine-tap ... our tap. You must have taken it home with you. You are such a one ... Lord, forgive us....'

Pyetushkov put on a dignified and chilly air.

'I will direct my man to look. Seeing that I was not here yesterday,' he pronounced significantly....

'Ah, why, to be sure, you weren't here yesterday.' Vassilissa squatted down on her heels, and began rummaging in the chest....

'Aunt, hi! aunt!'

'What sa-ay?'

'Have you taken my neckerchief?'

'What neckerchief?'

'Why, the yellow one.'

'The yellow one?'

'Yes, the yellow, figured one.'

'No, I've not taken it.'

Pyetushkov bent down to Vassilissa.

'Listen to me, Vassilissa; listen to what I am saying to you. It is not a matter of taps or of neckerchiefs just now; you can attend to such trifles another time.'

Vassilissa did not budge from her position; she only lifted her head.

'You just tell me, on your conscience, do you love me or not? That's what I want to know, once for all.'

'Ah, what a one you are, Ivan Afanasiitch.... Well, then, of course.'

'If you love me, how was it you didn't come to see me yesterday? Had you no time? Well, you might have sent to find out if I were ill, as I didn't turn up. But it's little you cared. I might die, I dare say, you wouldn't grieve.'

'Ah, Ivan Afanasiitch, one can't be always thinking of one thing, one's got one's work to do.'

'To be sure,' responded Pyetushkov; 'but all the same ... And it's improper to laugh at your elders.... It's not right. Moreover, it's as well in certain cases ... But where's my pipe?'

'Here's your pipe.'

Pyetushkov began smoking.

VII

Several days slipped by again, apparently rather tranquilly. But a storm was getting nearer. Pyetushkov suffered tortures, was jealous, never took his eyes off Vassilissa, kept an alarmed watch over her, annoyed her horribly. Behold, one evening, Vassilissa dressed herself with more care than usual, and, seizing a favourable instant, sallied off to make a visit somewhere. Night came on, she had not returned. Pyetushkov at sunset went home to his lodgings, and at eight o'clock in the morning ran to the baker's shop.... Vassilissa had not come in. With an inexpressible sinking at his heart, he waited for her right up to dinner-time.... They sat down to the table without her....

'Whatever can have become of her?' Praskovia Ivanovna observed serenely....

'You spoil her, you simply spoil her utterly!' Pyetushkov repeated, in despair.

'Eh! my good sir, there's no looking after a girl!' responded Praskovia Ivanovna. 'Let her go her way! So long as she does her work.... Why shouldn't folks enjoy themselves? ...'

A cold shudder ran over Pyetushkov. At last, towards evening, Vassilissa made her appearance. This was all he was waiting for. Majestically Pyetushkov rose from his seat, folded his arms, scowled menacingly.... But Vassilissa looked him boldly in the face, laughed impudently, and before he could utter a single word she went quickly into her own room, and locked herself in. Ivan Afanasiitch opened his mouth, looked in amazement at Praskovia Ivanovna.... Praskovia Ivanovna cast down her eyes. Ivan Afanasiitch stood still a moment, groped after his cap, put it on askew, and went out without closing his mouth.

He reached home, took up a leather cushion, and with it flung himself on the sofa, with his face to the wall. Onisim looked in out of the passage, went into the room, leaned his back against the door, took a pinch of snuff, and crossed his legs.

'Are you unwell, Ivan Afanasiitch?' he asked Pyetushkov.

Pyetushkov made no answer.

'Shall I go for the doctor?' Onisim continued, after a brief pause.

'I'm quite well.... Go away,' Ivan Afanasiitch articulated huskily.

'Well? ... no, you're not well, Ivan Afanasiitch.... Is this what you call being well?'

Pyetushkov did not speak.

'Just look at yourself. You've grown so thin, that you're simply not like yourself. And what's it all about? It's enough to turn one's brain to think of it. And you a gentleman born, too!'

Onisim paused. Pyetushkov did not stir.

'Is that the way gentlemen go on? They'd amuse themselves a bit, to be sure ... why shouldn't they ... they'd amuse themselves, and then drop it.... They may well say, Fall in love with Old Nick, and you'll think him a beauty.'

Ivan Afanasiitch merely writhed.

'Well, it's really like this, Ivan Afanasiitch. If any one had said this and that of you, and your goings on, why, I would have said, "Get along with you, you fool, what do you take me for?" Do you suppose I'd have believed it? Why, as it is, I see it with my own eyes, and I can't believe it. Worse than this nothing can be. Has she put some spell over you or what? Why, what is there in her? If you come to consider, she's below contempt, really. She can't even speak as she ought.... She's simply a baggage! Worse, even!'

'Go away,' Ivan Afanasiitch moaned into the cushion.

'No, I'm not going away, Ivan Afanasiitch. Who's to speak, if I don't? Why, upon my word! Here, you 're breaking your heart now ... and over what? Eh, over what? tell me that!'

'Oh, go away, Onisim,' Pyetushkov moaned again. Onisim, for propriety's sake, was silent for a little while.

'And another thing,' he began again, 'she's no feeling of gratitude whatever. Any other girl wouldn't know how to do enough to please you; while she! ... she doesn't even think of you. Why, it's simply a disgrace. Why, the things people are saying about you, one cannot repeat them, they positively cry shame on me. If I could have known beforehand, I'd have....'

'Oh, go away, do, devil!' shrieked Pyetushkov, not stirring from his place, however, nor raising his head.

'Ivan Afanasiitch, for mercy's sake,' pursued the ruthless Onisim. 'I'm speaking for your good. Despise her, Ivan Afanasiitch; you simply break it off. Listen to me, or else I'll fetch a wise woman; she'll break the spell in no time. You'll laugh at it yourself, later on; you'll say to me, "Onisim, why, it's marvellous how such things happen sometimes!" You just consider yourself: girls like her, they're like dogs ... you've only to whistle to them....'

Like one frantic, Pyetushkov jumped up from the sofa ... but, to the amazement of Onisim, who was already lifting both hands to the level of his cheeks, he sat down again, as though some one had cut away his legs from under him.... Tears were rolling down his pale face, a tuft of hair stood up straight on the top of his head, his eyes looked dimmed ... his drawn lips were quivering ... his head sank on his breast.

Onisim looked at Pyetushkov and plumped heavily down on his knees.

'Dear master, Ivan Afanasiitch,' he cried, 'your honour! Be pleased to punish me. I'm a fool. I've troubled you, Ivan Afanasiitch.... How did I dare! Be pleased to punish me, your honour.... It's not worth your while to weep over my silly words ... dear master. Ivan Afanasiitch....'

But Pyetushkov did not even look at his servant; he turned away and buried himself in the corner of the sofa again.

Onisim got up, went up to his master, stood over him, and twice he tugged at his own hair.

'Wouldn't you like to undress, sir ... you should go to bed ... you should take some raspberry tea ... don't grieve, please your honour.... It's only half a trouble, it's all nothing ... it'll be all right in the end,' he said to him every two minutes....

But Pyetushkov did not get up from the sofa, and only twitched his shoulders now and then, and drew up his knees to his stomach....

Onisim did not leave his side all night. Towards morning Pyetushkov fell asleep, but he did not sleep long. At seven o'clock he got up from the sofa, pale, dishevelled, and exhausted, and asked for tea.

Onisim with amazing eagerness and speed brought the samovar.

'Ivan Afanasiitch,' he began at last, in a timid voice, 'your honour is not angry with me?'

'Why should I be angry with you, Onisim?' answered poor Pyetushkov. 'You were perfectly right yesterday, and I quite agreed with you in everything.'

'I only spoke through my devotion to you, Ivan Afanasiitch.'

'I know that.'

Pyetushkov was silent and hung his head.

Onisim saw that things were in a bad way.

'Ivan Afanasiitch,' he said suddenly.

'Well?'

'Would you like me to fetch Vassilissa here?'

Pyetushkov flushed red.

'No, Onisim, I don't wish it. ('Yes, indeed! as if she would come!' he thought to himself.) One must be firm. It is all nonsense. Yesterday, I ... It's a disgrace. You are right. One must cut it all short, once for all, as they say. Isn't that true?'

'It's the gospel truth your honour speaks, Ivan Afanasiitch.'

Pyetushkov sank again into reverie. He wondered at himself, he did not seem to know himself. He sat without stirring and stared at the floor. Thoughts whirled round within him, like smoke or fog, while his heart felt empty and heavy at once.

'But what's the meaning of it, after all,' he thought sometimes, and again he grew calmer. 'It's nonsense, silliness!' he said aloud, and passed his hand over his face, shook himself, and his hand dropped again on his knee, his eyes again rested on the floor.

Intently and mournfully Onisim kept watch on his master.

Pyetushkov lifted his head.

'Tell me, Onisim,' he began, 'is it true, are there really such witches' spells?'

'There are, to be sure there are,' answered Onisim, as he thrust one foot forward. 'Does your honour know the non-commissioned officer, Krupovaty? ... His brother was ruined by witchcraft. He was bewitched to love an old woman, a cook, if your honour only can explain that! They gave him nothing but a morsel of rye bread, with a muttered spell, of course. And Krupovaty's brother simply lost his heart to the cook, he fairly ran after the cook, he positively adored her—couldn't keep his eyes off her. She might tell him to do anything, he'd obey her on the spot. She'd even make a joke of him before other people, before strangers. Well, she drove him into a decline, at last. And so it was Krupovaty's brother died. And you know, she was a cook, and an old woman too, very old. (Onisim took a pinch of snuff.) Confound the lot of them, these girls and women-folk!'

'She doesn't care for me a bit, that's clear, at last; that's beyond all doubt, at last,' Pyetushkov muttered in an undertone, gesticulating with his head and hands as though he were explaining to a perfectly extraneous person some perfectly extraneous fact.

'Yes,' Onisim resumed, 'there are women like that.'

'There are,' listlessly repeated Pyetushkov, in a tone half questioning, half perplexed.

Onisim looked intently at his master.

'Ivan Afanasiitch,' he began, 'wouldn't you have a snack of something?'

'Wouldn't I have a snack of something?' repeated Pyetushkov.

'Or may be you'd like to have a pipe?'

'To have a pipe?' repeated Pyetushkov.

'So this is what it's coming to,' muttered Onisim. 'It's gone deep, it seems.'

VIII

The creak of boots resounded in the passage, and then there was heard the usual suppressed cough which announces the presence of a person of subordinate position. Onisim went out and promptly came back, accompanied by a diminutive soldier with a little, old woman's face, in a patched cloak yellow with age, and wearing neither breeches nor cravat. Pyetushkov was startled; while the soldier drew himself up, wished him good day, and handed him a large envelope bearing the government seal. In this envelope was a note from the major in command of the garrison: he called upon Pyetushkov to come to him without fail or delay.

Pyetushkov turned the note over in his hands, and could not refrain from asking the messenger, did he know why the major desired his presence, though he was very well aware of the utter futility of his question.

'We cannot tell!' the soldier cried, with great effort, yet hardly audibly, as though he were half asleep.

'Isn't he summoning the other officers?' Pyetushkov pursued.

'We cannot tell,' the soldier cried a second time, in just the same voice.

'All right, you can go,' pronounced Pyetushkov.

The soldier wheeled round to the left, scraping his foot as he did so, and slapping himself below the spine (this was considered smart in the twenties), withdrew.

Pyetushkov exchanged glances with Onisim, who at once assumed a look of anxiety. Without a word Ivan Afanasiitch set off to the major's.

The major was a man of sixty, corpulent and clumsily built, with a red and bloated face, a short neck, and a continual trembling in his fingers, resulting from excessive indulgence in strong drink. He belonged to the class of so-called 'bourbons,' that's to say, soldiers risen from the ranks; had learned to read at thirty, and spoke with difficulty, partly from shortness of breath, partly from inability to follow his own thought. His temperament exhibited all the varieties known to science: in the morning, before drinking, he was melancholy; in the middle of the day, choleric; and in the evening, phlegmatic, that is to say, he did nothing at that time but snore and grunt till he was put to bed. Ivan Afanasiitch appeared before him during the choleric period. He found him sitting on a sofa, in an open dressing-gown, with a pipe between his teeth. A fat, crop-eared cat had taken up her position beside him.

'Aha! he's come!' growled the major, casting a sidelong glance out of his pewtery eyes upon Pyetushkov, and not stirring from his place. 'Sit down. Well, I'm going to give you a talking to. I've wanted to get hold of you this long while.'

Pyetushkov sank into a chair.

'For,' the major began, with an unexpected lurch of his whole body, 'you're an officer, d'ye see, and so you've got to behave yourself according to rule. If you'd been a soldier, I'd have flogged you, and that's all about it, but, as 'tis, you're an officer. Did any one ever see the like of it? Disgracing yourself—is that a nice thing?'

'Allow me to know to what these remarks may refer?' Pyetushkov was beginning....

'I'll have no arguing! I dislike that beyond everything. I've said: I dislike it; and that's all about it! Ugh—why, your hooks are not in good form even;—what a disgrace! He sits, day in and day out, at the baker's shop; and he a gentleman born! There's a petticoat to be found there—and so there he sits. Let her go to the devil, the petticoat! Why, they do say he puts the bread in the oven. It's a stain on the uniform ... so it is!'

'Allow me to submit,' articulated Pyetushkov with a cold chill at his heart, 'that all this, as far as I can make out, refers to my private life, so to say....'

'No arguing with me, I tell you! Private life, he protests, too! If it had been a matter of the service I'd have sent you straight to the guard-room! Alley, marsheer! Because of the oath. Why, there was a whole birch copse, maybe, used upon my back, so I should think I know the service; every rule of discipline I'm very well up in. And I'd have you to understand, I say this just for the honour of the uniform. You're disgracing the uniform ... so you are. I say this like a father ... yes. Because all that's put in my charge. I've to answer for it. And you dare to argue too!' the major shrieked with sudden fury, and his face turned purple, and he foamed at the mouth, while the cat put its tail in the air and jumped down to the ground. 'Why, do you know ... why, do you know what I can do? ... I can do anything,

anything, anything! Why, do you know whom you're talking to? Your superior officer gives you orders and you argue! Your superior officer ... your superior officer....'

Here the major positively choked and spluttered, while poor Pyetushkov could only draw himself up and turn pale, sitting on the very edge of his chair.

'I must have' ... the major continued, with an imperious wave of his trembling hand, 'I must have everything ... up to the mark! Conduct first-class! I'm not going to put up with any irregularities! You can make friends with whom you like, that makes no odds to me! But if you are a gentleman, why, act as such ... behave like one! No putting bread in the oven for me! No calling a draggletail old woman auntie! No disgracing the uniform! Silence! No arguing!'

The major's voice broke. He took breath, and turning towards the door into the passage, bawled, 'Frolka, you scoundrel! The herrings!'

Pyetushkov rose hurriedly and darted away, almost upsetting the page-boy, who ran to meet him, carrying some sliced herring and a stout decanter of spirits on an iron tray.

'Silence! No arguing!' sounded after Pyetushkov the disjointed exclamations of his exasperated superior officer.

IX

A queer sensation overmastered Ivan Afanasiitch when, at last, he found himself in the street.

'Why am I walking as it were in a dream?' he thought to himself. 'Am I out of my mind, or what? Why, it passes all belief, at last. Come, damn it, she's tired of me, come, and I've grown tired of her, come, and ... What is there out of the way in that?

Pyetushkov frowned.

'I must put an end to it, once for all,' he said almost aloud. 'I'll go and speak out decisively for the last time, so that it may never come up again.'

Pyetushkov made his way with rapid step to the baker's shop. The nephew of the hired man, Luka, a little boy, friend and confidant of the goat that lived in the yard, darted swiftly to the little gate, directly he caught sight of Ivan Afanasiitch in the distance.

Praskovia Ivanovna came out to meet Pyetushkov.

'Is your niece at home?' asked Pyetushkov.

'No, sir.'

Pyetushkov was inwardly relieved at Vassilissa's absence.

'I came to have a few words with you, Praskovia Ivanovna.'

'What about, my good sir?'

'I'll tell you. You comprehend that after all ... that has passed ... after such, so to say, behaviour (Pyetushkov was a little confused) ... in a word ... But, pray, don't be angry with me, though.'

'Certainly not, sir.'

'On the contrary, enter into my position, Praskovia Ivanovna.'

'Certainly, sir.'

'You're a reasonable woman, you'll understand of yourself, that ... that I can't go on coming to see you any more.'

'Certainly, sir,' Praskovia Ivanovna repeated slowly.

'I assure you I greatly regret it; I confess it is positively painful to me, genuinely painful ...'

'You know best, sir,' Praskovia Ivanovna rejoined serenely. 'It's for you to decide, sir. And, oh, if you'll allow me, I'll give you your little account, sir.'

Pyetushkov had not at all anticipated such a prompt acquiescence. He had not desired acquiescence at all; he had only wanted to frighten Praskovia Ivanovna, and above all Vassilissa. He felt wretched.

'I know,' be began, 'this will not be disagreeable to Vassilissa; on the contrary, I believe she will be glad.'

Praskovia Ivanovna got out her reckoning beads, and began rattling the counters.

'On the other hand,' continued Pyetushkov, growing more and more agitated, 'if Vassilissa were, for instance, to give an explanation of her behaviour ... possibly.... Though, of course ... I don't know, possibly, I might perceive that after all there was no great matter for blame in it.'

'There's thirty-seven roubles and forty kopecks in notes to your account, sir,' observed Praskovia Ivanovna. 'Here, would you be pleased to go through it?'

Ivan Afanasiitch made no reply.

'Eighteen dinners at seventy kopecks each; twelve roubles sixty kopecks.'

'And so we are to part, Praskovia Ivanovna.'

'If so it must be, sir. Things do turn out so. Twelve samovars at ten kopecks each ...'

'But you might just tell me, Praskovia Ivanovna, where it was Vassilissa went, and what it was she ...'

'Oh, I never asked her, sir.... One rouble twenty kopecks in silver.'

Ivan Afanasiitch sank into meditation.

'Kvas and effervescing drinks,' pursued Praskovia Ivanovna, holding the counters apart on the frame not with her first, but her third finger, 'half a rouble in silver. Sugar and rolls for tea, half a rouble. Four packets of tobacco bought by your orders, eighty kopecks in silver. To the tailor Kuprian Apollonov ...'

Ivan Afanasiitch suddenly raised his head, put out his hand and mixed up the counters.

'What are you about, my good man?' cried Praskovia Ivanovna. 'Don't you trust me?'

'Praskovia Ivanovna,' replied Pyetushkov, with a hurried smile, 'I've thought better of it. I was only, you know ... joking. We'd better remain friends and go on in the old way. What nonsense it is! How can we separate—tell me that, please?'

Praskovia Ivanovna looked down and made him no reply.

'Come, we've been talking nonsense, and there's an end of it,' pursued Ivan Afanasiitch, walking up and down the room, rubbing his hands, and, as it were, resuming his ancient rights. 'Amen! and now I'd better have a pipe.'

Praskovia Ivanovna still did not move from her place....

'I see you are angry with me,' said Pyetushkov.

'I've offended you, perhaps. Well! well! forgive me generously.'

'How could you offend me, my good sir? No offence about it.... Only, please, sir,' added Praskovia Ivanovna, bowing, 'be so good as not to go on coming to us.'

'What?'

'It's not for you, sir, to be friends with us, your honour. So, please, do us the favour ...'

Praskovia Ivanovna went on bowing.

'What ever for?' muttered the astounded Pyetushkov.

'Oh, nothing, sir. For mercy's sake ...'

'No, Praskovia Ivanovna, you must explain this! ...'

'Vassilissa asks you. She says, "I thank you, thank you very much, and from my heart; only for the future, your honour, give us up."'

Praskovia Ivanovna bowed down almost to Pyetushkov's feet.

'Vassilissa, you say, begs me not to come?'

'Just so, your honour. When your honour came in to-day, and said what you did, that you didn't wish, you said, to visit us any more, I felt relieved, sir, that I did; thinks I, Well, thank God, how nicely it's all come about! But for that, I should have had hard work to bring my tongue to say it.... Be so good, sir.'

Pyetushkov turned red and pale almost at the same instant. Praskovia Ivanovna still went on bowing....

'Very good,' Ivan Afanasiitch cried sharply. 'Good-bye.'

He turned abruptly and put on his cap.

'But the little bill, sir....'

'Send it ... my orderly shall pay you.'

Pyetushkov went with resolute steps out of the baker's shop, and did not even look round.

X

A fortnight passed. At first Pyetushkov bore up in an extraordinary way. He went out, and visited his comrades, with the exception, of course, of Bublitsyn; but in spite of the exaggerated approbation of Onisim, he almost went out of his mind at last from wretchedness, jealousy, and ennui. Conversations with Onisim about Vassilissa were the only thing that afforded him some consolation. The conversation was always begun, 'scratched up,' by Pyetushkov; Onisim responded unwillingly.

'It's a strange thing, you know,' Ivan Afanasiitch would say, for instance, as he lay on the sofa, while Onisim stood in his usual attitude, leaning against the door, with his hands folded behind his back, 'when you come to think of it, what it was I saw in that girl. One would say that there was nothing unusual in her. It's true she has a good heart. That one can't deny her.'

'Good heart, indeed!' Onisim would answer with displeasure.

'Come, now, Onisim,' Pyetushkov went on, 'one must tell the truth. It's a thing of the past now; it's no matter to me now, but justice is justice. You don't know her. She's very good-hearted. Not a single beggar does she let pass by; she'll always give, if it's only a crust of bread. Oh! And she's of a cheerful temper, that one must allow, too.'

'What a notion! I don't know where you see the cheerful temper!'

'I tell you ... you don't know her. And she's not mercenary either ... that's another thing. She's not grasping, there's no doubt of it. Why I never gave her anything, as you know.'

'That's why she's flung you over.'

'No, that's not why!' responded Pyetushkov with a sigh.

'Why, you're in love with her to this day,' Onisim retorted malignantly. 'You'd be glad to go back there as before.'

'That's nonsense you're talking. No, my lad, you don't know me either, I can see. Be sent away, and then go dancing attendance—no, thank you, I'd rather be excused. No, I tell you. You may believe me, it's all a thing of the past now.'

'Pray God it be so!'

'But why ever shouldn't I be fair to her, now after all? If now I say she's not good-looking—why, who'd believe me?'

'A queer sort of good looks!'

'Well, find me,—well, mention anybody better-looking ...'

'Oh, you'd better go back to her, then! ...'

'Stupid! Do you suppose that's why I say so? Understand me ...'

'Oh! I understand you,' Onisim answered with a heavy sigh.

Another week passed by. Pyetushkov had positively given up talking with his Onisim, and had given up going out. From morning till night he lay on the sofa, his hands behind his head. He began to get thin and pale, eat unwillingly and hurriedly, and did not smoke at all. Onisim could only shake his head, as he looked at him.

'You're not well, Ivan Afanasiitch,' he said to him more than once.

'No, I'm all right,' replied Pyetushkov.

At last, one fine day (Onisim was not at home) Pyetushkov got up, rummaged in his chest of drawers, put on his cloak, though the sun was rather hot, went stealthily out into the street, and came back a quarter of an hour later.... He carried something under his cloak....

Onisim was not at home. The whole morning he had been sitting in his little room, deliberating with himself, grumbling and swearing between his teeth, and, at last, he sallied off to Vassilissa. He found her in the shop. Praskovia Ivanovna was asleep on the stove, rhythmically and soothingly snoring.

'Ah, how d'ye do, Onisim Sergeitch,' began Vassilissa, with a smile; 'why haven't we seen anything of you for so long?'

'Good day.'

'Why are you so depressed? Would you like a cup of tea?'

'It's not me we're talking about now,' rejoined Onisim, in a tone of vexation.

'Why, what then?'

'What! Don't you understand me? What! What have you done to my master, come, you tell me that.'

'What I've done to him?'

'What have you done to him? ... You go and look at him. Why, before we can look round, he'll be in a decline, or dying outright, maybe.'

'It's not my fault, Onisim Sergeitch.'

'Not your fault! God knows. Why, he's lost his heart to you. And you, God forgive you, treated him as if he were one of yourselves. Don't come, says you, I'm sick of you. Why, though he's not much to boast of, he's a gentleman anyway. He's a gentleman born, you know.... Do you realise that?'

'But he's such a dull person, Onisim Sergeitch....'

'Dull! So you must have merry fellows about you!'

'And it's not so much that he's dull: he's so cross, so jealous.'

'Ah, you, you're as haughty as a princess! He was in your way, I dare say!'

'But you yourself, Onisim Sergeitch, if you remember, were put out with him about it; "Why is he such friends?" you said; "what's he always coming for?"'

'Well, was I to be pleased with him for it, do you suppose?'

'Well, then, why are you angry with me now? Here, he's given up coming.'

Onisim positively stamped.

'But what am I to do with him, if he's such a madman?' he added, dropping his voice.

'But how am I in fault? What can I do?'

'I'll tell you what: come with me to him.'

'God forbid!'

'Why won't you come?'

'But why should I go to see him? Upon my word!'

'Why? Why, because he says you've a good heart; let me see if you've a good heart.'

'But what good can I do him?'

'Oh, that's my business. You may be sure things are in a bad way, since I've come to you. It's certain I could think of nothing else to do.'

Onisim paused for a while.

'Well, come along, Vassilissa, please, come along.'

'Oh, Onisim Sergeitch, I don't want to be friendly with him again ...'

'Well, and you needn't—who's talking of it? You've only to say a couple of words; to say, Why does your honour grieve? ... give over.... That's all.'

'Really, Onisim Sergeitch ...'

'Why, am I to go down on my knees to you, eh? All right—there, I'm on my knees ...'

'But really ...'

'Why, what a girl it is! Even that doesn't touch her! ...'

Vassilissa at last consented, put a kerchief on her head, and went out with Onisim.

'You wait here a little, in the passage,' he said to her, when they reached Pyetushkov's abode, 'and I'll go and let the master know ...'

He went in to Ivan Afanasiitch. Pyetushkov was standing in the middle of the room, both hands in his pockets, his legs excessively wide apart; he was slightly swaying backwards and forwards. His face was hot, and his eyes were sparkling.

'Hullo, Onisim,' he faltered amiably, articulating the consonants very indistinctly and thickly: 'hullo, my lad. Ah, my lad, when you weren't here ... he, he, he ...' Pyetushkov laughed and made a sudden duck forward with his nose. 'Yes, it's an accomplished fact, he, he, he.... However,' he added, trying to assume a dignified air, 'I'm all right.' He tried to lift his foot, but almost fell over, and to preserve his dignity pronounced in a deep bass, 'Boy, bring my pipe!'

Onisim gazed in astonishment at his master, glanced round.... In the window stood an empty dark-green bottle, with the inscription: 'Best Jamaica rum.'

'I've been drinking, my lad, that's all,' Pyetushkov went on. 'I've been and taken it. I've been drinking, and that's all about it. And where've you been? Tell us ... don't be shy ... tell us. You're a good hand at a tale.'

'Ivan Afanasiitch, mercy on us!' wailed Onisim.

'To be sure. To be sure I will,' replied Pyetushkov with a vague wave of his hand. 'I'll have mercy on you, and forgive you. I forgive every one, I forgive you, and Vassilissa I forgive, and every one, every one. Yes, my lad, I've been drinking.... Dri-ink-ing, lad.... Who's that?' he cried suddenly, pointing to the door into the passage; 'who's there?'

'Nobody's there,' Onisim answered hastily: 'who should be there? ... where are you going?'

'No, no,' repeated Pyetushkov, breaking away from Onisim, 'let me go, I saw—don't you talk to me,—I saw there, let me go.... Vassilissa!' he shrieked all at once.

Pyetushkov turned pale.

'Well ... well, why don't you come in?' he said at last. 'Come in, Vassilissa, come in. I'm very glad to see you, Vassilissa.'

Vassilissa glanced at Onisim and came into the room. Pyetushkov went nearer to her.... He heaved deep, irregular breaths. Onisim watched him. Vassilissa stole timid glances at both of them.

'Sit down, Vassilissa,' Ivan Afanasiitch began again: 'thanks for coming. Excuse my being ... what shall I say? ... not quite fit to be seen. I couldn't foresee, couldn't really, you'll own that yourself. Come, sit down, see here, on the sofa ... So ... I'm expressing myself all right, I think.'

Vassilissa sat down.

'Well, good day to you,' Ivan Afanasiitch pursued. 'Come, how are you? what have you been doing?'

'I'm well, thank God, Ivan Afanasiitch. And you?'

'I? as you see! A ruined man. And ruined by whom? By you, Vassilissa. But I'm not angry with you. Only I'm a ruined man. You ask him. (He pointed to Onisim.) Don't you mind my being drunk. I'm drunk, certainly; only I'm a ruined man. That's why I'm drunk, because I'm a ruined man.'

'Lord have mercy on us, Ivan Afanasiitch!'

'A ruined man, Vassilissa, I tell you. You may believe me. I've never deceived you. Oh, and how's your aunt?'

'Very well, Ivan Afanasiitch. Thank you.'

Pyetushkov began swaying violently.

'But you're not quite well to-day, Ivan Afanasiitch. You ought to lie down.'

'No, I'm quite well, Vassilissa. No, don't say I'm not well; you'd better say I've fallen into evil ways, lost my morals. That's what would be just. I won't dispute that.'

Ivan Afanasiitch gave a lurch backwards. Onisim ran forward and held his master up.

'And who's to blame for it? I'll tell you, if you like, who's to blame. I'm to blame, in the first place. What ought I to have said? I ought to have said to you: Vassilissa, I love you. Good—well, will you marry me? Will you? It's true you're a working girl, granted; but that's all right. It's done sometimes. Why, there, I knew a fellow, he got married like that. Married a Finnish servant-girl. Took and married her. And you'd have been happy with me. I'm a good-natured chap, I am! Never you mind my being drunk, you look at my heart. There, you ask this ... fellow. So, you see, I turn out to be in fault. And now, of course, I'm a ruined man.'

Ivan Afanasiitch was more and more in need of Onisim's support.

'All the same, you did wrong, very wrong. I loved you, I respected you ... what's more, I'm ready to go to church with you this minute. Will you? You've only to say the word, and we'll start at once. Only you wounded me cruelly ... cruelly. You might at least have turned me away yourself— but through your aunt, through that fat female! Why, the only joy I had in life was you. I'm a homeless man, you know, a poor lonely creature! Who is there now to be kind to me? who says a kind word to me? I'm ut- terly alone. Stript bare as a crow. You ask this ...' Ivan Afanasiitch began to cry. 'Vassilissa, listen what I say to you,' he went on: 'let me come and see you as before. Don't be afraid.... I'll be ... quiet as a mouse. You can go and see whom you like, I'll—be all right: not a word, no protests, you know. Eh? do you agree? If you like, I'll go down on my knees.' (And Ivan

Afanasiitch bent his knees, but Onisim held him up under the arms.) 'Let me go! It's not your business! It's a matter of the happiness of a whole life, don't you understand, and you hinder....'

Vassilissa did not know what to say.

'You won't ... Well, as you will! God be with you. In that case, good-bye! Good-bye, Vassilissa. I wish you all happiness and prosperity ... but I ... but I ...'

And Pyetushkov sobbed violently. Onisim with all his might held him up from behind ... first his face worked, then he burst out crying. And Vassilissa cried too.

XI

Ten years later, one might have met in the streets of the little town of O—a thinnish man with a reddish nose, dressed in an old green coat with a greasy plush collar. He occupied a small garret in the baker's shop, with which we are familiar. Praskovia Ivanovna was no longer of this world. The business was carried on by her niece, Vassilissa, and her husband, the red-haired, dim-eyed baker, Demofont. The man in the green coat had one weakness: he was over fond of drink. He was, however, always quiet when he was tipsy. The reader has probably recognised him as Ivan Afanasiitch.

THE NOVELS OF IVAN TURGENEV

Rudin.

A House of Gentlefolk.

On the Eve.

Fathers and Children.

Smoke.

Virgin Soil. 2 Vols.

A Sportsman's Sketches. 2 Vols.

Dream Tales and Prose Poems.

The Torrents of Spring and other Stories.

A Lear of the Steppes and other Stories.

The Diary of a Superfluous Man and other Stories.

A Desperate Character and other Tales.

The Jew and other Stories.

www.ingramcontent.com/pod-product-compliance
Lightning Source LLC
Chambersburg PA
CBHW071915220626
47052CB00002B/359